#13 in the
Brady Coyne
Series

## OTHER NOVELS BY WILLIAM G. TAPPLY

*THE SNAKE EATER*

*TIGHT LINES*

*THE SPOTTED CATS*

*CLIENT PRIVILEGE*

*DEAD WINTER*

*A VOID IN HEARTS*

*THE VULGAR BOATMAN*

*DEAD MEAT*

*THE MARINE CORPSE*

*FOLLOW THE SHARKS*

*THE DUTCH BLUE ERROR*

*DEATH AT CHARITY'S POINT*

## NONFICTION

*SPORTSMAN'S LEGACY*

*HOME WATER NEAR AND FAR*

*OPENING DAY AND OTHER NEUROSES*

*THOSE HOURS SPENT OUTDOORS*

*WILLIAM G. TAPPLY*

# THE SEVENTH ENEMY

*A BRADY COYNE MYSTERY*

OTTO PENZLER BOOKS
New York

OTTO PENZLER BOOKS
129 West 56th Street
New York, NY 10019
(Editorial Offices only)

Simon & Schuster Inc.
Rockefeller Center
1230 Avenue of the Americas
New York, NY 10020



Designed by Songhee Kim

Manufactured in the United States of America

1 3 5 7 9 10 8 6 4 2

Library of Congress Cataloging-in-Publication Data

Tapply, William G.

The seventh enemy/William G. Tapply.

p. cm.—(A Brady Coyne mystery)

1. Coyne, Brady (Fictitious character)—Fiction. 2. Lawyers—Massachusetts—Boston—Fiction. 3. Boston (Mass.)—Fiction. I. Title. II. Series: Tapply, William G. Brady Coyne mystery.

PS3570.A568S48 1995

813'.54—dc20

94–29386

CIP

ISBN 1-883402-99-9

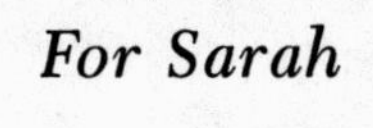
For Sarah

# THE SEVENTH ENEMY

# ◎ ACKNOWLEDGMENTS ◎

I am grateful to my candid and perceptive critics Rick Boyer, Vicki Stiefel, and Otto Penzler, who helped me beat this story into submission.

I owe thanks as well to many unwitting consultants, who, in a variety of social, public, and private settings over the years, have engaged me in enthusiastic debate and discussion on the subject of gun control. I have concluded that the issue is far more complicated than it seems.

# ◎ FOREWORD ◎

On May 5, 1994, Congressman Douglas Applegate (D–Ohio) voted "aye," and by the margin of that single vote the United States House of Representatives passed a bill banning the manufacture and sale of nineteen specified semiautomatic assault guns.

The battle to control paramilitary weapons such as the Uzi and the AK-47 had been waged for years in American governments at all levels. Before Congressman Applegate voted "aye," the gun lobby had won every skirmish.

My own education in the politics of gun control came two years before the passage of the House bill. It began on a quiet Sunday evening in May when my boyhood chum Wally Kinnick called me from Logan Airport, and I have to believe that the events that ensued in Massachusetts in 1992 helped to inform the debate in the United States Congress in 1994 and contributed to Douglas Applegate's historic "aye" vote.

Brady L. Coyne
Boston, Massachusetts
December 1994

**MAN WITH ASSAULT GUN SLAYS WIFE AT LIBRARY**

by

Alexandria Shaw

Globe Staff

Harlow—The silence of the public library in this little central Massachusetts community was shattered by gunshots on Wednesday afternoon. Maureen Burton, 32, a part-time librarian, was pronounced dead at the scene. Two others are in intensive care at the University of Massachusetts Medical Center.

According to eyewitnesses, David Burton, 37, an unemployed electrician and the estranged husband of the librarian, entered the building at approximately 3:45 in the afternoon carrying an AK-47, commonly known as a "paramilitary assault weapon." Witnesses report that Burton approached the desk where Mrs. Burton was seated, shouted, "I've had it!" and opened fire.

At least three bullets struck Mrs. Burton in the chest, killing her instantly. Police estimate that twelve to fifteen shots were fired altogether, some of which struck two bystanders.

Burton's body was later found in his pickup truck on the outskirts of town, dead of a single gunshot wound to the head, apparently self-inflicted.

According to state police records, the incident in Harlow marks the fourteenth death in Massachusetts this year directly attributable to semiautomatic assault weapons such as the AK-47, which are characterized by their capacity to fire a large number of shots as rapidly as the trigger is pulled.

Six of those victims have been police officers.

Massachusetts has no restrictions on the purchase or ownership of assault weapons beyond those that apply to target or sporting weapons. "If you have an FID [Firearms Identification Card] you can walk into a gun shop and buy an Uzi," says State Police Lieutenant Victor McClelland. "It's as easy as that."

Neighbors of the Burtons report that the couple were often heard arguing and had not been living together for over a year. Mr. Burton, they say, had recently been despondent over losing his job.

"Maureen had no children of her own," Geri Hatcher, sister of the victim, told the Globe, "which was one of the reasons she loved to work at the library after school. David refused to have children, and they argued about it a lot. That's why she left him. She planned to get divorced. I guess he couldn't stand it."

The names of the other two victims have not been released.

I was sitting out on the steel balcony that clings to the side of my apartment building and savoring the evening air, which was warm for early May. It was an excellent evening for balcony sitting, and I had left thoughts of newspaper reading and television watching inside. A skyful of stars overhead and a harborful of ship lights six stories below me mirrored each other. At Logan across the Inner Harbor a steady stream of airplane lights landed and took off, and I could see the streetlights from East Boston and, way off to my left, headlights moving across the Mystic River Bridge. Harbor smells wafted up, seaweed and dead fish and salt air and gasoline fumes diluted and mingled by the easterly breeze—not at all unpleasant.

I had tilted my aluminum lawn chair back on its hind legs. My heels rested on the railing of the balcony and a glass of Jack Daniel's rested on my belly, and when the phone began to ring I contemplated letting the machine get it.

I knew it wasn't Terri. It had been six months. Since Terri, I often found myself watching the harbor lights with a glass of Daniel's.

But it could have been one of my boys. They often call on Sunday evenings, Billy from U Mass needing money, or Joey from his mother's home in Wellesley just wanting to chat with his dad.

So I unfolded myself and padded stocking-footed into the kitchen.

"Brady Coyne," I said into the phone.

"Hey, guy."

"Wally," I said. "What hostile wilderness outpost are you calling me from this time?"

"About as hostile as you can get. Logan Airport."

"Just passing through?"

"Actually, I could use a lift," he said. "I've been waiting here for an hour. The guy who was supposed to meet me didn't show up."

"Need a place to crash for the night?"

"If you don't mind, it looks like I do."

"Hey," I said, "that's what lawyers are for. Cab service. Emergency accommodations. Sharing their booze. What terminal are you at?"

"Northwest. I'll wait at the curb."

"I can practically see you from here," I said. "I'll be there in fifteen minutes."

There's always somebody from our childhood who becomes famous, about whom we say, "I knew him—or her—when we were kids. You'd never have predicted it." It's the skinny girl in seventh-grade geography class who always kept her lips clamped tight over her mouthful of braces, and who ten years later smiles dazzlingly from the cover of *Cosmopolitan.* Or the stumbling overweight grammar school boy who goes on to play linebacker for Notre Dame, or the computer nerd who gets elected to Congress.

Most of us knew a kid who became an author or athlete or politician or actor or criminal, and we feel a kind of pride of ownership, as if we were the first to recognize his talent.

Wally Kinnick was that kid from my youth.

Nobody would ever have predicted fame for Wally. He was a quiet, unambitious teenager, a modest student with a very short list of activities on his college applications. He preferred hunting and fishing to playing sports or running for Student Council. Hell, he wanted to become a forest ranger. A more anonymous career I couldn't imagine.

After high school, I lost track of Wally for a while. When he popped up again he was famous. Outdoorsmen knew him as an expert. To environmentalists he was an ally.

Politicians considered him a nuisance.

It started with an innocuous local Saturday morning cable television program out of Minneapolis. At first it was called simply "Outdoors," a derivative good-old-boy hunting and fishing show featuring Wally and his guest celebrity of the week. But as Wally refined his television personality and style, he became "Walt" and his show became "Walt Kinnick's Outdoors." ESPN picked it up and sent him on hunting and fishing excursions to remote corners of the globe. He used the show as a forum for taking dead aim at the enemies of wildlife and their habitat.

Nobody could figure out whether Walt Kinnick was a liberal or conservative, Democrat or Republican. He defied labels. He sought the truth. He cut through the bullshit. He stepped on toes. Indiscriminantly.

Walt Kinnick's name and face and voice became as well known—though certainly not as beloved—as that of Julia Child.

By the early 1990s, Walt Kinnick had become the Ralph Nader of the environment. He submitted to questioning by Larry King, traded jokes with Letterman, testified before blue-ribbon commissions, wrote magazine articles. He even endorsed an insect repellent on television commercials.

He made enemies. He got sued. I was his Boston lawyer. He had other lawyers in other cities.

He had a cabin in the Berkshires in western Massachusetts near the Vermont border, a retreat where he went to fish and hunt and escape the rigors of public life. He'd invited me out several times, but our schedules never seemed to mesh.

Like most of my clients, Wally was also a friend. Otherwise I wouldn't have been so willing to go pick him up at the airport at eleven o'clock on a Sunday evening in May.

◎

When I got to the Northwest terminal, I spotted him instantly in the crowd that was clustered by the curb. He was wearing a sportcoat and necktie, his idea of a disguise. On television he always wore a flannel shirt and jeans with a sheath knife at his hip. But Wally Kinnick stood about six-three and sported a bushy black beard, and he would have been hard to miss regardless of what he was wearing.

I parked in the no-stopping zone, got out of my car, and walked up to him. I grabbed his shoulder.

He whirled around. "Oh, Brady," he said. "Thank God. Let's get the hell out of here. I hate airports."

He was bending for the overnight bag that sat beside him on the pavement when a man appeared behind him. He touched Wally's shoulder and said, "Walt Kinnick? Is that you?"

Wally turned. "McNiff?"

"God," said the man, "I'm sorry I'm late. My kid had the car this afternoon and left the tank empty and I had to drive all over Clinton to find a gas station that was open on a Sunday night and there was a detour on Route 2 . . ." He flapped his hands in a gesture of helplessness.

"Sure," shrugged Wally. "It's okay. Oh, I'm sorry," he said quickly. "Brady Coyne, Gene McNiff."

I shook hands with McNiff. He was a beefy guy with thinning red hair and small close-set eyes.

"Gene's the president of SAFE," said Wally.

"SAFE?"

"Second Amendment For Ever," said McNiff. "We're sort of the New England arm of the NRA. Walt's here to testify for us."

"We need the Second Amendment to keep us safe," said Wally. "SAFE, get it?"

I smiled. "Cute."

"Brady's my lawyer," said Wally.

McNiff arched his eyebrows. "Lawyer, huh?" He nodded. "Well, it's always good to have a lawyer, I guess. You'll be there tomorrow, then, Brady?"

"Oh, sure," I said, wondering what the hell he was talking about. "Absolutely. Wouldn't miss it."

"Good, good," he said. He turned to Wally. "Look, I'm really sorry I was so late. You must be pooped. So shall we . . .?"

Wally glanced at me, then turned to McNiff. "I figured we'd gotten our signals crossed, Gene. So I called Brady. He invited me for the night. You don't mind, do you?"

McNiff frowned. He clearly minded. But all he said was, "Sure. No problem. Really sorry I kept you waiting. I should've at least tried to call or something."

"That's okay," said Wally. "Brady and I have some work to do anyway, so it worked out fine. Just too bad you had to come all the way in here."

McNiff shook his head. "My own damned fault."

Wally reached for his hand and shook it. "See you in the morning, then, Gene."

McNiff forced a smile. "Right. See you there. Um, I'll meet you in the rotunda a little before ten. Okay?"

Wally nodded. "Sure. I'll be there."

McNiff turned and trudged away. Wally and I got into my car. He said, "Boy, that's a relief."

"Why?"

"I was supposed to spend the night with him. Dreaded the thought of it. All the local SAFE guys'll be waiting there in his living room, all primed to tell me about the big buck they nailed last year and how much they hate liberals. They'll want to stay up all night drinking Budweiser and shooting the shit with the big television personality. So now McNiff comes home without me, he's a bum. I'm sorry for him, but I'm thrilled for me. I know it's part of the job, but I really hate that shit."

"You told him you and I had some work to do."

"Nah. Not really. A little peace and quiet's all I want."

"You mind telling me what you're doing in Boston?"

"There's a bill up before a subcommittee of the state Senate. SAFE flew me in to testify."

"What kind of bill?"

"Assault-weapon control. The hearing's tomorrow morning. I'll go and do my thing, then head out to Fenwick for a glorious week at the cabin, reading old Travis McGee novels, sipping Rebel Yell, chopping wood, and casting dry flies on the Deerfield."

"You're testifying against this bill, I assume."

"Hell," said Wally, "SAFE doesn't pay expenses for someone to testify in *favor* of gun control, you know."

"How can you testify against controlling assault weapons?"

I heard him chuckle from the seat beside me. "It's complicated."

"This is something you want to do?"

"Telling people what I believe in?" he said. "Yeah, I kinda like it, to tell you the truth. The upside of being a public figure is you can say what you think and people actually listen to you. Sometimes you get to believe you can make a difference. The downside is they take you so damn seriously that you have to be very careful about what you say."

"You don't want my advice on this, I gather."

"I never ignore your advice, Brady."

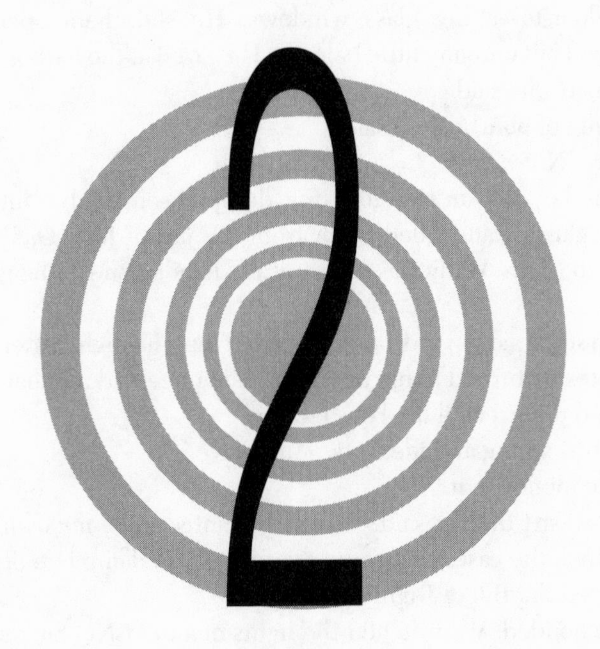

Wally and I had always done our business in my office or over a slab of prime rib at Durgin Park. He'd never been to my apartment. When we walked in, he looked around, smiled, and said, "Pretty nice."

I tried to see my place the way he did. To me it was comfortable. I have an understanding with my apartment. I give it plenty of freedom to express itself, and it doesn't impose too many obligations on me. The furniture can sit wherever it likes. I can leave magazines and neckties on it, and it doesn't complain. Fly rods hide in closets and newspapers find sanctuary under the sofa. I let my shoes go where they want. It's their home, too.

I expect, to Wally, it looked messy.

He dropped his overnight bag onto the floor and went over to the floor-to-ceiling glass windows. He slid them open and stepped out onto my little balcony. He gazed at the harbor. "This ain't bad," he said.

"Slug of bourbon?" I said.

"Ice. No water."

I broke open an ice-cube tray, dumped some cubes into two short glasses, and filled them from my jug of Jack Daniel's. I went to where Wally was standing and handed one of the glasses to him.

We stood side by side and stared out into the night. After a few minutes he turned to me and said, "You once told me that you'd wanted to be a civil liberties lawyer."

"I was young and idealistic. And naive."

"No money in it?"

"It wasn't that," I said. "I mainly wanted to be my own boss. So I took the cases that came my way. Not a damn one of them involved the Bill of Rights."

He nodded. We watched the lights of a big LNG tanker inch across the dark horizon. After a few moments, Wally said, "So what's your take on the Second Amendment?"

"What do you mean?"

"The right to bear arms. Is it absolute?"

"Well, the Supreme Court has said many times that no right is absolute. The individual's rights are limited by the rights of society. You know, you can't yell 'Fire!' in a crowded theater, even though the First Amendment says you've got the right to free speech. I'm not up-to-date on Second Amendment cases, but I do know that there are federal and state laws regulating handgun sales that have withstood court challenges."

"But the Second Amendment seems to be based on the rights of society, not the individual," he said. "It's not so much that I have the right to bear an arm as that we all have the right to protect ourselves and each other."

"'A well-regulated militia, being necessary to the security of a free state,'" I quoted, pleased with myself. "Yes. Except the idea of a militia is pretty antiquated."

"Damn complicated," Wally mumbled.

"The nature of the law," I said. "It's why we have lawyers."

I casually flipped my cigarette butt over the railing and watched it spark its way down to the water below. When I glanced at Wally, he was grinning at me. Wally preaches the importance of keeping our environment pristine. We should pick up trash, not dump it. I agree with him. And I had just thrown a cigarette into the ocean.

"Look," I said, "it's the filthiest, most polluted harbor in the world."

Wally shrugged. "I wonder how it got that way."

"Yeah," I mumbled. "Valid point." We stared into the night for a while. Then I said, "I thought those things were already regulated."

"What things?"

"Assault guns."

"You're thinking of automatic weapons. You know, the kind where you hold down the trigger and they keep firing. This bill is about semiautomatics. They shoot a bullet each time you pull the trigger."

"That's what they mean by paramilitary, then?"

He nodded. "They're modeled after military weapons. Your Uzi, your AK-47. Assault guns've got large magazines, but they're not fully automatic."

"A lot of sporting guns are semiautomatic, aren't they?"

"Sure," said Wally. "Shotguns, hunting rifles."

"So what's the difference?"

"Functionally, the only difference is the size of the magazine. Except, of course, your assault gun *looks*—well, it *looks*—like a military weapon. And they're pretty easy to modify into fully automatic." Wally turned and smiled at me. "You're not that bad at cross-examination, Brady, you know that?"

"I was just interested," I said. "Sorry."

"No, don't be. Talking about it helps me clarify it."

"So this *is* a consultation."

He turned to me and smiled. "You gonna put me on the clock?"

"I guess I should. Julie would be pleased. Want another drink?"

He shook his head. "Mind if I use your phone?"

"You don't have to ask." I flapped my hand at the wall phone in the kitchen. "Help yourself."

He went into the kitchen, took the phone off the hook, and sat at the table. He pecked out a number from memory. I turned my back to him, sipped my drink, and watched the clouds slide across the sky. I wasn't trying to listen, but I couldn't help hearing.

"Hey, it's me," said Wally into the phone. "Here, in Boston. . . . With my lawyer. . . . Just one night, then to the cabin. Gonna be able to make it? . . . Yeah, good. Terrific. I'll meet you at your place tomorrow, then. . . ." His voice softened. "Yeah, me, too. Um, how's? . . . Oh, shit. Well, look. Keep all the doors locked and don't be afraid to call the cops. . . . I know, but you should still do it. . . . Christ, babe, don't do that. I'll see you tomorrow, okay? It'll wait. . . ." He chuckled softly. "Right. You, too. Bye."

I heard him hang up. He came into the living room and slumped onto the sofa. I went over and took the chair across from him. We both put our feet up on the newspapers that were piled on the coffee table.

"That's a friend of mine," he said. "She's having problems with her husband."

"You fooling around with married ladies?"

"She's in the middle of a messy divorce. The guy's not handling it with much class."

"You didn't answer my question."

"I'm not fooling around with her," he said. "I'm serious about her."

"Sounds like a good situation to stay out of."

"My lawyer's advice?"

"Your friend's advice."

He shrugged. "You can't always pick 'em. You'd like Diana. She and I are gonna spend the week at the cabin. Hey, why don't you join us?"

"Sure," I said. "Just what you want. A threesome."

"No, really," he said. "We've got a spare bedroom. Diana would love it. So would I."

I shook my head. "I can't spare a week."

"A few days, at least. How about it? The Deerfield should be prime."

"Boy," I said, "I haven't had any trout fishing to speak of all spring. I could maybe take Thursday and Friday."

"Done!" said Wally.

"I gotta check with Julie."

"Assert yourself."

"It's not easy with Julie. But I'll try."

We sipped our drinks, chatted aimlessly, then began to yawn. I pulled out the sofa for Wally, found a blanket and pillow for him, and got ready for bed. When I went back to the living room, he was sitting at the kitchen table reading through a stack of papers and making notes on a legal-sized yellow pad. A pair of rimless reading glasses roosted on the tip of his nose.

"What's that?" I said.

"A copy of the bill I'm supposed to testify on tomorrow and some of the SAFE propaganda. I haven't had a chance to look it over."

"You probably ought to before you talk about it," I said. "Lawyer's advice."

"And that," said Wally, "is why I pay you those outrageous fees."

Whether it was the booze, or visions of Deerfield brown trout eating my dry flies, or just seeing Wally again, I don't know, but I lay awake for a long time. It all must have affected Wally the same way, because even as I finally drifted off to sleep I could still hear him pacing around in my living room mumbling to himself.

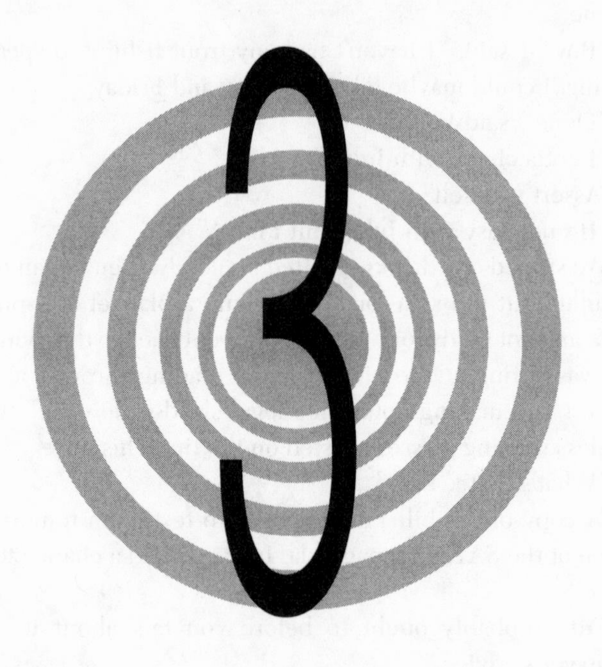


When I stumbled into the kitchen the next morning, Wally was slouched in the same chair at the table, scratching on his yellow legal pad. I poured two mugfuls of coffee and slid one beside his elbow. "You been sitting there all night?" I said.

He took off his reading glasses, laid them on the table, and pinched the bridge of his nose. Then he reached for his coffee and took a sip. "I slept for a while."

"This must be important," I persisted, gesturing at what looked like an entire pad's worth of balled-up sheets of yellow paper scattered on the floor behind him.

Wally leaned back and rolled his shoulders. "Actually it's just a little subcommittee hearing, one of those deals where you slip in and slip out and nobody listens to what you say because they've already got their minds made up, but the law requires a public hearing. So they set it up for Monday morning before the press rolls out of bed and everybody just wants to get it over with."

"Then why. . . ?" I gestured at the litter of paper balls on the floor.

"I just like to do things right," said Wally with a shrug. "It's a character flaw."

I waited until nine to call Julie. "Brady L. Coyne, Attorney," she said. "Good morning."

"It's me."

"Where are you?"

"Home. I'm gonna be late."

"How late?"

"Couple, three hours."

"No, you're not. Mrs. Mudgett has a ten o'clock."

"Call her. Reschedule."

"Aha." I could visualize Julie squinting suspiciously. "Who is it? The Hungarian or the Italian?"

"I'm not with a woman, Julie. I'm with a client, and we should be done sometime before noon."

"Don't try to bullshit me, Brady Coyne," said Julie.

"No. Listen—"

"I know you," she said. "You don't set up meetings with clients. Especially on Monday mornings. You avoid meeting with clients. You hate meeting with clients. I'm the one who sets up meetings. Then I have to keep kicking your butt to make you show up for them. Look. If you're hung over, or if you're calling from some fishing place in New Hampshire, or if you've got your legs all tangled up with some woman and just can't summon up the strength of character to kick off the blankets, okay, fine. I mean, not fine, but at least I know you're telling the truth."

"It's Wally Kinnick. He flew in unexpectedly last night. He's got a problem. I'm his lawyer. My job is to help my clients with their problems. So—"

"Ha!" she said. "I know the kinds of problems you and Mr. Kinnick discuss. Like how to catch big trout on those little bitty flies you use."

"No, listen," I said. "This is lawyer stuff. We're here at my place, and we've been conferring, and we've got more work to do, and I'll be there by noon. And don't give me any more shit about it or I'll fire you."

"Ha!" she said. "You'd go broke in a week."

"I know. I won't fire you. I'll give you a raise. Call Mrs. Mudgett and reschedule her. Oh, and, um, you better clear my calendar for Thursday and Friday."

"Fishing, right?"

"Well, yeah, but—"

"Boy," sighed Julie. "To think, I could've been an emergency room nurse, run the control tower at O'Hare, something easy on the nerves."

"Thanks, kiddo," I said. "Love ya." I made kissing noises into the phone.

After I hung up, Wally said, "From this end it sounded like you were taking a bunch of shit from a wife."

"Worse. A secretary."

Wally grinned. "That Julie's a piece of work."

His testimony before the Senate Subcommittee on Public Safety was scheduled for ten. It was a gorgeous May morning, so we decided to walk over from my apartment on the harbor. I carried my briefcase and Wally lugged his overnight bag. We talked about fishing and baseball and micro-breweries and girls we knew when we were in high school. We did not discuss gun control.

We got to the Common at about nine forty-five and took the diagonal pathway that led to the State House. Halfway across, Wally stopped and said, "Oh-oh."

"What's the matter?"

"Look."

I looked. The golden dome atop the State House gleamed in the morning sunlight. On the sidewalk in front a mass of people were milling around in a slow circle. I saw that many of them were carrying placards.

Several of them, in fact, were dressed in cartoonish animal costumes. I saw a Bambi, a couple of Smokey-the-Bears, and several person-sized rabbits.

They were chanting. At first I couldn't distinguish what they were saying. Then it became clearer.

"Kinnick's a killer."

That was the chant: "Kinnick's a killer."

I turned to Wally with raised eyebrows.

"Animal rights activists," he said. "For some reason, they don't like hunters."

"Ah," I said. "The good folks who splash red paint on fur coats. Does this happen often?"

He nodded. "Yep. Some places you expect it. Washington, of course. Denver, New York, San Francisco. Dallas, on the other hand, or Cheyenne or Billings? Never. Boston, or, best of all, Cambridge? Definitely."

"I love their costumes," I said.

Wally shrugged. "Part of their schtick. Come on. Let's go."

We climbed the steps that took us from the Common up to Beacon Street. The demonstrators patrolled the sidewalk across the street. From where Wally and I stood I could read the signs they carried.

LET'S MAKE HUNTERS THE NEXT ENDANGERED SPECIES, read one.

A Smokey look-alike carried a placard that said, SUPPORT YOUR RIGHT TO ARM BEARS.

HUNTERS MAIM WITH NO SHAME. A big rabbit held that one.

PEOPLE FOR THE ETHICAL TREATMENT OF ANIMALS. An uncostumed pregnant woman.

KILLERS JOIN SAFE.

FUND FOR ANIMALS.

STOP THE WAR ON WILDLIFE.

HUNTING: THE SPORT OF COWARDS.

ANIMAL LIBERATION.

COMMITTEE TO ABOLISH SPORT HUNTING.

OPEN SEASON ON KINNICK.

KINNICK'S A MURDERER.

REMEMBER BAMBI.

There were thirty or forty demonstrators, I guessed, an equal mix of men and women, various ages, costumed and not, moving slowly back and forth, chanting "Kinnick's a killer" and waving their placards. A policeman stood off to the side watching them.

"I didn't realize you were so popular," I said to Wally.

He grinned. "Like it or not, I've become the nation's most visible hunter."

"I would've said you were an outdoorsman, a conservationist."

"Sure," he said. "Me, too. But to some people, if you hunt, that's what you are. A hunter. None of the rest matters. You're a murderer, and it doesn't matter what else you do, what else you stand for."

"How'd they know you'd be here?"

"Gene McNiff probably told the media that I was testifying. That's McNiff's main thing. Politics, lobbying, public opinion. He speaks to any group that'll listen. Watchdogs the six New England legislatures. Prints his newsletter. Keeps gun issues alive in the media. That's SAFE's whole purpose. If they didn't do these things, they believe the Second Amendment would be doomed." He touched my arm. "Well, shall we?"

"Lead on," I said.

We crossed the street and approached the milling crowd of demonstrators. "Excuse us," said Wally. "Please let us through."

Some of them paused and stepped back to let us pass. We began to edge through the crowd. Then someone shouted, "That's him! The big guy with the beard! That's the killer!"

Others echoed the cry. "That's Kinnick! That's him!"

"Come on, folks," said Wally. "Get a life, huh?"

They closed in around us. The chant rose up, loud, frenzied voices. "Kinnick's a killer. Kinnick's a killer." Their bodies bumped ours. They were yelling into our ears. I felt an elbow ram into my ribs. Something thudded against the back of my shoulder. I felt a hand grab my arm and yank me. I stumbled forward.

Wally was tugging me up the steps and the crowd was behind us. "Wait, now," said Wally. "Be cool."

We stopped at the first landing on the stairway, flanked by the statues of Horace Mann and Daniel Webster on the State House lawn. I turned to look back. The demonstrators, people and ersatz animals, were all staring up at us, waving their placards and yelling. I could read the passionate hysteria of their conviction in their faces. Their chant was out of sync now, so that their words mingled into an undifferentiated swirl of hate-filled noise.

One tenderhearted animal lover in a rabbit costume was giving us the paw.

The policeman hadn't moved. The expression of resigned cynicism on his face hadn't changed.

"Jesus," I said.

"True believers," said Wally. "Goes to show what happens to people with too much time on their hands."

"Are they here for the hearing?"

"Naw. They don't care about assault weapons. They care about animals. They're here for me."

"They're kinda scary."

"All true believers are."

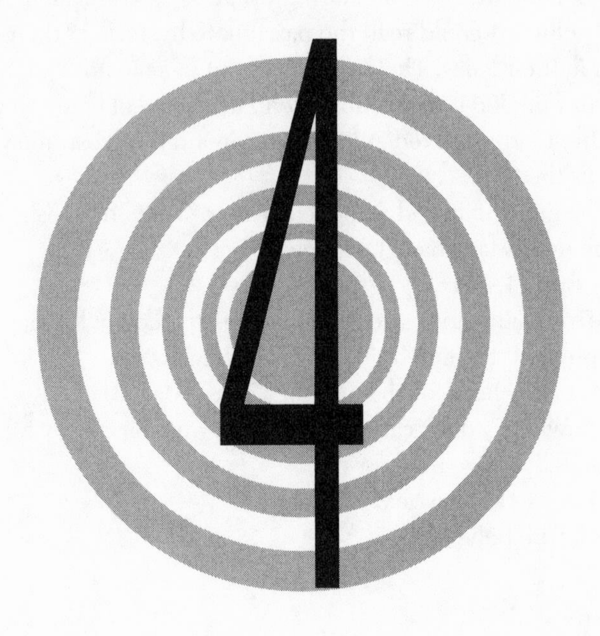


We continued up the long flight of steps and entered into the lobby of the State House. It was packed with tourists on this Monday morning. A teacher was addressing a knot of elementary school children in front of a glass-covered display case. I wondered if she was explaining the example of democracy at work that Wally and I had just experienced outside.

Wally and I wove our way among the people into the second lobby, which was equally mobbed. More school children. Tourists. A busload of senior citizens. Harried tour guides and teachers. We passed through into the third round room, this one directly under the golden dome. It was an oasis of relative quiet.

Old murals encircled the arched ceiling. Historic flags were illuminated behind glass cases.

We stood there for a moment before Gene McNiff appeared. He grabbed Wally's hand, shook it, and said, "You guys okay?"

"Fine," said Wally.

"Speak for yourself," I said.

"Did they hurt you?" said McNiff to me.

"I'm fine."

"If they did, we can sue their assess. Right, Mr. Coyne? You're a lawyer. I'd love to be able to sue those animal nuts."

"They seemed pretty harmless," I said.

"Don't count on it," said McNiff. He turned to Wally. "Right?"

Wally shrugged. "They've got friends in high places, they've got money, and they've got one of those deceptively convincing arguments. I never underestimate them." He grinned. "They're something like SAFE."

McNiff glanced at Wally and frowned. "Well," he said with a shrug, "they're not our concern today. The Second Amendment. That's today's agenda. Let's go."

Wally and I followed McNiff to a flight of stairs that descended into the bowels of the State House. We turned down a corridor and came to a door marked "Hearing Room." Someone had written "S-162" in black felt-tip on a piece of typing paper and taped it onto the door. McNiff pulled it open and we stepped inside.

We found ourselves standing at the rear of a narrow rectangular room. In front was a long table behind which sat four men and two women with microphones in front of them. A smaller table in front of the committee had one chair and one microphone. A uniformed policeman sat there facing the committee, mumbling into the microphone. I couldn't distinguish his words above the drone of voices in the acoustically primitive room, because behind the witness were rows of folding chairs—a hundred, minimum, I guessed—and it looked as if every one of those chairs was occupied. The narrow aisle down the side of the room was blocked with standees. This was a public hearing, and, at ten o'clock on this Monday morning in May, the public had turned out for it.

I scanned the audience. I saw only a few women in it. Ninety-percent men. Some were wearing business suits, but most of them wore shirts open at the neck, working clothes, blue jeans, boots. None of them had on an animal suit. It was a predominantly blue-collar crowd, and their unspoken message was clear: We are the voters, the masses, the majority that refuses to be silent. We hold the power to fill or to vacate legislative seats. We are watching you.

Many of them, I noticed, were glancing around at Wally and mumbling out of the sides of their mouths to the people around them. They seemed to be ignoring the policeman who was testifying up front.

Wally, Gene McNiff, and I stood at the side of the room leaning our backs against the wall.

"Who are all these people?" I said to McNiff.

"Ours," he said.

"SAFE?"

"Yep." He smiled. "We turn 'em out. The sacred right to bear arms is under attack everywhere. We've got to be vigilant."

True believers, I thought. Paranoia rampant.

"Why don't you try to find a seat, Mr. Coyne?" said McNiff. "Walt, we've got to get up front with the witnesses."

He led Wally toward the front of the room. I spotted an empty seat. I edged my way down the aisle and squeezed in between two flannel-shirted men.

A minute later the guy on my left thrust a clipboard into my hands. It held several mimeographed sheets of paper. Each sheet had "S-162" and the date printed across the top and columns marked "name," "address," "pro," and "con." I flipped through them. The "pro" column had been checked by none of those who had signed the sheet. The "con" column was solid with checkmarks.

I scratched my name and address. I checked neither pro nor con. I hadn't read the bill. Then I passed the clipboard back to the man on my left. I noticed that he looked at it, checking me out.

The policeman finished his testimony and was dismissed. Another witness was called. He wore glasses and a three-piece suit. He took the witness seat and laid a slender attaché case on the table in front of him. He opened it and slid a few sheets of paper from it. I heard him clear his throat into his microphone, and for a moment the low din in the hearing room subsided. "My name is Earl Clements," he said. "I'm a professor at the New England School of Law. My field is constitutional law, my specialty the Bill of Rights."

Around me, the men in the audience, SAFE members all, resumed their talking and chuckling, paying no further attention to the professor up front. I guessed that they'd heard him before. They weren't there to become informed anyway. They were there simply—to be there.

The amplification system in that room was as primitive as the acoustics, and the noise continued as the law professor began to speak, so I only caught snatches of the beginning of his statement.

". . . well-regulated Militia . . . security . . . shall not be infringed. . . . intended as an individual, not collective, right. . . . Significant that it comes second only to free speech. . . . Militia historically means the citizens at large, not the organized armed force of the state. . . . Federalist 29 . . . Hamilton refers to the militia as a check against the potential despotism of a standing army, which the Founding Fathers feared, with good reason. . . . in Federalist 46 Hamilton emphasized the 'advantage of being armed' . . . a 'barrier against the enterprises of despotic ambition.'"

As he spoke, his voice became clearer and more confident, and as it did, he seemed to win the attention of those seated in the audience. The noise subsided enough for me to hear the testimony more clearly.

Professor Clements cited several Supreme Court decisions which, he argued, tended to be misinterpreted by those who promoted gun control.

From my seat I could observe the six committee members up front. One of them was fiddling with his wristwatch. Another seemed to be studying some papers on the table in front of him. The two female senators, seated side by side, were whispering to each other. The other two members were staring blankly at the professor.

He concluded by quoting the familiar aphorism of John Philpot Curran: "'The condition upon which God hath given liberty to man is eternal vigilance; which condition if he break, servitude is at once the consequence of his crime and the punishment of his guilt.'" The professor looked up at the committee. "I urge you to reject this bill. It contradicts the spirit of liberty and both the intent and the words of the Constitution. Thank you for hearing me today."

After a pause, a few of the men in the audience clapped. The scattered applause died quickly.

The chairman of the committee said, "Any questions for Professor Clements?"

None of the committee members had any questions.

"Well, thank you, then, sir," said the chairman. "Please leave us a copy of your statement." He waited while the professor stood up, handed him the papers from which he had been reading, and left the room. Then the chairman said, "Our next witness is Walter Kinnick."

As Wally moved to the witness chair, somebody from the back of the room shouted, "You tell 'em, Walt." Several people applauded.

Wally removed a sheet of yellow paper from his jacket pocket and unfolded it onto the table in front of him. He looked up at the committee. The chairman smiled at him and nodded, and I saw Wally return the nod. The room grew quiet. Wally cleared his throat into the microphone. Then he began to read.

"My name is Walter Kinnick," he said slowly, in that familiar television voice. "I grew up in Massachusetts. Although my primary residence is now in Minnesota, I also own a place in the western part of the Commonwealth. It's a retreat, and I come here frequently to hunt and fish. I have been a hunter all my life, and I own several guns. I'm the host of a weekly television program that promotes hunting, fishing, camping, conservation, and outdoor recreation in general. I speak today strictly as a Massachusetts property owner and taxpayer, a private citizen, a concerned citizen."

Wally paused to glance up at the six senators. They wore the same blank expressions they'd showed during the previous testimony. Boredom. They already knew what he was going to say. The public hearing was pro forma, something that the law required but which they didn't expect to inform them.

"I have studied this proposed legislation, S-162," Wally continued. "I have studied it from the standpoint of a sportsman, a gun owner, one who enjoys recreation with firearms. I have looked for its flaws." He hesitated, cleared his throat, again peered at the committee people. He waited until each of them was looking at him. Then he said, "I find no flaw in this legislation. I think it's time that responsible gun owners acknowledged the right of the state to regulate and limit the distribution of certain weapons whose only purpose is to abet the commission of crimes and kill other people. This is good legislation. It's clear, specific, limited. I'm for it. I urge you to pass it. Thank you."

The room was dead silent for a moment. Then a murmur arose from the audience. I looked around at the rows of men who had come to show their numbers. They were whispering among themselves, frowning, shaking their heads. I could read their lips. What did he say? Did I hear that right? Was that Kinnick?

The chairman cocked his head and stared at Wally for a moment, his eyebrows arched in an expression of surprise. "Well," he said. "Thank you, Mr. Kinnick." Then he glanced at the five other committee members and said, "Any questions for Mr. Kinnick?"

One of the women said, "Ah, Mr. Kinnick, you mean you're in favor of this bill, then, is that right?"

"Yes."

"You think assault weapons should be regulated?"

"I think they could be regulated in the manner set down in this legislation without violating any basic rights. Yes."

"Do you belong to the NRA, sir?"

"I speak as a private citizen," said Wally, sidestepping the question.

"Do you own an assault weapon?" she persisted.

"If I did, and if this bill were passed, I would obey the law," said Wally, avoiding that one, too.

"Your testimony comes as a surprise, Mr. Kinnick," she said. "Are there many gun owners who feel the way you do?"

"I have no idea, Senator," said Wally.

She smiled, then shrugged. "No more questions," she said to the chairman.

"Anybody else?" he said.

When none of the other senators ventured a question, the chairman said, "Mr. Kinnick, we thank you for your testimony. You're excused. Please leave a written copy of your statement with me for the record."

I stood up, intending to follow Wally out of the hearing room. But a crowd blocked my way as many members of the audience rose from their seats and headed toward the door. Anger and confusion registered on their faces and in their voices, and they bumped and pushed against each other, jamming the narrow aisle. So I settled back into my seat to wait for them to pass.

Above the angry undercurrent came the amplified voice of the chairman calling the next witness. I didn't catch his name or see where he came from, but a moment later a small, bespectacled man in a brown suit took the seat where a few minutes earlier Wally Kinnick had been sitting.

The man chose to wait for the noise in the room to subside

before he began speaking. It took several minutes, because the people in the audience weren't paying any attention to him. He sat there patiently, waiting them out, while the committee chairman banged his gavel.

Finally the witness cleared his throat and said, "My name is Wilson Bailey and I live in Harlow, which is a small town west of Worcester that you may not have heard of. I teach chemistry in the regional high school there. I'm no expert on guns or law enforcement or anything, so I want to thank the chairman for the opportunity to tell you my story here today. I hope it will help you decide to vote in favor of this bill."

As he spoke, I leaned forward to see Wilson Bailey more clearly. He had no written statement or notes in front of him. He gazed from one committee member to the other as he talked. His voice was soft and confident. If he had memorized his speech, he had done it well. He made it appear that he was speaking directly from his heart.

"Two years ago last April," Bailey continued, "my wife and daughter were checking out books at the Harlow Public Library. It was a Wednesday, a rainy spring afternoon just after school had let out for the day. My wife was thirty-four years old. We had learned only a week earlier that she was pregnant with our second child. Her name was Loretta, and we had been married for nine years. She taught Sunday school. Elaine, my little girl, was seven. A first-grader. She loved to read and draw pictures of rainbows and trees that looked like lollipops and people with big smiles on their faces. She was planning to try out for Little League when she was old enough. She had a pet hamster named Bobo. She was afraid of frogs. We were planning to go to Disney World in June, right after school got out. We already had our airplane tickets."

Bailey paused and cleared his throat into the microphone. The sound of it echoed in the room. Many of the SAFE members from the audience had left after Wally's testimony. Those who remained were silent, listening.

"I learned afterward that the librarian who was at the desk that day had, a week earlier, gone to court for a restraining order on her husband. He beat her and she was afraid of him. Just at the time when my little Elaine was checking out her books at the desk, the librarian's husband appeared. He was, apparently, very drunk and very angry. He had in his hand an Avtomat Kalashnikov semiautomatic rifle. An AK-47. He held it at his hip and began shooting. I don't know what the magazine of an AK-47 holds. But he emptied it in the library. He killed his wife and he killed Elaine and he killed Loretta and he killed our unborn child, and then he went outside and climbed into his pickup truck and drove down to the river and killed himself."

Bailey stopped, met the eyes of each of the subcommittee members in turn. "Senators," he said, "I suppose that man might have murdered his wife with a knife or a clothesline or a conventional firearm. Perhaps no legislation could have prevented that. But this man owned an AK-47. He kept it behind the seat in his truck. It was available to him any time he wanted to use it. As a result Loretta Bailey, aged thirty-four, and Elaine Bailey, aged seven, and her unborn sibling are senselessly dead, and my life is worse than death. It shouldn't have happened. I don't want to hear that it's the price we must pay for liberty. Nobody construes the Constitution to permit such things. I know the Second Amendment For Ever people and the NRA would have you believe that. But they are wrong. I know their votes and their money have defeated legislation such as this one in the past. That's why Loretta and Elaine died. Senators, please. The job of the government is to protect its citizens. To ensure domestic tranquillity. And don't pretend that the certainty of severe punishment would have deterred this man from bringing his AK-47 into that library. It's very clear that if he did not have that weapon handy in his truck at the time when he got drunk and his fury at his wife took control of him, Loretta and Elaine Bailey and another Bailey child would be alive today. This legislation you are considering could save the life of a pregnant woman or an innocent child who only wants to check a Curious George story out of the library. If it saves one life, it's good legislation. I urge you—I beseech you—to support it."

Wilson Bailey slumped back in his chair. The room was silent. Even the SAFE members in the audience were obviously moved by the man's story. For a long moment, nobody spoke.

Then the chairman cleared his throat and said, "Uh, thank you, sir, for your testimony." He glanced at the other committee members. "Any questions?"

They all shook their heads.

"Well, if you have a copy of your statement, Mr. Bailey, please leave it with me."

"I have no statement, Mr. Chairman," he said. "It's my story, and I don't need to write it down. But with your permission, I'd like to leave a photograph of Loretta and Elaine Bailey with you."

Bailey stood up, handed a photograph to the chairman, and left through the door that Wally had taken. I edged out into the aisle and followed behind him.

The corridor outside the hearing room was a chaos of shouting voices, elbowing bodies, and flashing cameras. It took me a moment to realize that Wally stood at the center of it. I wedged my way among the bodies until I was close to him. He was speaking with several reporters.

". . . not a constitutional lawyer," he was saying. "I don't pretend to know what the Founding Fathers had in mind."

"But aren't you afraid," said a female reporter, "that by disagreeing with the NRA you will alienate your allies?"

"I'm afraid of plenty of things, miss," said Wally. "But that's not one of them. The NRA holds the Second Amendment sacred. I guess right now I'd just refer you to the amendment that comes right before it, which is also a pretty good one. I have an opinion, and I stated it, and thank God we live in a country where a man can do that."

"The Second Amendment For Ever organization invited you here, is that correct?" asked a different reporter.

"SAFE arranged for me to testify, yes."

"Did they know what you were going to say?"

"I say what I believe. Nobody tells me what to say."

"But did they understand that you would testify in favor of this bill?"

Wally smiled at the reporter. "Don't be silly," he said.

Another reporter wedged forward. "Mr. Kinnick, are you concerned that your television show will lose its supporters because of your testimony today?"

Wally shrugged. "No. I don't worry about things like that."

"Do you intend to campaign for gun-control legislation?"

"I testified today in favor of this one particular bill. If I learn of other pieces of legislation that I have an opinion about, and if I am given the opportunity to testify, I will. On gun control or any other issue. It's what they call democracy."

Wally glanced in my direction. "Ah, Brady," he said. "Let's get out of here." To the reporters he said, "That's all, folks. I've got an appointment with my lawyer."

The reporters all began to yell at once.

"Wait."

"Mr. Kinnick, one more question."

"But, Walt, what about—"

But Wally had shouldered his way past them. I caught up with him, and we moved quickly down the corridor and up the stairs. Several of the reporters were following behind us, shouting questions. Wally didn't stop, and neither did I, until we reached the top of the steps outside the building.

Down at the foot of the wide stairway, the animal people were still marching with their signs. Wally leaned back against a pillar and looked down at them. "Jesus," he mumbled.

Three or four reporters came puffing up to us. Wally straightened up and turned to face them. "Okay, you guys. Enough. Give me a break."

"Just one more—"

"No more questions," he said.

The reporters backed off but remained there, as if they were waiting for something else to happen.

I fished out a cigarette and lit it. "Quite a performance," I said to Wally.

"Nah," he said, shaking his head. "It wasn't any performance."

"You shocked the hell out of them."

"I guess I shocked the hell out of me, too." He smiled wryly at me.

"Those SAFE guys are kinda pissed."

Wally nodded. "Guess I don't blame them. But if they think I was being frivolous, they're dead wrong. It would've been a helluva lot easier to say what everybody expected me to say, believe me." He shrugged. "I was awake most of the night, thinking about it. I came to Boston intending to speak against this bill. I still don't like gun control. I've testified on the issue plenty of times. I've never supported any kind of gun control before. I believe that weapons are neutral, and you've got to deal with the people who misuse them. That's the NRA line, the SAFE line, and in general I buy it. I just think that if we're going to have any credibility in this climate of opinion today, we've got to show that we're reasonable and thoughtful, that we're willing to compromise a little. This bill won't hurt anybody. Probably won't help anybody, either. We can give on this one without really giving anything away. I figure just maybe I can crack the stereotype. You know, that gun owners and hunters are all single-minded idiots, or reactionary fascists, or sadistic murderers, or even just irresponsible citizens. Give 'em something to think about. Can't hurt." He touched my shoulder and smiled. "Sorry. Guess this thing's got me a little wound up."

I shrugged. "It was great theater."

"It wasn't supposed to be theater, Brady. I just keep struggling with the fact that I've gotta go on living with myself."

"I was proud of you."

"You ain't got much company today."

"You ready to get going?" I said.

He gazed down again at the animal demonstrators, who were still chanting, "Kinnick's a killer." He nodded. "In a minute. They sound like they're running out of steam."

So we stood there. I smoked and Wally rested his back against the brick pillar, and the reporters eyed us, and the people in animal costumes marched and chanted at the foot of the stairway.

I had just taken the last drag on my cigarette when Wilson Bailey emerged from the building. He blinked in the May sunshine. The reporters, who had missed his testimony in order to quiz Wally, ignored him. Bailey spotted Wally and came up to him. He held out his hand. "Mr. Kinnick," he said. "I'm Wilson Bailey. I testified right after you."

Wally shook his hand. "Good to meet you," he said without enthusiasm.

A couple of reporters, I noticed, were edging closer. One of them snapped a photo of Wally and Bailey shaking hands.

"We were on the same side," said Bailey. "I liked what you said."

Wally shrugged. "Thanks."

Bailey's head bobbed up and down with his enthusiasm. "Well, sir, it was great, and I thank you." He turned to the reporters. "Did you folks hear my testimony?" he said to them.

They stared at him and shrugged.

"Please," said Bailey. He fumbled in his jacket pocket and came up with a sheaf of photographs. "My wife and daughter. I'd like you to know what I had to say today."

He handed out the photos. The reporters closed around him.

"Good chance to get out of here," mumbled Wally.

"That man had quite a story to tell," I said. "His wife and daughter were killed by an AK-47."

"They were killed by a person," said Wally.

I shrugged. "I stand corrected."

We were halfway down the steps when a voice called, "Hey, Kinnick! Wait!"

We stopped and turned around. Gene McNiff was hurrying toward us. His eyes blazed and his mouth was an angry slash across his red face.

"Who the fuck do you think you are?" he snarled at Wally.

"A United States citizen, I guess," said Wally mildly.

"I arrange this whole thing," growled McNiff, "agree to take care of your expenses, and you—you fucking betray me. You killed us in there. I hope you know that every member of the NRA in the country will hear about this. You're dead meat, Kinnick. Trust me."

"Don't worry about the expense money, Gene," said Wally with a smile. "I appreciate all you've done."

"Well, I ain't done with you," said McNiff.

Wally touched my elbow. "Come on, Brady. Let's go get some coffee."

We started down the stairs. Behind us, McNiff yelled, "This ain't the end of it, Kinnick."

"He's going to be in trouble for bringing me here," said Wally. "That's what he's upset about."

"I don't blame him."

"Me, neither." He shrugged. "Tough."

The demonstrators spotted us. "There he is," several of them shouted, and they all turned to look at us.

"Excuse us," said Wally. "Come on, now, folks. Some of us have things to do today. Let us through." We moved directly toward them, and they parted to let us pass. They mumbled slogans at us, but they seemed to have lost their energy, or their enthusiasm, for it.

"That," I told him after we had crossed Beacon Street, "was quite a morning. In one fell swoop you made enemies of both the animal rights crowd and the NRA."

"Well," he said, "if you're still my friend, I'm happy. I could use a cup of coffee."

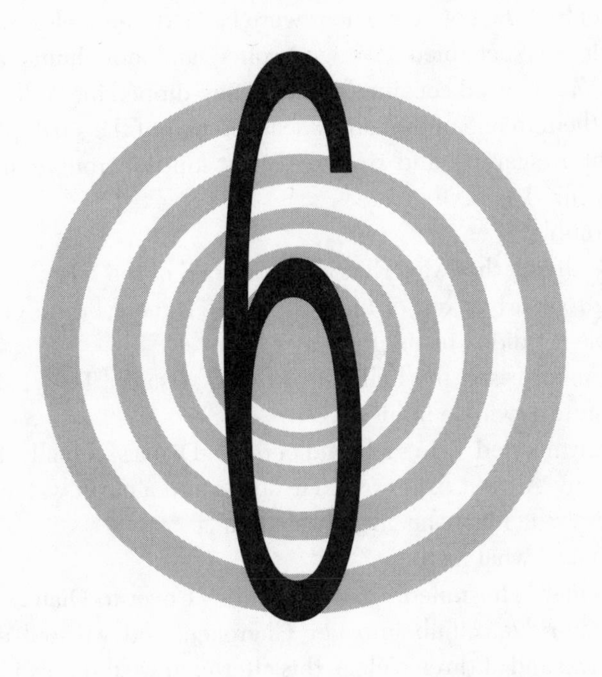


"Well," I said, "we can go down to Charles Street or cut over to Newbury. Plenty of little European-type cafés where we can get a cup of raspberry-chocolate–flavored coffee and a croissant."

"Or?"

"The Parker House in the other direction. Best coffee in town."

"Or?"

"Well, there's a Dunkin' Donuts right over there on Tremont Street."

"Dunkin' for me," said Wally.

I smiled. "Somehow I knew you'd say that."

We strolled down Park Street to Tremont, crossed over, and

went into the Dunkin' Donuts. Five or six people were perched on stools at the counter. There were half a dozen tables, none of which was occupied. We got coffee and doughnuts at the counter—toasted coconut for me, honey-dipped for Wally—and took them to one of the tables near the rear of the small place.

I lit a cigarette and sipped. "What kind of trouble are you really in?" I said.

"Trouble?"

"Testifying that way. Everybody's afraid of the NRA."

He took a bite out of his doughnut. "I guess I'd be in more trouble if I didn't testify the way I believed."

"You surprised the hell out of them," I said. "The chairman had quite a twinkle in his eye."

Wally nodded. "He's a friend of mine. Diana's, actually. Pretty good guy. A trout fisherman. He sponsored a clean water bill a year or so ago that she got involved in."

"So now what happens?"

"To me?" He smiled. "Now I take the T over to Diana's place in Cambridge, climb into her Cherokee, and we tool out to Fenwick, and at three o'clock this afternoon we'll be casting dry flies on the Deerfield River. And you'll join us later, huh?"

"I can probably break away Thursday."

"You'll make it a long weekend, at least, I hope. It should be—" Wally stopped, glanced over my shoulder to the front of the shop, and said, "Oh, oh."

I turned around. Three men had entered. They stood inside the doorway. They were staring in our direction.

"Friends of yours?" I said to Wally.

"SAFE boys. I remember the fat one."

I watched them as they sidled up to the counter. They gave their order, then turned to stare at me and Wally. One of them was, indeed, fat, although he was also tall, an over-the-hill offensive tackle with a pockmarked face and a pale untrimmed beard. The second man was equally tall, rail-thin, with bushy black eyebrows and dark hair clipped to a buzz. Right out of *Deliverance*. Both of them appeared to be in their late thirties. The third man was younger, twenty or so. He wore a ponytail and an earring. His cheeks were pink.

All three of them wore blue jeans and flannel shirts. The SAFE uniform.

They paid for their coffee and headed our way. "Don't say anything," whispered Wally.

They came directly to our table. The fat guy slammed against it with his hip. Wally's coffee mug tipped and spilled.

"Oh, sir, I'm terribly sorry," said the fat man, his voice dripping with mock politeness. "Please, let me help you."

He grabbed a napkin and began to smack Wally's chest with it. Wally grabbed both of the man's wrists and held them immobile. He smiled mildly up into the fat guy's face. "Thanks, anyway," he said quietly. "Apology accepted. I'm fine."

The fat man wrenched his hands free and stood there dangling his arms and glaring down at Wally.

The dark-haired man stepped forward. He put his coffee mug in front of Wally. "Here, sir. Take mine." Then he hit it with the back of his hand so that its entire contents spilled onto the table and flowed into Wally's lap. "Oh, how careless of me," said the dark guy.

I found my fists clenched. I started to stand up, but Wally frowned at me. I sat down.

"Take it easy, boys," he said quietly. "You've made your point."

"Fuckin' traitor," said the young guy. "Who the fuck do you think you are?"

"I *know* who I am," said Wally.

The kid grabbed a handful of Wally's jacket. "You better watch your ass," he said.

"And you better let go," said Wally softly.

The kid yanked at Wally's jacket and the next thing I knew he was staggering backward holding his stomach. He ended up sitting on the floor gasping for air.

Then Wally stood up and so did I. The other two, the fat guy and the dark-haired guy, held their ground. Their arms hung at their sides as if they were gunfighters ready to draw. Their eyes were narrowed and their mouths worked soundlessly at finding words to express their feelings.

"Does Gene McNiff know you're here?" said Wally to them.

"McNiff's an asshole," mumbled the fat man.

"Hasta be, bringing you here," said the other one.

"You want to start a brawl in a public place, it's not going to help your cause any," Wally said. "Why don't you boys go home and think about it?"

"You get the message?" said the dark guy.

"I would infer that you aren't happy."

"'I would infer,'" mimicked the fat guy. "Fuckin' big shot."

"Your ass is grass, man," said the other one.

The young guy had regained his breath. He got to his feet. "I want a piece of him," he said.

The fat guy put his hand on his shoulder. "Not now, Dougie." He turned to me. "You, too, Mr. Lawyer. We know you."

I dipped my head. "My pleasure."

By now the waitress had come out from behind the counter. She was young and pretty in her soiled white uniform. "I've called the police," she said.

"Shit," said the fat guy. "Let's get out of here."

He turned and walked away. The other two followed behind him. The young guy, Dougie, turned at the doorway. "This ain't done with," he said. Then they all left.

The waitress smiled at us. "Are you all right?"

"No problem," said Wally. "Little misunderstanding."

"Let me get you more coffee."

"Thank you."

She went back behind the counter. Wally and I sat down. She returned a moment later with two cups of coffee and a big wad of napkins. "I probably *should've* called the police," she said.

Wally was dabbing at the coffee stains on the front of his shirt and pants. He grinned at her. "You didn't?"

She shook her head. "You looked like you could handle it."

Wally touched her arm. "You did just right. Thanks."

She shrugged. "Stuff like this happens here now and then. We're open late. Guys come in, drunk, mad at the world. I can get a cop in about thirty seconds if I need one." She gestured at the coffee. "This is on the house."

She went back to the counter. Wally sipped his coffee. I lit a cigarette. "You handled yourself rather well," I said. "I'm glad you were here."

"Hell," he said, "if I hadn't been here you wouldn't have had a problem."

"Good point."

At that moment a woman appeared at our table. "Alex Shaw, Boston *Globe*," she said. "I saw what just happened. Can we talk?"

Wally glanced at me, then said to the woman, "My friend and I are just having a quiet cup of coffee, miss."

"It didn't look that quiet to me."

"There's no story," said Wally. "Just a misunderstanding among friends."

Alex Shaw pulled out a chair, sat down, and hitched it up to our table. Her reddish-brown hair was cut chin length, and it framed her face like a pair of parentheses. She wore big round eyeglasses, which kept slipping down her nose. "I know better," she said, poking at her glasses. "You're Walt Kinnick, and I just heard you testify, and those three guys are members of SAFE and they threatened you. They believe you betrayed them."

Wally didn't say anything.

"I followed you here," she persisted, "hoping for an interview."

"An interview," said Wally. He turned to me. "She followed us here, Brady." To her he said. "This is Mr. Brady Coyne. He's my lawyer. He advises me on things. Brady," he said, turning to me again, "I thought back there after the hearing I told all of those journalists I didn't want to answer any questions."

"That you did," I said.

"And just now I think I said that there was no story."

"You are correct, sir," I said in my best Ed McMahon imitation.

"Implying, I thought, that I just wanted to sit here and relax and sip this delicious coffee with you in privacy."

"As a lawyer," I said, "I would interpret it precisely that way."

"Because I said all I have to say at the hearing."

"You said it concisely and clearly," I said.

"And I have a certain mistrust of journalists."

"Not without reason, sir," I said.

"Journalism," said Wally, "being nothing more than the ability to meet the challenge of filling space."

"As Rebecca West so shrewdly observed," I said. "Journalism also being the profession that justifies its own existence by the great Darwinian principle of the survival of the vulgarest."

"Oscar Wilde," said Alex Shaw, who was grinning. "Are you guys having fun?"

"My lawyer advises me to refrain from comment on my statement at the hearing," said Wally.

"What about what just happened here?"

Wally glanced at me, then said, "Nothing happened here, Miz Shaw."

"Looked to me like you were both victims of an assault. I heard what they said to you. They threatened you. Do you take their threats seriously? I mean, these are guys who love guns. Are you frightened?"

Wally caught my eye and gave me a small headshake. Neither of us said anything.

"I'd like to hear your side of the story," she persisted.

"If you heard my testimony, you got it all," said Wally.

"I mean on what just happened here."

"Nothing happened," said Wally.

"It was pretty obvious where they were coming from."

Wally shrugged. "We'd just like to drink our coffee, if you don't mind."

She stood up. "Okay. Maybe you'll give me an interview this afternoon?"

"Sorry. I'm leaving momentarily. After I drink my coffee."

She turned to me. "Mr. Coyne, how about you?"

I shook my head. "I've got to get to the office."

She nodded. "Too bad. Guess I'll have to do the best I can with the story without your input."

"Fill up that space," said Wally.

She stood there for a moment, frowned at Wally, then peered at me through her big glasses. "Lawyers," she said, "are the only persons in whom ignorance of the law is not punished."

"Jeremy Bentham?" I said.

"You are correct, sir," she said, and hers wasn't a bad Ed McMahon imitation, either. She grinned wickedly, then turned and left.

We watched her go. She was wearing a short narrow skirt, and Wally said, "Admirable legs, Coyne."

"Jesus, Wally. You can't say things like that."

"Why not? It's true."

"Doesn't matter. It's offensive."

"Oh," said Wally, touching his fingertips daintily to his mouth. "How insensitive of me. I've offended you."

"Not me, asshole."

"Who, then?"

"The vast majority of women who don't happen to have admirable legs, I guess. You're supposed to admire their brains."

"Oh, sure. How porcine of me."

I smiled. "Well, you're right about her legs, of course."

"That one has admirable brains, too, I suspect."

"Dangerous combination," I said, "admirable legs *and* brains."

He nodded, sipped his coffee, then sighed. "I really don't need this kind of publicity, Brady. I can see it. WALT KINNICK IN COFFEE SHOP BRAWL. Or KINNICK ASSAULTS SAFE MEMBER."

"Maybe you should've given her an interview," I said.

He shrugged. "I just want to go fishing."

# 7

Wally wrote out the telephone number and sketched a map to his cabin in Fenwick on a Dunkin' Donuts napkin. It looked complicated. Fenwick was way out in the northwest corner of the state. Numbered highway to paved road to gravel road to a maze of dirt roads. The cabin was up in the hills at the end of a pair of ruts. Significant landmarks along the route included a wooden bridge, a lightning-struck oak tree, a stone wall, and a spring-fed brook.

I told him I'd get there sometime Thursday morning. He said he and Diana would be expecting me. He told me that the Fife Brook Dam usually drops the water around two in the afternoon that time of year, and that's when the fishing gets good. So I should be sure to get there by noon to give us time to have some lunch and get geared up. It would be about a three-hour drive from Boston.

We finished our coffee. Wally left a five-dollar tip on the table, which was more than we'd paid for our coffee and doughnuts. Then we walked out onto Tremont Street.

We shook hands outside the Park Street T station. Wally descended into the underground and I set off down Beacon Street. I cut across to Newbury at Clarendon so I could peek into the shop windows and art gallerys along the way, and it was a few minutes before noon when I walked into my office.

Julie was hunched over a stack of papers. She glanced up at me, said, "Hi," and returned her attention to the papers.

"Hi, yourself," I said. I frowned at her. "You're not mad?"

"Mad?"

"Having to handle everything yourself this morning? Not having the exquisite pleasure of my company?"

"Hey, it's your office, you're the lawyer." She sat up and arched her back. "I'm just the secretary. You pay me a salary. I make my money whether you're here or not. What do I care that Mrs. Mudgett is looking for a new attorney to handle her divorce, that Mr. Carstairs of the ABA called long distance the way you told him to, or—"

"Oh, shit," I said. "I forgot about Carstairs."

"—or Mr. McDevitt canceled your lunch plans. What do I care? I did my job."

"I had to meet with Wally Kinnick. I told you that. He was testifying at the State House."

"What's the case?"

"There's this bill on assault weapons, and—"

"What's our case, I mean?"

I shrugged. "There's no case. He just wanted his lawyer there."

"Moral support, huh?"

"Well, legal support, too, you might say."

Julie sniffed. "Well," she said, "you better get back to

Carstairs, and you better try to soothe Mrs. Mudgett's savage breast. She wants legal support, too, you know. And I know you'll call Mr. McDevitt."

I snapped her a salute and went into my office, where I lit a cigarette and called Phil Carstairs. He wanted me to give a speech in Houston. I declined. Charlie McDevitt was at lunch, so I flirted with Shirley, his grandmotherly secretary, for a few minutes. Then I called Mrs. Mudgett, managed to appease her, and rescheduled.

I persuaded Julie to hang out the Gone Fishin' sign and sweet-talked her out of the office. We headed for Marie's in Kenmore Square. It was lunchtime already. We had both put in a hard morning.

I stayed at the office until nearly seven that evening, in an abortive effort to convince myself that I was a responsible and hard-driving attorney. I stopped for a burger and beer at Skeeter's on the way home, watched a little of the Monday night baseball game with my coffee, and it was after nine when I got back to my apartment.

The red light on my answering machine was winking at me. I pressed the replay button as I wrenched off my necktie. The machine whirred, clicked, and then Wally's voice said, "Hey, Brady. It's Wally, up here in Fenwick. Give me a call." He left his number.

I went into the bedroom and shucked off my office clothes. I pulled on my apartment sweat pants and T-shirt, lay down on my bed, and dialed Wally's number. It rang three times, and then his answering-machine voice said, "Sorry. I guess I'm not here. Leave your number and I'll get back to you."

I waited for the beep, then said, "It's Brady, returning your call. I'm home. I hope everything's—"

There was a click, and then a woman's cautious voice said, "Hello? Brady?"

"Yes, hi."

"Hang on for a sec. Let me turn off the machine. There.

Sorry. Walter's been letting the machine take his calls."

"Anything wrong?"

"I'll let him tell you," she said. "But listen. Walter says you're going to come out and do some fishing with us."

"I'd like to, if the invitation still stands."

"Oh, absolutely. We'd both love it. I'm looking forward to meeting you. The fishing's been lovely. Listen, I'll put him on."

A moment later Wally said, "Nice little caddis hatch this afternoon, Coyne. We had a couple hours of glorious dry-fly fishing. You missed it."

"I don't need that from you," I said. "What's this about not answering your phone?"

I heard him blow out a big breath. "Those boys don't waste any time."

"Who? SAFE?"

"You got it. Kinnick's betrayed the cause, and they're threatening to boycott our sponsors. The producers are getting jumpy. My damn phone's been ringing off the hook."

"So what're you going to do?"

"Do? Shit. I'm going to let my machine answer the phone while I go fishing, that's what. You expect me to retract?"

"No," I said. "I certainly wouldn't expect that. But what's going to happen?"

"Oh, it'll die down. I'm not worried. Pain in the ass, that's all."

"Is that why you called?"

"Nah. I don't need a lawyer for this. I just called to tell you about the fishing. You are coming, aren't you?"

"If you still want me to."

"We both do."

"Thursday, then."

I beat Julie to the office on Tuesday morning, and when she walked in at precisely nine o'clock, as she always did, the coffee was ready. I poured a mugful for her and took it to her desk. She reached into her big shoulder bag and pulled out a newspaper. "Did you see this?" she said, waving it at me.

"Nope."

She opened it onto her desk. "Take a look."

A small headline at the bottom left of the front page read, ASSAULT WEAPON BILL HEARD BY SENATE SUBCOMMITTEE.

A box in the middle of the text read, "News Analysis, p. 6."

I skimmed the front-page article. It summarized the intent of the bill and highlighted the testimony of some of the witnesses. It continued on page six. I opened the paper to that page. There was a photograph of the animal rights protestors. Their signs were clearly legible, and in their Bambi and Smokey and Bugs Bunny costumes they looked silly. The State House loomed in the background. The caption read, "Animal Rights Groups Picket Senate Appearance of Walt Kinnick."

Another photograph, this one smaller, showed Walt shaking hands with Wilson Bailey, the poor guy from Harlow whose wife and child had been killed in the library. I was standing there behind Wally's shoulder. The caption read, "Walt Kinnick Congratulated by Admirer After Assault-Weapon Testimony."

An article entitled "Assault Weapons Explosive Issue—News Analysis" began on that page. Its author was Alexandria Shaw, the reporter who had witnessed the confrontation in Dunkin' Donuts.

> Emotions ran high as the Senate Subcommittee on Public Safety heard testimony on S-162, a bill which will, if passed, severely restrict the ownership and distribution of certain paramilitary guns labeled "assault weapons" in the Commonwealth.
>
> Assault weapons are defined in the bill as all semiautomatic rifles and shotguns with large magazines (a semiautomatic weapon fires a shot as fast as the trigger can be pulled). The Uzi and the AK-47 are among the twelve weapons specifically designated for control in the bill.
>
> Representatives of the Police Chiefs Association of Massachusetts testified in favor of the legislation, citing the danger to policemen from criminals armed with the semiautomatic weapons.
>
> Second Amendment For Ever (SAFE), a branch of

the National Rifle Association (NRA) and staunch opponents of all forms of gun control, presented testimony citing the Second Amendment (the right to bear arms) and argued that stiffer penalties, not gun control, are the appropriate remedy for assault-weapon–related crimes.

Perhaps most controversial of all was the testimony of Walt Kinnick, the popular host of the ESPN television series "Walt Kinnick's Outdoors." Kinnick has been an outspoken advocate of outdoor sports, including hunting. Kinnick testified in favor of the regulation of assault weapons, surprising both the subcommittee and the observers in the hearing room, who were predominantly members of SAFE.

It is believed that Kinnick's appearance before the subcommittee was arranged by SAFE. It is certain that the nature of his testimony took the pro-gun organization by surprise.

Gene McNiff, president and executive director of SAFE, refused to comment on Kinnick's testimony.

"It surprised me, I admit it," said Senator Marlon Swift (R–Marshfield), the chairman of the subcommittee. "Coming from someone like Walt Kinnick, it's really something to think about."

Angry words were exchanged between Kinnick and McNiff outside the State House. Later, Kinnick and his attorney, Brady L. Coyne of Boston, were accosted by SAFE members in the Dunkin' Donuts on Tremont Street. Neither Kinnick nor Coyne would comment on the incident.

It is clear that the Massachusetts gun lobby, which has generally had its way with the legislature in recent years, was dealt a severe blow this morning by Walt Kinnick's unexpected testimony. The Subcommittee on Public Safety is expected to report on S-162 by the end of the month.

I looked up at Julie. She was grinning. "You're famous," she said. "Nice picture, too."

I shrugged. "I didn't realize it was such a big deal."

"Check the editorial," she said.

I leafed through the paper and found the page. The lead editorial was titled, "Time to Get Tough on Guns." It read:

> The Second Amendment For Ever supporters have had it their way too long. Stubborn, single-minded, hopelessly out of touch with prevailing opinion, SAFE has opposed any and all efforts to regulate the ownership and distribution of guns, including paramilitary assault weapons, in the six New England states.
>
> Backed by powerful allies and a well-stocked war chest, SAFE has intimidated advocates of even the most modest efforts to control gun-related crime. Legislators have bowed and scraped before the SAFE bombast. Time after time we have seen gun-control legislation die in subcommittee, shot down by the high-caliber SAFE arsenal.
>
> Yesterday, the courageous testimony of Walt Kinnick punctured the SAFE bubble, and it will never be the same again. The nation's most famous hunter, and himself a gun owner, Kinnick issued an appeal that rings true to all who would listen.
>
> Very simply, the time has come for hunters and gun owners to be reasonable, Kinnick told the subcommittee. We agree.
>
> We don't argue with the right of sportsmen to possess their shotguns and hunting rifles. But assault weapons have only one function: to kill people. They do not belong in the hands of private citizens. It's time for SAFE to join the rest of us at the brink of the twenty-first century. SAFE must take to heart the testimony of its most respected spokesman, Walt Kinnick. Be reasonable, compromise, or cease to exist.

For someone who just wanted to get away and do some quiet trout fishing, Wally had made quite a splash. If Gene McNiff had been upset after the hearing, I wondered how he felt now.

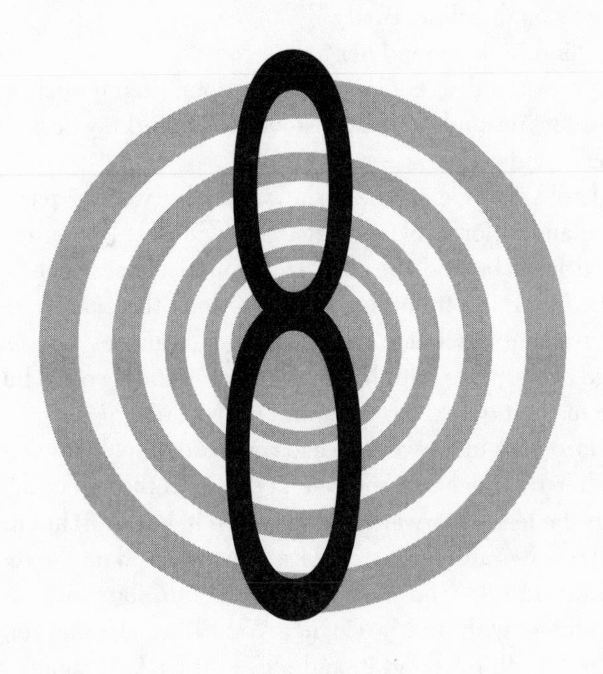

I spent most of Tuesday morning on the telephone, and Julie and I had chicken salad sandwiches at my desk for lunch. Sometime in the middle of the afternoon, while I was trying to outline the article I had promised Phil Carstairs out of my guilt for refusing to make a speech to the ABA in Houston, my intercom buzzed. I picked up the phone and said, "Yeah?"

"Brady," said Julie, "there's a Miz Shaw here to see you."

"Who?"

"She's a reporter for the *Globe*."

Julie wanted me to talk to her. Otherwise she wouldn't have buzzed me. I generally do what Julie wants.

"I'm right in the middle of something," I told her. "Why

don't you give her an appointment?"

"She's on deadline, Brady."

I sighed. "Okay. Send her in."

There was a discreet knock on my door, then it opened. Julie held it for Alexandria Shaw. I stood up behind my desk. "Come on in," I said.

"Thanks for seeing me," she said. She wore a pale green blouse and tailored black pants. Her wide-set blue-green eyes peered from behind the oversized round glasses that perched crookedly on the tip of her nose. She took the chair beside my desk without invitation. She poked her glasses up onto the bridge of her nose with her forefinger. "I know you're busy. I'll try to make it quick. Do you mind if I record it?"

Before I could answer she had removed a small tape recorder from her shoulder bag and plunked it onto the top of my desk. When she leaned forward to fiddle with it, her short auburn hair fell like wings around her cheeks. She switched on the recorder and said into it, "Tuesday, May nineteenth, four forty-five P.M. I'm talking with Brady Coyne, Walt Kinnick's lawyer." She snapped it off, rewound it, and played it back. It sounded fine. She dug into her bag again and came up with a notebook and a pen. "Okay," she said, "a couple questions."

I held up both hands. "Hey, slow down," I said. "Do you want coffee or something?"

"I don't know about you," she said, "but I gotta get this story in by seven. Fill the space, you know? Survival of the vulgarest." She grinned quickly. "So if you don't mind, let's get to it."

I smiled. "I don't really have anything to say."

"About that incident at the Dunkin' Donuts yesterday—"

"No comment," I said quickly.

"Are you a member of SAFE?"

"Me?"

She grinned. "I guess that answers my question."

"Who cares, anyhow?"

"Hey," she said. "I gotta fill the space, remember?"

"Well," I said, "I am a member of the ABA and Trout Unlimited and the Sierra Club. But I don't belong to SAFE. Or the NRA. Or lots of other worthy organizations."

"You think they're worthy?"

"Who, SAFE?" I shrugged. "I don't know much about them."

"Do you sympathize with them?"

"Excuse me," I said, "but really. Who cares about me?"

"You're Walt Kinnick's lawyer."

I shrugged.

"Right?" she said.

"Yes."

"Are you defending him in any litigation?"

"Come on. No comment. You know better. Really."

"Did you advise him on his testimony yesterday?"

I smiled. "You obviously don't know Wally."

"You're his boyhood friend, right?"

She had done her homework. "Yes. We went to high school together."

"And you and he were threatened yesterday at Dunkin' Donuts."

I shook my head. "No comment, okay?"

She jabbed her finger at her eyeglasses. "Mr. Coyne," she said, "I don't know what your opinion is of SAFE, but there's a major story here and I want it."

"I already told you I don't know anything about SAFE."

"Sure you do. They're mobilizing against Walt Kinnick, did you know that?"

"What have you heard?"

"They've got the NRA working with them, and they're trying to mount a boycott against the sponsors of his show. They're investigating him. They've got lots of resources. Any skeletons, they'll find them. If they can discredit him, they will. Seems obvious, if you're his lawyer you're going to be involved in this."

Skeletons. Like the fact that Wally was shacking up with a woman who was still technically married. "How do you know these things?" I said to Alexandria Shaw.

She smiled. "It's my job."

"And if they find some of these—skeletons?"

She shrugged. "It's the job of the newspaper to print it. And," she added, glancing sharply up at me, "I assume it will be your job to protect him."

"So you want . . ."

"Balance," she said.

"Well, I just don't see how I can help you. I don't know about any skeletons in Walt Kinnick's closets, and if I did, I'd hardly tell you about them. As his friend, and especially as his lawyer, I am not the one to help you. I'm sorry. I shouldn't have seen you."

"I'm just trying to get the whole story, Mr. Coyne. SAFE has been very forthcoming with the media."

"Organizations can do that. It's trickier for individuals."

"When the individuals are public figures," she said, "like Walt Kinnick, they're fair game." She tilted her head and grinned at me. "Hunting metaphor, huh? Fair game?" She shrugged. "Now you're on their list. Walt Kinnick and you. If you're not for them, you're against them. A turncoat is the worst kind of enemy. Right? Those people are told how to think by their leadership, and that's how they've been instructed to think, so—"

"What do you mean, their list?"

"SAFE publishes a list of their so-called enemies in their newsletter. Prominent people who oppose their party line. The word is that you and Walt Kinnick will be high on their next list. How do you feel about that?"

"Flattered. Humble. Unworthy."

She smiled quickly. "Come on, Mr. Coyne. Any comment?"

I shrugged. "I appreciate the warning, Ms. Shaw."

"It wasn't a warning. Just some information that'll be in my story tomorrow. I wish you'd give me a hand with the rest of it."

"Sorry. I can't."

She stared at me for a moment, then nodded. She reached into her bag and came out with a business card. She put it onto my desk. "If you change your mind, hear anything else . . ."

"Right," I said. "Sure."

"Oh, one more thing."

"Yes?"

"How can I reach Walt Kinnick?"

I shook my head. "Sorry. Can't tell you. Privileged information."

She smiled. "Didn't think so." She snapped off the tape recorder and stuffed it into her bag. Her notebook followed it.

She stood up and held out her hand to me. "Thanks," she said.

Her grip was firm. She actually shook my hand. "I'm afraid I wasn't much help," I said.

"Everything helps," she said. "You'd be surprised."

I spent Wednesday doggedly trying to clear enough odds and ends off my desk to appease my conscience so that I wouldn't feel compelled to lug my briefcase to Fenwick. Julie, of course, would pack it up for me, as she did every day, and I'd dutifully take it home with me when I left the office. I'd prop it against the inside of the door to my apartment, the way I always did, so I wouldn't forget to take it back to the office with me.

But I wasn't going to bring the damn thing on my fishing trip. Briefcases and fly rods don't belong in the same car together.

So I skipped lunch and stayed at the office until nearly eight and felt wonderfully masochistic and virtuous. I was a man who had earned a few days of trout fishing.

That evening I assembled my gear, not an easy task since I found it scattered all around my apartment. My fly rods were in their aluminum tubes in the back of my bedroom closet. My waders lay rumpled in the corner of the living room. I found my reels on the bottom shelf of the linen closet. I discovered fly boxes on my desk, in the kitchen cabinet with the canned soup, in the drawer of my bedside table.

I nearly abandoned the search for my favorite fishing hat, the stained and faded Red Sox cap that my friend Eddie Donagan, the one-time Sox pitcher, had given me. It was studded with bedraggled flies, each of which had caught me a memorable fish, and I needed it for luck. I finally found it in the last place I expected—hanging on a hook in the front closet.

When I got all the stuff assembled, it looked as if I had enough equipment for a two-month African safari. When I got it packed in my car there certainly wouldn't be any room for a clunky old briefcase.

I showered, brushed my teeth, and climbed into bed. I started to turn off the light, then changed my mind. I picked up the phone on the bedside table and pecked out the familiar Wellesley number.

It rang five times before Gloria mumbled, "H'lo?"

"Sorry. You sleeping?"

"Oh. Brady. No."

"Busy?"

"Not really."

"I'm sorry. Didn't mean to interrupt anything."

"I said I wasn't busy."

"You said, 'Not really.'"

"That means no."

"Well, but you said, 'Not really.' What did you mean, 'Not really,' if you didn't mean you really were busy?"

"Brady, dammit, do you always have to cross-examine me? You don't have to play lawyer with me. If I was busy, I would've said I was busy. Okay?"

I sighed. "Okay."

I heard Gloria sigh, too. "Shit, anyway," she said.

"I'm sorry."

"Yeah. Fine."

"Everything okay?"

"Except for Perry Mason phone calls, fine."

"Well, good."

"That why you called? To find out if I was busy?"

"Well, no." I cleared my throat. "I'm going to be away for a few days. Thought you should know."

"Why?"

"Well, I've got a chance to go fishing with—"

"No. I mean, why did you think I should know?"

"Oh." I hesitated. "The truth is, I guess it feels better, thinking that there's someone who should know when I go somewhere. I mean, everybody should have somebody who knows when they're going away. Does that make any sense?"

"No," said Gloria. But I heard her chuckle. She knew me. She understood.

"Somebody who—cares," I said.

"I'm not stupid, you know," she said softly. "You're looking for someone to play wife for you."

"No, I just—"

"I'm not your wife, Brady. I was your wife. When I was your wife, it was appropriate, your telling me when you were going somewhere. Which you used to do a great deal, if you remember. I don't recall that you ever actually asked. You told me. Then you went."

"I asked," I said. "I always asked."

"Yeah. You'd say, 'I'm off to Canada with Charlie Saturday, remember?' Some question."

"I didn't—"

"Or you'd say, 'You don't mind if Doc Adams and I spend the weekend out on the Beaver River, do you?' Like that. Asking."

"It's the Beaverkill. Lovely trout river."

"Whatever." Gloria laughed softly. "Brady, if you want to tell me when you're going somewhere, that's fine. If you want me to be a telephone wife now and then, I can handle it. Go fishing. I don't care. Have fun. Don't fall in. Whatever you want out of it. Okay?"

I lit a cigarette. I took a deep drag, let it dribble out. "I don't know why I called," I said.

"Me neither," she said. "When Terri was on the scene you didn't call that much."

"I guess not."

"I'm not your girlfriend, you know."

"I know."

"So why are you calling me?"

"I don't know. I mean, family . . ."

"You made your choices, Brady."

"Billy's at school, Joey's in his own world. You . . ."

"I'm divorced. So are you. We're divorced from each other, as a matter of fact."

"I don't like the idea of being out of touch."

"That's the choice you made."

"Yeah."

"You can't have it both ways."

"I guess not."

"That was always your problem," she said. "Wanting it both ways."

"It was more complicated than that."

"Not really."

"Yeah," I said. "Maybe you're right."

"Look," she said. "If it'll make you feel better, leave a number with me."

"Just in case something . . ."

"Right," she said.

I read Wally's phone number to her.

She repeated it. "This is Walt Kinnick?" she said.

"Yes."

"I've been reading about him in the paper. You, too, actually."

"Yeah, well we're just going to do some fishing."

She hesitated a minute. "Are you okay?"

"Sure. Fine."

"I don't know," she said. "It sounds . . ."

"Nothing to worry about."

"I didn't say I was worried." She paused. "Maybe a little concerned."

"Yeah?"

"Um."

"Thanks," I said.

"Sure," said Gloria. "It's what we ex-wives are for."

"And that," I said, "is why every man needs one."

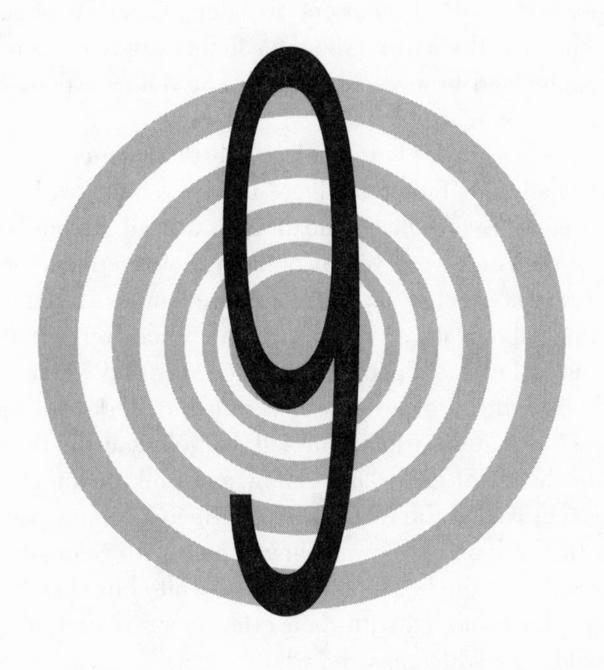

I was on the road a little before seven. I beat the westbound commuters onto Storrow Drive, angled onto Route 2 by the Alewife T station, and had clear sailing. Morning fog hovered over the swampy places alongside the highway. It would burn off by mid-morning. It promised to be a perfect May day in New England.

Sixty miles or so west of Boston Route 2 narrows from a divided superhighway to a twisting two-laner. Here it is called the Mohawk Trail. It dips and wiggles through towns like Erving, which prospers on its paper mill and its waste treatment plant, and Farley and Wendell Depot and Miller's Falls, which don't appear to prosper at all.

On an October Saturday, the Mohawk Trail is crammed with leaf peepers, most of them out-of-staters. Caravans of automobiles pull onto the narrow shoulder so that gaudy vistas of crimson maples and bronze oaks and bright yellow aspens can be recorded on Kodacolor.

It's pretty as hell. Photographs rarely do it justice.

Personally, I'd rather meditate upon a single scarlet maple leaf, preferably one that is floating on a trout stream past my waders, than on several billion of them all washed together over hillsides that stretch on for a hundred miles. I agree with Thoreau: All of Nature's mysteries are revealed on a single leaf.

Actually, I'm a leaf peeper myself in May, and when the trail began its acute northwest ascent into the Berkshire foothills west of Greenfield, I found myself marveling at the thousands of pale shades of green and yellow and pink in the new May leaves that walled the roadside and formed a canopy overhead. Even the bark on the new saplings rioted with color—the gold of the willows, the black of the alders, white birch, gray aspen. The maples exploded with their crimson springtime blossoms. The wild cherry blooms were white.

Nature's colors are more understated and subtle in May than they are in October. In May they're fresh, young, natural, full of vigor and confidence. October foliage is the desperate makeup of old age, trying too hard to recapture the beauty that has irreversibly passed.

May's my favorite month.

The fact that the best trout fishing New England offers comes in May could have something to do with it.

I pulled to the side of the road where it picked up the Deerfield River just west of Shelburne Falls. I consulted the map Wally had drawn for me on the back of the Dunkin' Donuts napkin. Nine miles past the old inn in Fenwick, according to Wally's sketch, an unmarked gravel road angled off the paved road to the right. The gravel road forked exactly two-point-two miles past a wooden bridge. The left fork followed the river. I was to go right. A lightning-struck oak tree stood at the point of the fork.

The right fork began as gravel but, after two hundred yards, turned to dirt. It twisted up into the hills. Wally had indicated several other roads branching off it. At exactly one-point-nine miles from the dead tree I was to follow the ruts to the left. A brook paralleled the wrong road. A stone wall and an old cellar hole marked the correct one. From there, a one-mile ascent would take me to Wally's cabin. That's where the road ended. Wally had drawn a picture of his place. Smoke twisted from its chimney.

I suspected Wally liked his cabin because no one could find it without one of his maps.

I found the unmarked gravel road. I recognized the fork by the dead oak. From there it got confusing. The road was narrow and rocky. The previous night's rain puddled in the ruts. What on Wally's map appeared to be small tributaries off a central roadway were, in fact, branches of equally untraveled dirt roads. It would've driven Robert Frost crazy. I drove slowly, glancing frequently at the Dunkin' Donuts napkin. Finally the ruts narrowed and brush began to scrape against both sides of my car.

I stopped. This felt wrong. I looked again at the map. It didn't help.

I stepped out and leaned against the side of my car. I didn't know where the hell I was. But, I decided, wherever it was, it was a perfectly fine place to be on a May morning. I was in the woods. All around me birds were whistling and cooing and flirting with each other. From somewhere above the canopy of new leaves came the squeal of a circling hawk. He was hunting, not flirting. A gray squirrel cussed me from the trunk of a beech tree. Off to my right I heard a brook burbling its way downhill over its boulder-strewn watercourse.

Maybe in one sense I was lost. But I knew exactly where I was.

The road was too narrow for turning the car around, so I had to back down to where it branched. I got out and walked up the left tine of the fork, where I found the stone wall and the cellar hole. According to Wally's map, I was no longer lost.

So I stood there and told myself what a cunning woodsman I was, and after a minute or two I noticed the smell of woodsmoke. I climbed into my car and chugged in second gear to Wally's cabin.

◎

It was made from weathered logs. A roofed porch spanned the entire front. Rocking chairs were strategically placed to encourage the loafer to prop his heels up on the railing and sip bourbon at sunset and watch the bats fly and the deer creep into the clearing. Big picture windows bracketed the front door. Smoke did indeed wisp from the chimney.

It was more than a cabin and less than a house. From the outside, it looked spacious and inviting.

I parked beside a mud-splattered black Cherokee, shut off the ignition, and stepped out. My BMW was mud-splattered, too.

Before I had taken two steps toward the cabin, a liver-and-white Springer spaniel came bounding to me. I scootched down to scratch his ears, and he rolled onto his side and squirmed and whined.

Suddenly there came a shrill whistle, the kind that basketball coaches make by jamming two fingers into the corners of their mouth. I never learned to whistle that way.

A woman's voice yelled, "Corky!"

Instantly the Springer scrambled to his feet, trotted back to the porch, and flopped down beside the woman who was standing there waving at me. Her blond hair was pulled back into a careless ponytail. She was wearing a white T-shirt and faded blue jeans and bare feet. She was slim and tall. She looked about sixteen. She was smiling at me.

"Hey, Brady," she called.

I waved back at her. "Diana. Hi."

I went to the porch. Up close, I saw that she was closer to thirty-six than sixteen. Tiny lines webbed the corners of her dark eyes and bracketed her mouth and lent character to her face. She looked even better up close.

The legend on her T-shirt read, "I FISH THEREFORE I AM."

She was holding out her hand. I took it. Her grip was firm. "You made it," she said.

"Only took one wrong turn."

"That's par. I hope you're ready to go fishing. Time for one cup of coffee. Let's get your stuff."

We headed back to my car. Corky scrambled up and heeled behind her.

"Where's Wally?"

She jerked her head backward in the direction of the cabin. "On the phone."

"Problems?"

"He doesn't seem particularly concerned. He'll be out in a minute."

We unloaded my stuff and lugged it to the cabin. As we stepped onto the porch the front door opened and Wally stood there. He grinned and held up one hand like an Indian. "Howdy."

"Hiya," I said.

He held the door for me and Diana. It opened into a brightly lighted space that encompassed the kitchen, dining area, and living room. A huge fieldstone fireplace took up the entire side wall. Brass-bottomed cookware and sprigs of dried herbs hung from the kitchen beams and framed wildlife prints hung on the raw cedar walls.

"You're in here," said Diana. She pushed open a door with her foot. It was a small bedroom. One queen-sized bed, a dresser, bedside table, chair. The single window looked out back into the woods. "Bathroom's through there," she added, indicating a doorway.

We dumped my stuff on the bed, then went back into the living room. Wally handed me a mug of coffee. "We oughta be on the river in an hour," he said. "Drink up."

"Let the poor man relax," said Diana.

"How can I relax?" I said. "I want to go fishing."

I sat on the sofa in front of the fireplace, where embers were burning down to ash. Wally sat beside me and Diana took a rocking chair. Corky flopped onto the bare wood floor beside her. She reached down absentmindedly to scratch his ears.

"Who was it this time?" she said.

Wally waved his hand dismissively. "One of the assistant producers."

"Is this serious?" I said.

He shrugged. "The word's gotten around. Kinnick has betrayed the cause. I guess SAFE's got the NRA boys calling the station from all over the country. But, shit, we've always had stuff like that. Today the NRA, tomorrow People for the Ethical Treatment of Animals or the congressman from New Jersey. I don't know, I just seem to piss people off. The producers complain and worry and create disastrous scenarios, but I think they actually kinda like it when I offend. Controversy. That's the ratings game, I guess. They like to say, bad reviews are one helluva lot better than no reviews. No, he was just wondering what I said in Boston that got the switchboard all lit up. I told him, just like I've been telling everyone else. He said it sounded okay to him."

"You seen a newspaper recently?" I said.

"Absolutely not. Newspapers are not allowed in this place. Or televisions, either. We get some ink?"

"The *Globe* thinks you're a hero."

"Sure. They would." He stretched elaborately. "Ready to go?"

I gulped the dregs of my coffee and stood up. "I'm ready."

"Me, too," said Diana. The instant she stood, Corky scrambled to his feet and scurried to the front door. He whined and pushed at it with his nose. "Okay, okay," she said to the dog. "You can come."

Corky turned and sat, resting his haunches back against the door. I'd have sworn that dog was smiling.

The four of us piled into Diana's Cherokee—she drove and Wally sat beside her in front, while Corky and I shared the backseat. After twenty minutes—and at least that many forks in the dirt roads—we pulled onto the grassy parking area on the banks of the Deerfield just downriver from the hydroelectric dam. Only one other car was there, a late model green Volvo wagon with Vermont plates and a Trout Unlimited sticker on the back window.

When I stepped out I could hear the river gurgling down in the gorge beyond the screen of trees. Here and there through the leaves I caught the glint of sunlight on water. I was familiar enough with the sounds of the Deerfield to know that the dam had reduced its flow and the water was running low. The sun was warm and mayflies and caddis flitted in the air—perfect fly-fishing conditions.

I glanced at the sign tacked onto a fat oak tree, identical to the signs that were spaced every fifty feet along the river.

In bold red letters, it read:

**WARNING**
**RISING WATERS**

Then, in more sedate black lettering:

**Be constantly alert for a quick**
**rise in the river. Water**
**upstream may be released**
**suddenly at any time.**
***New England Power Company***

I smiled to myself. On two occasions in the years I had fished the Deerfield I had failed to be "constantly alert." Twice I had been lifted from my feet and swept downstream on the crest of the rising water.

The first time it happened I was trying to make a long cast to a large trout. Charlie McDevitt fished me out.

The second time, two men with guns were chasing me and a boy named E. J. Donagan. That time a bullet grazed my buttock, and it was E.J. who saved me.

I had no desire to try it again.

Another sign on an adjacent tree, also one of many, read:

CATCH AND
RELEASE
AREA
ARTIFICIAL
LURES ONLY
NO FISH OR BAIT IN
POSSESSION

A guy from North Adams named Al Les had worked mightily to persuade the state to set aside these several miles of beautiful trout water for no-kill fishing. The trout here were bigger and more abundant than elsewhere in the river, the logical result of their being allowed to continue their lives after being caught by a fisherman. If your idea of good fishing did not require you to bring home trophies, this was the place.

More than fifty years ago Lee Wulff said, "A good gamefish is too valuable to be caught only once." Thanks to people like Wally Kinnick and Al Les, Wulff's wisdom has been gradually catching on, and those of us who love fishing for its own sake have been the beneficiaries.

The three of us pulled on our waders and rigged up our rods, while Corky sniffed the shrubbery and lifted his leg in the prime spots.

Wally was ready first. "I'm heading down," he said.

"We'll be right along," said Diana.

After Wally disappeared down the steep path, Diana smiled at me. "He's like a kid when he's going fishing. I love his passion for it."

"I knew him when he was a kid," I said. "Nice to see he hasn't changed."

She was tying a fly onto her leader tippet. She squinted at it, clamping the tip of her tongue in her teeth. She was, I thought, very beautiful in her floppy man's felt hat and bulging fishing vest and baggy chest-high waders.

We started down the path, me first, Diana behind me, and Corky at her heel. It was narrow and descended abruptly, so that I had to grip saplings to keep from slipping. Halfway down, I came upon Wally. He was crouched there in the pathway, peering through the trees down at the river.

Without turning around, he held up one hand and hissed, "Shh."

I stopped right behind him.

"Look," he whispered, pointing down at the river.

I peeked through the foliage. A fishermen was standing knee-deep in the water. His rod was bent. He was bringing a fish to his net. It looked like a large one.

"Hey," I said. "A good—"

"Shh!"

The angler had stepped directly out of the Orvis catalog. His vest was festooned with glittering fishing tools and gadgets, and his neoprene waders looked new and custom-fitted. His slender split-bamboo rod was bent in a graceful arc. He netted the fish and then knelt in the water to remove the fly from its jaw. He was turned away from me so that through the foliage I couldn't clearly see what he was doing.

Suddenly Wally muttered, "Bastard!"

"What?" I said.

"The son of a bitch killed the fish. He slipped it into the back of his vest."

"You sure?"

"Damn right I'm sure."

"But it's—"

"Of course. They're all supposed to be released. He's a fucking poacher."

We hunkered there in the path for another minute or two. Then Wally said, "Let's go."

We scrambled the rest of the way down the slope and found ourselves standing on the cobbled bank of the river where, in high water, we'd be up to our knees in surging currents. Big boulders along the edges were still wet from where, not too much earlier in the morning, they had been underwater.

The fisherman had resumed casting. Wally called, "Hey! How're they biting?"

The angler turned, hesitated, then smiled. "Oh, hi. They've just started to rise."

"Catch any?" said Wally.

He shrugged. "A couple."

Wally waded toward him. Diana and I followed along a few steps behind. Corky sat on the bank.

The fisherman stopped casting. He cocked his head, squinting at Wally. "Hey," he said. "I know you."

Wally smiled at him.

"Walt Kinnick, right? Damn! I watch your show all the time. I heard you had a place near here. Jesus, what a treat!"

He held out his hand to Wally, who took it.

"You know," said the guy, "I'm a real fan of yours. A couple years ago I drove all the way down from Brattleboro to hear you speak at the Boston Fly Casters club."

Wally nodded and said, "That's a nice-looking fly rod."

The angler grinned. "Neighbor of mine in Vermont custom made it for me. I love it. Guess I ought to. Cost me fourteen hundred bucks." He held it out to Wally. "Give it a try."

Wally handed his own rod back to Diana and took the man's split-bamboo fly rod. He examined the workmanship, nodding his approval. He waved it in the air a few times. "Sweet," he said. "I bet it casts like a dream." Wally glanced at the man. "Come here often?"

"Couple times a week. It's only an hour or so from home, and it's better than any of the rivers in my own state."

"It's been terrific since they made it catch and release, huh?"

The guy nodded.

"I hear," said Wally, "that sometimes guys'll sneak in with bait, catch a bunch and kill them. It's a shame that the wardens don't patrol it better." He waved the man's rod in the air, admiring its flex. "The way I figure it," he continued, "we've got to more or less patrol it for ourselves." Wally turned around to Diana and me and showed us the fly rod. "This is a beautiful piece of work, Brady," he said. "Damn shame that this guy doesn't deserve it."

The fisherman was frowning now. "Just a minute, there—" he said.

Wally turned back to him. "I saw you kill that trout," he said quietly.

"What—?"

"How long did it take the guy in Vermont to make this rod for you?"

The guy frowned. "Almost two years from the time I ordered it. But I—"

Wally gripped the rod with both hands. "It took five years to grow that trout you killed," he said softly.

"I don't know what you're talking about," the guy muttered.

Wally held the man's rod up at eye level and began to bend it.

"Hey—!"

It cracked halfway up the butt section. Wally twisted the two broken parts until the splintered halves separated. He handed the mangled rod back to the wide-eyed fisherman. "That's the price for killing that fish," he said.

The guy dumbly took his rod. He stared at it for a moment. Then he looked up at Wally. He was shaking his head slowly back and forth. "You broke my rod," he finally said.

Wally nodded.

"You *bastard*. You broke my rod. Who the *hell* do you think you are?"

Wally shrugged. "Try obeying the rules, friend," he said. He turned his back on the guy. To Diana and me he said, "Let's head upstream where the water's not polluted."

The three of us began to wade away. The man with the broken rod yelled, "God *damn* it, Kinnick. That's fourteen hundred bucks. I'll sue you, you son of a bitch."

"This is my lawyer," said Wally, gesturing to me. "Talk to him."

I turned to face the man. "Brady Coyne," I said, dipping my head cordially. "My number's in the Boston book."

The guy glared at me but said nothing.

We headed upstream. "That was a little extreme, don't you think?" I said.

Wally shrugged. "Bastard deserved it."

"It's obvious you're not interested in a lawyer's advice."

"Nope."

"You can't just run around breaking people's fly rods, for God's sake."

"I know," he said. "It's a terrible habit of mine."

Diana smiled. "Walter's a real diplomat. He makes enemies wherever he goes."

"Yeah, just what he needs," I said. "More enemies."

"Judge a man by his enemies," said Wally. "I'm going fishing."

He waded in and began casting. Downstream from where we stood, the fisherman with the broken fly rod was standing there knee-deep in the Deerfield River staring at us. As I watched, he trudged out of the water and disappeared up the path toward the parking lot.

Diana and I continued to pick our way upstream through the

calf-deep water over the slippery rocks. We hooked elbows with each other for our mutual balance. Corky followed along on the bank. "He's a very impetuous man," said Diana. "You must know that. It makes him lovable and impossible, all at the same time."

"It's actually kind of admirable, in an Old Testament sort of way."

"Yeah, but he scares me sometimes."

"We grew up together, you know," I said. "We used to fish and hunt when we were kids. We haunted a place on the other side of town we called the Swamp. Several hundred acres of forest and wetland. Full of game. Rabbits, squirrels, grouse, pheasants. We hunted every Saturday during the season and hardly ever managed to kill anything. A pretty little brook with native trout ran through it. Wally and I loved the Swamp. It was our playground. When the other kids were on the baseball diamond or the football field, Wally and I played in the Swamp. Anyway, we went there one April to fish and we began to find these surveyor's stakes in the ground. You know the kind, with orange paint on top and lot numbers written on them. Wally went absolutely berserk. Screaming and cussing at the top of his lungs. Started to race through the woods ripping up those stakes and heaving them as far as he could. I tried to tell him that he couldn't do things like that, but he paid no attention to me, and after a few minutes I got into the spirit of it myself. I think we ended up finding about fifty of those surveyor's stakes. We yanked every one of them out of the ground, and I've got to admit, it felt good." I shrugged. "Of course, it didn't do any good. Within a year the bulldozers were there, and a year after that they had that pretty little brook flowing through a concrete culvert and roads were cut through the woods and foundations were all poured and I guess there wasn't a grouse or a rabbit left."

Diana looked at me and smiled. "And he's been metaphorically ripping up surveyor's stakes ever since. He's managed to make a career of it."

"Like I said. It's admirable. Of course," I added, "as his lawyer, I'd advise against it. But he never consults me."

Diana and I picked out likely stretches of river to fish, and soon I was lost in the rhythms of fly casting. Little cream-colored caddis flies were dancing over the surface of the water, and here and there trout swirled and splashed at them. I had to change flies a few times before I found one that the fish liked. I missed a couple of strikes, and then I managed to hook one, a fat rainbow of about fourteen inches. He jumped clear of the water three or four times before I was able to bring him to my side. I slipped my hand down the leader and twisted the barbless hook from his mouth. He finned in the water beside my leg for a moment before he darted away.

The river bubbled musically. Birds chirped in the trees. The May sunshine warmed my arms and face. I caught a few trout. Now and then I heard Wally grunt or Diana squeal, and when I glanced at them, their rods were bent. After three or four hours—my sense of time completely deserts me when I'm fishing—the insects disappeared from the water and the trout stopped rising. I waded to the bank, sat on a boulder, and lit a cigarette. Corky bounded over and sat beside me. I scratched his ears.

A few minutes later Wally and Diana reeled in and came over to join me. They sat beside each other on a large flat rock. Diana tilted up her face and nuzzled Wally's beard. "How you doin', big guy?" she said softly.

He smiled quickly. "I'm still pissed."

"Some day you're going to break the wrong guy's rod, you know."

He shrugged. "If the guy's been killing fish illegally, it'll be the right rod."

"You know what I mean," she said.

He hugged her against his side and looked at me. "Remember the Swamp, Brady?"

I nodded. "I was telling Diana about those surveyor's stakes."

"I'm *still* pissed about that," he said.

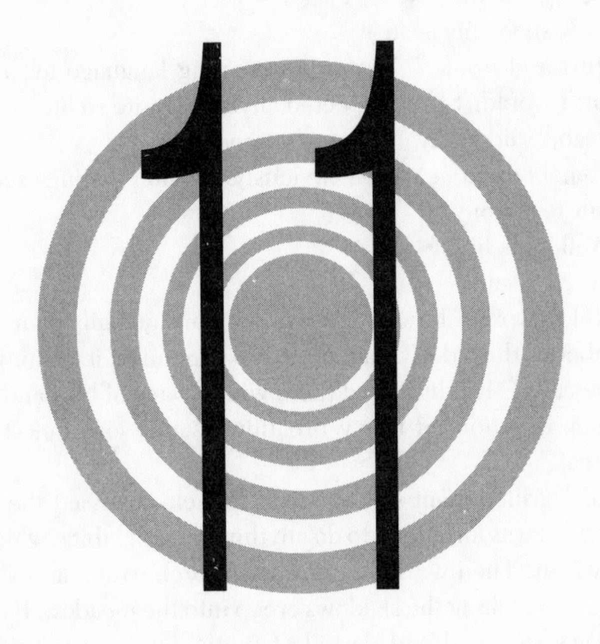

# 11

Back at the cabin, Diana took Corky out for a walk and I went into my bedroom to change out of my fishing clothes. When I walked into the living room, Wally said, "Listen to this."

He was standing by his answering machine. He pressed the button. It whirred for a moment, then a recorded voice said, "Walter Kinnick, you have betrayed the Second Amendment For Ever and you deserve to die a just and ironic death."

The machine clanked and rewound itself.

"Jesus, Wally," I said. "Have you had any other calls like that?"

He shrugged. "A few yesterday. They upset Diana. I figure they're just venting their frustrations. Harmless."

"This guy didn't sound harmless," I said. "Play it again."

Wally did.

"Recognize the voice?" I said.

Wally shook his head.

"'Just and ironic,'" I said. "Interesting language for a death threat. I wouldn't have expected anything quite so literate."

"Yeah," said Wally. "The guy's a poet."

"Somebody from SAFE, obviously," I said. "Taking exception to your testimony."

"Well, fuck him."

"Sure," I said.

"Not to worry," he said. "When someone actually plans to kill somebody, they don't call them to announce it. Anonymous phone calls?" He dismissed them with a wave of his hand. "Just another variation on heavy breathing. Come on. I'm starved. Let's eat."

Wally grilled giant steaks on his hibachi, I tossed the salad, and Diana was forbidden to do anything except kibitz, which she did, wittily. Then we sat on the front porch eating and sipping beer and watching the shadows creep into the meadow. Bats and swallows swooped and darted at moths and mosquitoes, and after the shadows had deepened from gray to purple a doe and her spindly-legged fawn tiptoed into the opening.

Once from inside the cabin we heard the phone ringing. "Let the machine get it," said Wally when Diana started to get up.

She shrugged and sat down.

I punched my palm. "Damn it," I said. "You should've saved that tape."

"Why?"

"That message you had. You should've saved it."

"What for?"

I shrugged. "I don't know."

He smiled. "Me neither. Anyway, too late now. It's been recorded over."

"What kind of message this time?" said Diana.

"Just another nut, honey," he said.

"I think it's scary."

He reached over and squeezed her hand.

We sat out there in the darkness for a while longer. Finally

Wally stretched, groaned, and stood up. "Gotta make a few calls," he said. He bent over, lifted Diana's hair, and kissed the back of her neck. "I'll meet you in the sack," he said to her. Then he went inside.

Diana and I sat in the darkness for a few minutes. Then she said, "Do you play cribbage?"

"I was the champion of Raven Lake Lodge up in Maine a few years ago. Wrested the title from a couple of very crafty Penobscot Indian guides. I'm probably too good for you."

"Let's find out."

She went inside. I lit a cigarette. A few minutes later the porch light went on and Diana shouldered open the screen door. She was carrying a tray which bore a cribbage board, a deck of cards, and two mugs of coffee.

We played cribbage and sipped coffee while the moths swirled around the porch light and the night birds called in the darkness. Once Diana paused in the middle of shuffling the deck and said, "Brady?"

"Um?"

"Those phone calls?"

I nodded.

"It's scary."

"I know," I said. "But Wally's probably right. Some people get off on phone calls. They're cowards."

"Mm," she said doubtfully.

A little later she suddenly began giggling.

"What is it?" I said.

"That man? Whose rod Walter broke? Did you see his face?"

"I think Wally's right," I said. "He deserved it."

She beat me three games to two. She got all the good cards.

As my penalty for losing, I went in to refill our mugs. Wally was seated at the kitchen table with the telephone wedged against his ear. He rolled his eyes at me.

I brought coffee out to Diana. "Doesn't he ever stop working?" I said.

"He pretends to. When we come out here, he always swears he's going to forget it. But every time I turn around, he's on the phone."

We sipped our coffee in comfortable silence for a couple of minutes. Then she leaned toward me and touched my arm. "You were probably wondering about us," she said. "Me and Walter, I mean."

I shrugged. "None of my business whatsoever."

"I want to tell you. Maybe you can give me some advice."

"Legal or personal?"

"Either," she said. "Both."

"As long as you don't value it too highly," I said. "Anybody can give advice."

"You're a friend. That makes it worth something."

"Thank you," I said.

"It's kind of a cliché," said Diana quietly, "now that I think of it. My husband works for a public relations firm, and one of their clients is this bank president or something who wanted to get onto Walter's show. Anyhow, there was some kind of reception at the Bostonian Hotel, and Howard had to go because his client was going. And Walter was there. Now, I had one of those marriages—well, Howard and I had been married for about six years, just drifting along. Nothing bad, but nothing much good, either. And when I met Walter—well, something happened. I just thought he was the sexiest, most down-to-earth guy I'd ever known. I mean, I talked to him for about three minutes and I just wanted him to wrap his arms around me and never let go." She shrugged. "I loved him instantly. I never believed that happened. But it does. It did."

"And Wally?" I said.

"He was charming. We talked. I couldn't take my eyes off him. I just wanted to grab him." She smiled. "I made the mistake of letting him know how I felt. I mean, looking back on it, it was something out of a romance novel. I don't even remember what I said, but it seemed outrageously bold at the time. Walter smiled at me, picked up my left hand, looked at my wedding ring in a meaningful way, dropped my hand, and without a word he turned around and walked away from me. That same night I told Howard I was leaving him. Which I did. Not for Walter. It had been coming for a long time. Meeting Walter, it just—it made me confront it. So I got my own place in Cambridge and filed for divorce. See, that response I had to Walter, it made me realize the truth about my marriage. Regardless of Walter, I just knew that the marriage had to end. It wasn't really that I left Howard West for Walter Kinnick. I just—I guess I left Howard for me. Anyway, I wrote Walter a long letter. I didn't really expect to hear from him. I mean, I'd met him just that once, and I had no reason to believe that he'd even remember me. But eventually he wrote back to me. It was just a short polite note, really. He answers all his fan mail, and that's all my letter was to him." She smiled. "But I wrote back to him, and he answered that one, too. We did that for nearly a year. Finally we got together, and . . ." She shrugged.

"I thought Wally told me you weren't divorced," I said.

She nodded. "Right. I'm not. Howard's still fighting it. He did not take it well." She laughed ironically. "There's an understatement for you. Howard went bananas is what happened. See, Brady, I've got nothing against Howard. I just don't want to be married to him. But somehow his entire self-image is at stake here. It's not that he loves me or needs me or can't live without me. Not *me*. I honestly don't think it's me he really cares about. It's the *idea* of me. He feels that if he loses me he's a failure. He just can't believe that somebody wouldn't want to be married to him." She paused, gazed up at the sky, took a deep breath, and whooshed it out. When she looked at me again, her eyes had brimmed with tears. "It's so *damn* frustrating. I thought we could be friends. You know, I figured we'd tell each other it was a pretty good six years and get on with our lives. Just to show you how naive I was, I even thought Howard would be happy for me, that I'd found someone I really loved."

"It hardly ever works that way," I said.

"You do divorces, right?"

"I do them. I also had one of my own."

"So you know what I mean. It's been three years. He calls me. Talks and talks. He yells, he cajoles, he cries, he begs, he threatens, he—"

"Threatens?" I said.

She laughed quickly. "Wrong word. He never leaves death-threat messages on my answering machine, if that's what you mean. Oh, he'd like me to believe that he's going to kill himself or something, that he can't live without me. Psychological threats like that. Just trying to make me feel guilty. I know him. He likes everything in its proper place. He hates surprises. This—I guess it surprised him. It's out of place. He doesn't know where it fits. It makes him a little crazy. I never saw that part of him before. It makes *me* crazy sometimes. I mean, it's unnerving, seeing something new in somebody after you've been married to him for six years."

"But he hasn't threatened you," I said.

She smiled. "No. Not physically, or financially, or anything. Not Howard. Oh, there are all those phone calls. When I'm not home, he'll fill the entire tape on my answering machine. Promising to change and in the same sentence threatening to jump off a bridge. It's all crazy. I've had my number changed, had it unlisted, but Howard's got connections. He finds it out. And sometimes he comes to my apartment building, banging on the door, yelling up from the street. He sat on my front steps all night a couple times when Walter was there. The only time I can relax is when I'm here or on a trip with Walter."

"He doesn't belong to SAFE, does he?"

"Howard?" She laughed. "As far as I know, he's never touched a gun."

"It still sounds pretty frightening," I said.

She shook her head. "Howard West doesn't frighten me. He makes me furious, and he drives me nuts sometimes. But I'm not afraid of him. He's—well, actually, he's probably like the guys who are leaving those messages. He's a coward."

"I don't know," I said. "I keep reading about these stalkers . . ."

She laughed. "He's not like that at all. I know Howard West."

"He doesn't know about this place?"

"Whew!" she said. "I hope not."

"It takes time."

"I know," she said.

"You've got a good lawyer?"

She nodded.

"I wasn't looking for business," I said quickly.

She patted my hand. "I didn't think you were."

# 

I was wide awake at six-fifteen the next morning. Back in the city, I tend to sleep late, probably because nothing there seems worth getting up for. Give me a taste of clean country air and a day on a trout river, and sleeping seems like a waste of time.

I pulled on my jeans and a T-shirt and stumbled into the kitchen. Diana was seated at the table sipping coffee and reading a magazine. She looked up and smiled at me. "Coffee?"

"You bet. I'll get it."

I went to the coffee machine and poured myself a mugful. I took it to the table and sat down across from her.

"Sleep well?" she said.

"Like a bear in January. Where's Wally?"

She jerked her head in the direction of the front door. "Walking with Corky. He hardly slept last night. He shrugs all this stuff off, but it eats at him. His producers, apparently, really are giving him a hard time. I guess some of their sponsors are getting fidgety."

"Boy," I said, "they don't waste any time."

"What's going on, Brady? These past few days . . ."

I shrugged. "The gun lobby is pretty upset. They figured Wally for a solid ally, which makes him the worst kind of traitor in their eyes. They've threatened to mobilize some kind of boycott of his TV sponsors."

"Can they do that?"

"I don't know," I said. "It'll probably all go away. The NRA, along with its local arms like SAFE, is one of the best-funded and most sophisticated pressure groups in the country. They've always been very successful. If that bill should become law, it would be like them to blame it on Wally. That's probably what's got him worried."

Diana smiled down into her coffee mug. "Walter never really worries. He sees things as challenges, not worries. About all he's told me about this assault weapon business is that he's satisfied he did the right thing, and if his sponsors drop him they'd be doing the wrong thing. I've gotten the impression that his producer would like him to make some kind of retraction on television, or at least say something that would fudge the issue. He would never do anything like that. So," she said with a smile, "he's walking in the woods. Going to church, he calls it." She looked up at me. "How do you like your eggs?"

"Over easy," I said. "But you don't—"

At that instant from somewhere outdoors came the sharp crack that I instantly recognized as a rifle shot. There was a pause, and then several more in quick succession.

Diana and I sat there for a moment looking at each other. Then she whispered, "Oh, Jesus."

She leaped up from the table, and I did too. We ran outside. I followed Diana around to the side of the house.

"Walter!" she screamed.

There was no answer.

She yelled again and again, and then Corky came bounding out of the bushes. He was wagging his tail, happy to see her. He rolled onto his back beside her, squirming in anticipation of having his belly scratched.

Diana scooched down beside him. "Where's Walter? Come on, Corky. Let's find Walter."

Corky scrambled to his feet and looked at her, and I would swear he understood exactly what she was saying. He turned and headed back into the woods. Then he stopped and looked at us, as if to say, "You guys coming, or what?"

We followed him through the thick undergrowth for about a hundred yards. Then we heard Wally moan.

"Walter!" Diana yelled.

We found him sitting on the ground, hunched over, hugging himself with his knees drawn up tight to his chest. Diana ran to him and knelt down beside him. "Honey?" she said.

Wally looked up at her. His face was wet with pespiration. "I'm okay," he mumbled.

"Let me see," I said. I squatted beside him. "Let's try to lie down," I told him.

Diana and I helped him onto his back. He groaned and squeezed his eyes shut. His breath came in quick shallow gasps.

A dark wet blotch was spreading across the front of his shirt. It looked like he'd gotten it in the stomach.

Diana leaned close to his face. "Honey?" she whispered.

"Hey, babe," he mumbled.

She looked at me. "What do we do?"

"Get a blanket. Call an ambulance."

She ran back to the house.

I wiped his face with my handkerchief. "How's it feel?" I said to him.

"Hurts like hell," he mumbled through clenched teeth.

I carefully unbuttoned his shirt and opened it. The bullet had struck him just above and to the left of his navel. It made a neat black hole from which blood was seeping steadily, and I didn't see how it could have missed vital organs on its way through him.

I helped Wally roll onto his side. The exit wound in his back was bigger and uglier and had bled profusely, judging by the black puddle that had already soaked into the leaves under him. I took off my own shirt, balled it up, and held it tight against the ragged hole in his back. "Hang on, old buddy," I told him.

Diana returned with a blanket, which we spread over Wally. She cradled his head on her lap. "The ambulance is on its way, honey," she said.

He opened his eyes and tried to smile. "They got me," he said.

"Who?" I said. "Did you see them?"

His eyes closed again. "Oh, shit," he moaned. He gagged, turned his head to the side, and vomited weakly.

Diana wiped his mouth and beard with the corner of the blanket. "Oh, baby," she whispered. "Don't die, baby."

I bent close to him. "Wally, did you see who shot you?"

"Gotta rip up all those fuckin' stakes, Brady," he mumbled. "Gotta save the Swamp."

His head lolled to the side. His eyelids drooped and his eyes rolled up and his mouth hung open slackly. Diana whispered, "Oh . . ."

I pressed my fingers against the side of his throat. It took me a moment to find the flutter of his pulse. It felt like the panicky beating of an insect's wings.

I looked up at Diana. Her eyes were wide.

"He passed out," I said. "He's lost blood. He's in shock. How soon before that ambulance will get here?"

She shook her head back and forth rapidly. "I don't know. I gave them directions. They seemed to know where we are. They said they were on their way." She bent down and kissed Wally's damp forehead. "Hang on, big fella," she whispered. She laid her cheek against his bushy black beard.

Far in the distance I heard the wail of a siren. I remembered all the wrong turns one could take, how even with Wally's map I had gotten lost trying to find his cabin. I recalled the ruts and mud of the roads. Wally could die while the ambulance wandered through the woods getting stuck in potholes.

I told Diana to hold the makeshift compress against the wound in Wally's back. Then I jogged back to the cabin and started down the dirt road.

It seemed forever, but it was probably only a couple of minutes later when the white van appeared. I waved my arm for it to follow me, then trotted back to the cabin. It pulled up on the lawn. Three EMTs in white jackets leaped out. "What've we got?" one of them said.

"Gunshot wound in the stomach. This way."

I led them into the woods to the place where Diana was kneeling beside Wally.

Within a minute or two they had him bandaged and on a stretcher and were carrying him through the woods back to the ambulance, one EMT on each end and the third holding up a bottle with a tube snaking down to Wally's arm. A plastic oxygen mask was strapped over his nose and mouth. They loaded him into the back. Two of the EMTs climbed in with him. The third slammed the door shut behind them and slid in behind the wheel. Then the vehicle spewed dirt from its rear tires and disappeared down the muddy road.

I stood there staring down the roadway. After a few minutes I heard the wail of the siren. It faded, then died.

Diana was beside me hugging my arm. "It was all so sudden," she said quietly.

"Where'd they take him, do you know?"

"North Adams. There's a hospital there. I'm going."

"I think we should wait. The police will be here."

"The hell with them," she said. "I'm going to be with Walter."

"You're right. The hell with them. Let's go."

I drove and Diana huddled against the door, and we didn't talk at all during the half-hour or so that it took us to drive down out of the hills to the hospital in North Adams. I figured we were both thinking the same thing.

Wally would be dead when we got there.

We jogged from the parking lot to the main entrance of the hospital. Inside, a young woman sat behind a counter chewing gum. She smiled and lifted her eyebrows when Diana and I approached her. I said to her, "Walter Kinnick."

She turned to face her computer terminal with her fingers poised over the keyboard. "Can you spell it?"

"He would've just got here. In an ambulance."

"Emergency?"

"Yes."

She pointed toward an elevator bank. "First floor. Go left and follow the signs."

"Thanks," I said.

Everybody in the emergency room seemed to be occupied with emergencies, but I finally got the attention of a gray-haired nurse.

"Walter Kinnick," I said to her. "He just came in by ambulance."

"I'm not—"

"Gunshot wound," I said.

She nodded and smiled quickly. She had a pumpkin-shaped face and a gap between her front teeth. She reminded me of Ernest Borgnine. "We didn't have his name," she said. She seemed much friendlier than most of the characters Ernest Borgnine played. "He's in surgery." She gestured off to her left. "You can wait in there. I'll make sure the doctor knows you're here."

"Is he okay?" said Diana.

The nurse shrugged. "I don't know, miss. I'm sorry. You'll have to wait."

A television was mounted on a wall bracket in the waiting room. A mid-morning soap opera was playing loudly on it. There were ten or a dozen other people in there, also waiting. Most of them were staring vacantly at the TV show.

Diana and I sat down. She let out a long breath. I put my arm around her shoulders. "All we can do is wait," I said.

"I'm very frightened," she said.

"I know. Me, too."

I found a six-month-old copy of *Sports Illustrated*. I paged through it from back to front, looking at the pictures, then put it down, glanced around, and spotted a coffeepot. I got up and poured two Styrofoam cupfuls. I handed one to Diana, who looked at me and nodded.

The coffee had the consistency of maple syrup.

I flipped through an old *New Yorker*, pausing at the cartoons, which didn't seem that funny.

We had been sitting there for an hour or so, me glancing through magazines and Diana staring up at the television, when a voice said, "Ah, excuse me?" I glanced up. He was a nondescript guy, receding hairline, plastic-rimmed glasses, middle-aged paunch, wearing baggy corduroy pants and a short-sleeved blue shirt.

"Yes?" I said.

"You're with the gunshot wound?"

"Yes. Is he—?"

"I'm the sheriff," he said. He held his hand out to me. "Mason."

"Brady Coyne," I said, shaking his hand. "This is Diana West."

Mason glanced at Diana and nodded. "Ma'am," he mumbled.

"How is he, do you know?" said Diana.

Mason shrugged. "No idea, miss," he said. "They tell me gunshot wound, I gotta come see what's up. They didn't say he was—" He cleared his throat. "Anyways, I need to know what happened. You can start by giving me his name."

"Walter Kinnick," I said. "He—"

The sheriff nodded quickly. "Okay. Sure. I know who he is. He's got the Palmer place up there in Fenwick, right?"

"Yes," said Diana.

Maybe they didn't have cable in that part of Massachusetts. Still, Mason must have known that Wally was a television personality. But I figured that, like most rural folks, he made it a point to be staunchly unimpressed with wealth or fame. Wealthy and famous people keep getting lost in the woods. They don't know how to change flat tires. They wear impractical clothes.

To the locals, Wally wasn't the television guy. Wally was the guy who bought the Palmer place up in Fenwick, and probably paid more for it than he should have, and just used it for vacations now and then. A city boy. An outsider.

Mason squatted down in front of us. "That where it happened?"

Diana nodded. "Outside. In the woods."

"Tell me about it."

"Wally was out walking with the dog," I said. "We were inside. We heard shots. When we got out there, he was on the ground. He was hit in the stomach."

"You see or hear anything besides the gunshots?"

“I don’t—”

“Anybody? Somebody running? Voices? Noises in the woods? A vehicle? The sound of a vehicle starting up?”

I shook my head.

“No,” said Diana.

“How many shots?”

“Three or four,” said Diana. “Real close together.”

“Actually,” I said, “I think there was one shot, then a pause, then three or four after that.”

Mason shrugged. “Who called it in?”

“I did,” said Diana.

“When you heard the shots?”

“We ran outside. Corky—that’s my dog—he led us to him. Walter was on the ground in the woods. When we realized he had been shot, I went back and called.”

“But you didn’t actually see anything.”

“No,” she said.

“Mr. Coyne?”

I shook my head.

“Was Mr. Kinnick conscious?”

“Yes. He passed out before the ambulance arrived.”

“Did he say anything?”

“He said, ‘They got me.’”

“Is that all?”

I nodded. “I asked him what he meant, who got him, but he didn’t say. He mumbled some things that made no sense. Then he passed out.”

“What things that made no sense?”

“I don’t exactly remember. References to things he and I did as boys. We grew up together. It seemed to me he was hallucinating.”

“But maybe he saw who did it.”

I shrugged.

Mason was still squatting down in front of us. He shifted his weight, then glanced from Diana to me. “And you two?”

I frowned. “What?”

“How are you related? To Kinnick, to each other.”

“I’m his lawyer,” I said. “Diana’s his . . .”

"Friend," she said.

"And what were you doing there?" he said to me.

"At the cabin? A little vacation. We were fishing."

"The three of you."

I nodded. "The three of us."

"The Deerfield, huh?"

"Yes."

He nodded. "I hear it's been fishing good. So what do you figure happened?"

"Somebody hid in the woods and tried to assassinate him," I said. "It's pretty obvious."

Mason smiled. "Who'd want to go do something like that?"

"Somebody who belongs to the Second Amendment For Ever," I said. "See, Wally testified in favor of a gun-control bill last Monday. SAFE brought him in to testify against it, but he ended up supporting it." I shrugged.

Mason scratched his chin. "That's quite a theory, Mr. Coyne."

"He's been getting anonymous phone calls. I heard one of them on his answering machine yesterday. Said he was a traitor to SAFE. It was a death threat."

"Really?"

"Yes. And Gene McNiff threatened him right after he testified and then a gang of SAFE guys followed me and Wally to the Dunkin' Donuts on Tremont Street and attacked Wally, and . . ." I let out a deep breath. "Jesus. It's obvious."

Mason put his hand on my arm. "Calm down, there, Mr. Coyne. Just relax."

"Look," I said, "if it's *not* one of the guys who threatened him on the phone, it's quite a coincidence, don't you think? The way I understand it, every gun-totin' member of SAFE figures Walt Kinnick's their biggest enemy in the world, and one of them figures he's going to serve the cause, so he calls up Wally and tells him he deserves to die for his treachery, and next thing you know Wally's been shot in the gut with a gun."

"Coincidence?" Mason rubbed his chin with the palm of his hand. "Yeah, I guess it could be at that. That's more'n likely what it is. A big coincidence. Fact is, coincidence explains most things. Listen, I ain't saying it *wasn't* some nutcake done it. But you're forgetting the most obvious thing, and you should never forget the obvious thing."

"What's the obvious thing?" I said.

Mason looked at me over the tops of his glasses. "Hunting accident, Mr. Coyne."

"Oh, for Christ sake."

He shrugged. "Don't be too quick to jump to conclusions, there," he said. "Listen. It's turkey season, right this very minute. This part of the state, we get a lot of gunshot wounds in turkey season. Last couple years, no fatalities, thank God. But accidents, you know? Those ridges up there by the Palmer place are prime for gobblers, and everybody around here knows it. The boys get out there way before dawn, hunker against a tree trunk in their camouflage jumpsuits with their tight-choked twelve gauges, and they work on their calls and they wait, and when they see one they let loose. Even if they don't see one, after a while they sometimes *think* they see one. Pretty nerve-racking, turkey hunting. You sit and you sit, morning after morning, just waiting. Imagination starts workin' on you. Little movement in the bushes?" Mason flapped his hand. "A charge of number-four shot hits a twig, it deflects, and the head of a gobbler's just about belt-high on a man . . ." He shrugged as if it was self-evident.

"They sounded like rifle shots to me," I said.

"You were inside when you heard them?"

I nodded.

"They came from out in the woods, right?"

"Yes. But a rifle sounds a lot different from a shotgun."

"It's illegal to hunt turkeys with a rifle, Mr. Coyne."

"Yes," I said. "That's my point."

"Sure." He smiled. "Good point."

"Well," I said, "I assume you intend to investigate it."

He nodded. "Why, sure. Have to investigate a gunshot accident. Law requires it. Accidents happen. But we can't have folks running away when they shoot somebody. It's like a hit and run. We don't put up with that."

"A hit and run?" said Diana.

"Same idea, miss."

She shook her head. "Hardly," she mumbled.

"You're planning to talk to Wally, aren't you?" I said.

Mason shrugged and said nothing. I caught his meaning. He'd talk to Wally if Wally didn't die.

"Somebody tried to kill him," said Diana quietly.

"Maybe so, miss," said Mason. "We'll go up to the Palmer place and have us a look, all right. And we'll inquire around, see who might've been hunting those ridges this morning. Maybe one of 'em'll admit to firing those shots. Maybe one of the boys saw something. Any vehicle parked by the roadside, they'd notice. Don't you worry. Let's just hope Mr. Kinnick comes out of it okay."

He stood up and arched his back with a small groan. "You folks take care, now," he said. "Maybe we'll talk again. Meantime, we'll all be prayin' for Mr. Kinnick."

Diana looked up at him. "Thank you," she said.

He started to walk away, then stopped and said, "He didn't happen to save that tape, did he?"

"Tape?" I said.

"On the answering machine. The threatening message."

I shook my head. "No."

Mason shrugged, then left the room.

Diana sighed heavily. "What do you think, Brady?"

"I think he really believes it was a hunting accident. I guess gunshot wounds are pretty common in these parts. So Sheriff Mason's had a lot of experience with men being dragged out of the woods bleeding with bullets in them. The big crime, from his point of view, isn't the shooting. It's that the shooter ran away. He thinks we're paranoid because probably everybody gets paranoid if they or their friends get shot."

"But the phone calls. . . ?"

"This is the country, Diana. It's not Cambridge. Everyone out here hunts and owns guns. Most of them probably belong to SAFE. Maybe Mason himself is a member. He wouldn't believe that anybody from SAFE would do this. He's got his mind made up, and I don't think he's likely to pursue a sophisticated investigation. Far as he's concerned, it was a hunting accident."

"What about the state police, or the FBI, or something?"

I touched her arm. "It's the sheriff's case," I said. "Those others won't be involved in it."

What I meant was that they wouldn't be involved if Wally recovered. If he died, it would become a homicide case. Then everybody would be involved.

I decided not to explain that to Diana just then.

# 14

After another hour or so I got up and went back to the emergency admitting area. I found the same gray-haired nurse seated at a computer monitor. "Excuse me . . ." I began.

She looked up at me and shook her head. "He's still in surgery," she said. "I'll be sure you know when there's any news."

"He's been in there a long time."

She shrugged. It meant he hadn't died yet.

Diana had been slumped in her chair with her eyes closed since Sheriff Mason had left. When I returned to the waiting room, I touched her arm and said, "How about something to eat?"

She opened her eyes and looked at me. "No. I feel like I'm going to throw up as it is."

“They told me he’s still in surgery.”

Her eyes closed. “He’s going to die.”

I didn’t say anything.

Sometime after three o’clock in the afternoon the gray-haired nurse appeared in the waiting room. A young doctor wearing hospital greens stood beside her. She caught my eye, turned to the doctor and spoke to him, then left. The doctor approached me and Diana. We both stood up.

“We can talk better outside,” he said, jerking his head in the direction of the corridor. Diana and I followed him.

I guessed he wasn’t yet thirty, but deep creases had already etched themselves into his forehead. His eyes were bloodshot. He needed a shave. “You’re with Mr. Kinnick,” he said.

“Yes. Is he—?”

“I’m Dr. Frankel. We’ve got him patched up. He’s . . . stable.”

Diana slumped against me. I put my arm around her.

“Stable?” I said.

The doctor sighed. “I won’t try to fool you. It was messy. It nicked his liver and intestine. He lost a lot of blood. But it could have been a lot worse. His vital signs are good. We got him cleaned out and sewn up. He’s a strong, healthy man.”

“Will he be okay?” asked Diana.

“The worry is always infection with something like this,” he said. “We’ve got him on antibiotics. I think he’ll be fine.”

“Thank God,” she whispered. “Can we see him?”

“Come back tomorrow, miss,” he said. “He’s in ICU, and he’s heavily sedated. You’ve got to go and give the desk some information.” He touched her shoulder and smiled wearily. “Okay?”

“I’d just like to see him.”

“You’re his wife?”

“No. His—friend.”

He nodded. “Talk to the nurse at the desk. Maybe she’ll sneak you in for a peek.”

We followed the doctor back into the admitting area. Diana answered some questions for the gray-haired nurse at the computer, then the nurse came out from behind her counter.

“You want to come, Brady?” said Diana.

I shook my head. “I’ll wait for you here.”

I had no desire to see Wally lying unconscious on a hospital bed with plastic tubes coming out of his nose and legs and arms and penis, with monitors ticking his heartbeat and measuring his blood pressure. Seeing him that way wouldn't do Wally any good, or me, either.

Diana was back in ten minutes. Her face was streaked with tears. "He looks so—so shrunken," she said.

I put my arm around her shoulders. "Let's go home," I said.

She nodded. "Yes. I've got to feed Corky."

I found a head of lettuce in the refrigerator. I tore it into a big wooden bowl, added half a jar of ripe olives, dumped a can of tuna fish onto it, and drenched it with Italian dressing. I tossed it with wooden salad forks until the tuna was all shredded and sticking to the lettuce. Then I took it out onto the porch and placed it ceremoniously on the table beside Diana.

She had been sitting there gazing out over the meadow since we returned from the hospital. Corky was lying beside her, and she was absentmindedly scratching his ears. I had poured her a glass of Zinfandel. It sat untouched beside her.

She looked up at me and tried a smile. It worked for just a moment. "Oh, nice," she said.

"I'll be right back." I went inside, found two salad bowls, forks, napkins, and my own wineglass. I carried everything out to the porch and filled Diana's bowl with lettuce, tuna, and olives.

I handed it to her. "Eat," I said. "This is my speciality. I call it Brady's Special Italian Salad Minus the Anchovies, Sweet Peppers, Tomatoes, and Bermuda Onion. We could also use a big loaf of hot garlic bread, actually. But I'll be offended if you don't love it."

She took a small bite. "It's great. I do. I love it." She put her fork down.

"Eat it. You haven't eaten since breakfast. You've got to eat."

"I'm really not that hungry, Brady. But this is delicious."

"It's not going to help Wally, you getting sick."

"I know. You're right." She picked up her fork and took another bite. She chewed thoughtfully, then looked at me. "Brady, remember the man whose rod Walter broke?"

"It was only yesterday, Diana."

She smiled softly. "Yes. It seems like a long time ago."

"You think he's the one who shot Wally?"

She shrugged. "He was pretty mad."

"I'll mention it to Mason when I see him. He was driving a green Volvo wagon with Vermont plates. Maybe somebody noticed a Volvo somewhere near here this morning." I hesitated for a moment, then said, "There was something else we didn't mention to the sheriff."

She looked up at me.

"Your husband," I said gently.

Diana frowned, then shook her head. "Howard isn't the type at all."

"You heard some of those threatening messages."

She nodded. "None of them was Howard."

"Wally played one for me when you were out with Corky yesterday. After we got back from fishing."

"I didn't hear that one," she said. "Too bad he didn't save it. I would certainly recognize Howard's voice on an answering machine."

"Too late for that."

"Well, you can mention Howard to that sheriff if you think you should. But it wasn't him. No way."

"Yeah," I said. "It's pretty obvious who it was."

"Turkey hunters," she said, and we both smiled.

The sun had fallen behind the mountains and shadows blanketed the meadow. Diana and I sat there picking at our salads and gazing into those shadows. Suddenly she sat forward and whispered, "Look!"

My first thought was that she had spotted a man with a gun.

Then I saw the shape, and then three other shapes, and I realized that four wild turkeys had tiptoed into Wally's meadow. I had never seen a wild turkey before. Just paintings of Pilgrims with blunderbusses and photographs in *Field & Stream.* Ben Franklin believed the turkey, not the bald eagle, should have been the national bird. When I was growing up in the Commonwealth, there were no wild turkeys. The Massachusetts Division of Fisheries and Wildlife began to reintroduce them into the state in the 1970s, and the birds had, from all I'd read, done well. They reproduced and eventually established themselves securely enough that they could be hunted.

Turkeys are the wariest of all wild creatures, the most worthy quarry for a human hunter.

It's a lot easier to stalk a man than a turkey.

These four were all hens. Gobblers travel alone, at least in the spring mating season when they're staking out their territory and trying to lure in hens that they can seduce.

I've always been fascinated with nature's various rituals of love and lust. Many of them are at once ceremonious and comical, violent and tender. Males strut, sing, and fight each other. Females flirt and blush and play hard-to-get and wait for the biggest toughest guy in the neighborhood to assert his dominance. It reminds me that people are creatures of nature, too, although a lot of us don't like to admit it.

As we watched the four hen turkeys, they abruptly ducked their absurd heads and scuttled back into the woods.

It was hard to imagine how a hunter could mistake a six-foot-three-inch man with a black beard for a turkey.

I turned to Diana. "That was—"

I stopped. Her head was bowed. She was crying.

I touched her shoulder. "What is it?"

"I feel like it's my fault," she said softly. "It's my punishment for trying to be happy. Sometimes I think—I don't deserve it. I don't deserve Walter, I don't deserve—anything. Sometimes when we're together I'm just happy all over, and it scares me. It makes me think that something's going to happen, because you can't just be happy. It never lasts. Something always happens."

I nodded. Diana was right. Something always happens. "I don't know about you," I said, "but I could sure use a hug."

She turned to me and tried to smile. “I could use one, too.”

She stood up, and I did, too. She leaned against me. I put both of my arms around her. She snuffled, then began to shudder. She sobbed loudly. I stood there holding her for a long time, while the shadows darkened in the meadow.

A knock on my bedroom door woke me up. "Come in," I mumbled.

Diana pushed open the door. "Are you decent?"

"Many people don't think so," I said.

She laughed and put a mug of steaming coffee on the table beside my bed. "I'm going to the hospital," she said.

"What time is it?"

"Seven. I'm leaving now. If you want to come . . ."

"I think I should hang around in case the sheriff shows up. Maybe later."

She bent down and kissed my forehead. "Thank you, Brady

Coyne. I'm awfully glad you're here. I don't know what I would've done . . ."

"I'll come along later. If there's any news, call me."

She looked solemnly at me and nodded.

After I drank my coffee, showered, and dressed, I whistled for Corky and we went outside. Dark clouds hung over the mountains. I could smell rain in the air. I pushed through the dense woods until I came to the little clearing where we had found Wally. I knelt down and found some dark splotches on the leaves where he had bled. I looked around. Surrounding the clearing was thick undergrowth. A mixture of birch saplings and alders and hemlocks and knee-high weeds separated the clearing from the forest. An assassin could hide himself nicely in that undergrowth. I supposed it was also the kind of place a turkey hunter might hide.

I stood up and pushed my way through the close-growing vegetation and began to look around. I didn't know what I expected to see—a footprint, a cigarette butt, anything—but I kept my eyes on the ground and tried to do it in an orderly way, studying every square foot. Corky snorted and snuffled here and there, hunting like a Springer spaniel is supposed to.

The woods were damp and dark and quiet, the way it gets when all the wild creatures know a storm is coming.

After what seemed like a long time I was aware that it had begun to rain. I heard the drops pattering softly on the leafy canopy over my head.

Soon the natural umbrella overhead would become saturated, and then the rain would begin to dribble down. But for now I was dry. I continued my search. I found ferns and mushrooms, clusters of tiny blue flowers, wild strawberries just breaking into blossom, a single pink lady slipper. But no footprints. No sign of an assassin.

Corky hadn't caught any interesting scents, either.

I had turned to go back to the cabin when something caught my eye, a dull metallic glitter. I knelt down. It was a rifle cartridge, an empty bronze-colored cylinder, half hidden under the leaves. I picked it up and held it in my palm. It was about an inch long, with a narrowed-down neck. The legend .223 REM was engraved on its round end.

I looked back in the direction of the clearing where Wally had fallen. It was about a hundred feet away. There was a small opening in the thick growth, no more than a foot in diameter, and about waist-high on a tall man. Through it I could see the place where Wally would have been standing.

I imagined a man kneeling here, training his rifle on that opening, patient, figuring that sooner or later his quarry would appear.

This was where the assassin had waited.

I prowled the area on hands and knees. The canopy over my head had become saturated. Rain came dripping down onto me, and I soon became drenched. I found no boot prints or cigar butts or matchbooks or driver's licenses. But I did find two more spent cartridges in the leaves, identical to the first one. These I picked up on the end of a twig and wrapped in my handkerchief. Maybe the shooter had left his fingerprints on them.

I knew I should turn the cartridges over to Sheriff Mason. I also knew I wouldn't do that. He'd smudge them and drop them into his pocket, and that would be the end of them. As long as Wally lived, it was simply a local incident. The man in charge had decided it was a hunting accident. He had neither the resources nor the inclination to consider other scenarios.

When I got back to Boston I'd call Horowitz. He'd know what to do.

I had changed into dry clothes and poured myself a fresh mug of coffee when the obvious thought hit me.

Any assassin who wanted to kill Wally probably wouldn't reject an opportunity to kill me.

And he probably wouldn't pass up the chance to take a shot at Diana, either. A crackpot with a rifle would undoubtedly subscribe to the theory of guilt by association.

She and I had spent the previous evening lounging on the porch watching the darkness seep into the meadow. It had been stupid.

I didn't want to spend any more time in Wally's cabin. I didn't want Diana to, either.

She called me a little after noon. "He was awake for a little while," she said. "Groggy, pretty out of it. But he recognized me. He has no idea what happened."

"Did you talk to the doctor?"

"Briefly. He seemed pleased. Walter had a fever in the night, but it's come down. He says that infection is still the main concern."

"Diana, listen," I said. "I want Wally transferred to Mass General as soon as possible. I'm going to make a few calls. Okay?"

"But—"

"The best medical care in the world is at Mass General. Anyway, I want him near us. And we're not staying here."

"You can go home, Brady. I'll be fine. I'm staying."

"No, you're not. It's not safe."

She was quiet for a minute. "You really don't think it was an accident, do you?"

"Of course it wasn't an accident."

"So you think. . . ?"

"You and I are going to find a motel tonight. Tomorrow we go home. Wait for me there. What do you need me to bring?"

"Brady—"

"We're going to do it my way, Diana."

"Just bring Corky, then."

I caught Doc Adams at his home in Concord. I explained to him what had happened. Doc knows every medical person in eastern Massachusetts and has an affiliation with Mass General. He said he'd handle the whole thing.

He called me back at four o'clock. "It's all arranged," he said. "There's a room waiting for him. They'll bring him by ambulance tomorrow morning."

"I appreciate it."

"I've seen Kinnick's show," said Doc. "He's my kind of guy."

I finally summoned up the nerve to peek in on Wally Sunday morning, just an hour before they were going to load him into the ambulance for his trip to Mass General. They'd cranked his bed into a half-sitting position. He bristled with tubes, just as I'd imagined. Some of them were introducing fluids into him, and others were evacuating them.

I sat down in the chair beside his bed and squeezed his shoulder. "How you feeling?" I said.

"Just pisser." One of the tubes snaked up through his nostril and down his throat. When he talked, it came out as a soft croak.

"Has the sheriff been in to see you?"

Wally rolled his eyes. I guessed it would hurt too much to shrug his shoulders. "Dunno. Been sleeping."

"Did you see anything?"

"Huh?"

"When you were shot."

"Nothing." He closed his eyes for a moment.

"Pain?" I said.

"Comes and goes."

"Who did it, Wally? What do you think?"

"Not SAFE. They're not that stupid."

"Who else, then?"

"Dunno."

I leaned close to him. "You have a suspicion?"

He sighed. "None. Sleepy."

Diana and I waited in Wally's room until they wheeled him out to the ambulance that would take him to Boston. Then she and Corky and I drove back to the cabin. We cleaned up and packed and loaded our cars. Then she climbed into her Cherokee and I got into my BMW, and I followed her down the hill.

When we got to the gravel road, Diana bore left to head back to Cambridge. I impulsively took a right. Saturday's rain had stopped sometime overnight. It was a sparkling Sunday afternoon in May, and I was reluctant to leave the woods and the clean air and the river.

I followed the dirt road that paralleled the Deerfield, crossed the narrow bridge, and pulled into the grassy area where Wally and Diana and I had parked a couple of days earlier. This time there were eight or ten cars there. None of them was a green Volvo wagon with Vermont plates and a Trout Unlimited sticker on the back window.

I didn't bother rigging up. I clambered down the steep path and found a boulder on the water's edge to sit on. From that vantage I could see three anglers casting flies. The one closest to me was a woman. She cast with fluid grace, and it relaxed me to sit and bathe my face in the sunshine and watch her. She was casting to a fish that was rising in a tricky location where the current eddied behind a rock. She changed flies a couple of times, shifted her position, and then I saw a little spurt of water engulf her fly. Her rod arced, and a minute later she knelt by the riverbank and unhooked what looked like a rainbow of fifteen or sixteen inches. She released it gently, stood, and noticed me. She grinned and waved and I waved back to her. Then she waded back into the river.

I sat there for a few minutes longer, then climbed the path to my car. I had found what I'd come here for—that "momentary stay against confusion" that Frost wrote about. Trout rivers—even when I don't fish in them—do that for me.

I got into my car, followed the dirt roads to Route 2, and turned left. I was headed east, back to the city. I kept it below the speed limit. I was in no hurry to get home. Tomorrow I'd have to go to the office. It always amazed me how a few days in jeans and moccasins blunted whatever enthusiasm I had for the practice of law.

Up ahead on the right I saw a sign that read GUNS. Why not? I thought. I pulled into the peastone parking area. Only two other vehicles were there, a blue Ford pickup and an old Buick sedan.

It was a low-slung square dark-shingled building. Hand-printed signs in the window advertised AMMO, BAIT, TACKLE, AND GUNS NEW AND USED.

I climbed the steps and went in. A bell jangled when the door opened. A beagle was sleeping on an old sweatshirt beside a cold woodstove in the corner. He opened his eyes, looked me over, decided I wasn't a rabbit, and closed them again. Two men were leaning toward each other over a glass-topped display case. The one behind it, I figured, ran the place. The other was a customer, or perhaps just a friend in for a chat.

On the wall behind the glass case stood a rack of guns. There must have been forty or fifty of them standing there on their butts. Guns of every description—double-barreled shotguns, pumps, autoloaders, bolt-action rifles, rifles with scopes.

The glass case under the two guys' elbows contained boxes of ammunition and an assortment of handguns.

I glanced around the rest of the place. Against the back wall stood the bait tanks. There was a free-standing rack of spinning and bait-casting rods. Rotating display racks held lures affixed to cardboard, vials of scent, spools of monofilament, hooks, bobbers, swivels, lead weights. There were knives and hunting bows, bowsights and broadheads, canteens and tents and sleeping bags, camouflage suits and boots.

It reminded me of an old-time Five and Ten, with a theme.

I prowled around while the two men talked at the counter. I took a small Buck knife from a shelf, slid it from its sheath, and tested it against the ball of my thumb. I'm a sucker for good knives. I collect them the way some people collect paintings. In fact, a well-made knife to me is beautiful, a work of art. I only actually use two or three of my knives. But I do like to own them.

I continued browsing until the customer left the store. Then I went up to the counter.

"How ya doin'?" he said. He had a bristly black mustache and watery blue eyes. Late thirties, early forties.

"I'd rather be fishing," I said.

He nodded. "Ain't that the truth."

I put the knife on the counter. He picked it up. "Want this one?"

I nodded. "It fills out my collection."

"Buck makes a good knife." He hit some keys on his old-fashioned cash register. "Forty-two bucks. Plus two-ten for the governor."

"Fine," I said. I jerked my head in the direction of the rack of guns. "What kind of rifle would you use for turkeys?" I said.

"Rifle?" He smiled. "No kind, that's what. Get yourself arrested, hunting turkey with a rifle. You want a tight-bored twelve-gauge autoloader for turkey. One of those Remingtons with the thirty-inch barrels, they'll send out a nice tight pattern of number fours. You want to shoot your turkey in the head, which ain't much bigger'n silver dollar. You wanna kill a turkey, you need all the help you can get. Shotgun's the thing for gobblers."

"You wouldn't use a rifle?"

"Not in Massachusetts, unless you want to break the law. Some guys go after turkeys with a bow. Helluva sport, bow and arrow hunting for turkey. You plannin' on goin' after a turkey?"

"I never did it. Sounds like fun." I fumbled in my pockets and brought out one of the empty cartridges I'd found in the woods, the one I'd already handled. I had sealed the other two in a plastic bag, hoping there were fingerprints on them.

I handed the cartridge to the guy. "You wouldn't use one of these for turkey, then, huh?"

He squinted at it for a moment, then handed it back to me. "Very common varmint load, the .223 Remington. Put a good scope on a .223 and it'd probably work real fine on a gobbler. Except, like I say, it's illegal."

"So I'd want a shotgun," I said.

He nodded. "You need camouflage, turkey call, maybe a spread of decoys. I got all that stuff. Also a video that'll teach you how to call. You've gotta know how to call 'em in. Kinda late to get started, actually. Spring season's about over now."

I nodded. "Maybe next year I'll try it." I took out my wallet and handed him my Mastercard. "I'll take this nice Buck knife, anyway."

He ran the card through his machine and gave me the slip to sign.

I peered up at the rack of guns behind him. "How's the market for assault guns these days?" I said.

"A little slow. I've sold maybe three or four this spring."

"If a man wanted to get himself, say, an Uzi . . ."

He shrugged. "No problem. I haven't got one in stock, but I could order it for you. I get 'em on trade-in now and then, too."

"As easy as that?"

He smiled. "So far, that's all there is to it. You want to buy a gun, if I've got what you're after here, you give me money, show me your FID card, and I give you the gun."

"That's it?"

"Yup. That's it."

"Any gun?"

“Any gun you want. If I ain’t got it in stock, I can order it for you. Whatever you want.”

“Even a military weapon?”

“You bet. Except for full automatic, of course.”

“There’s no waiting period or anything?”

“Thank God, not yet. Matter of time, I suppose, the way things are going.” He cocked his head at me. “You lookin’ for an Uzi?”

“Nope. Not today. This knife will do me for today.”

He dropped the knife into a bag, and I took it, thanked him, and headed for the door. A table just inside the entrance held a coffee machine and a stack of papers. I picked one up. The SAFE logo was blazoned across the top—a flintlock musket poking through the A in SAFE, and under it the slogan: “The right of the people to keep and bear arms shall not be infringed.”

“Can I take one of these?” I said to the guy behind the counter.

“Help yourself. They’re free. Just got ’em in Wednesday.”

I waved and went out to my car.

When I slid behind the wheel I looked at the four-page newsletter. The front page was taken up by a two-column article with the title, “Another Attack on Gun Owners.”

It was written by Gene McNiff, SAFE executive director. I skimmed it. It gave an acutely biased summary of each witness’s testimony on the assault-weapon bill, and concluded with a dire warning about the impact the legislation would have, if passed, on the liberties of the American people.

Walt Kinnick’s statement before the subcommittee was characterized as a “cynical betrayal.”

The second page, and the first column on page three, contained a series of short pieces reporting events at New England rod-and-gun clubs.

The right-hand column on the third page was called “Know Your Enemy.”

It was a list, and the words “Brady Coyne” jumped from the middle of it and smacked me in the face.

“The following people,” read the lead-in to the list, “want to take your guns away from you. Let them hear from you. Let them know how you feel. Let them know that all of us decent law-abiding gun owners are not going to lay back while they rip up our Constitution."

There were ten of us, complete with our mailing addresses and phone numbers. Walt Kinnick was number one. Second was Marlon Swift (R–Marshfield), the state senator who had chaired the subcommittee before which Wally had testified. Then came the governor of Connecticut, followed by both United States senators from Massachusetts and the congressman from Rhode Island's Second District.

Then, in seventh place, Brady Coyne. Me. Enemy number seven.

Seeing my name there in print made me shiver. I was an actual enemy. I was on a list. Name, phone number, address.

Wally was at the top of the list, and he had nearly been assassinated. Somebody had let Wally know how how he felt. The list, giving his phone number, came out on Wednesday, just two days after the hearing. That's when he began getting phone calls.

SAFE obviously didn't take their enemies lightly.

They shot them.

One week earlier I had never even heard of the Second Amendment For Ever organization. Now my friend had been shot in the stomach, and I was their seventh-ranked enemy.

I wasn't sure I had the courage to be a worthy enemy.

Then I thought, Hell, if they wanted an enemy that badly, they could have me. Like Boston Blackie from the early television days, I was willing to be an enemy of those who made me an enemy.

Blackie had been a friend to those who had no friends, and that suited me, too. Walt Kinnick seemed to be losing a lot of friends.

I glanced at the rest of the names that filled out the list of ten. Eighth was a United States senator from Vermont. Number nine was a congresswoman from Maine. Gun-control advocates, I assumed.

Number ten was Wilson Bailey, the poor guy whose wife and

child had been mowed down in a small-town library near Worcester by an angry man with an assault gun. Wilson Bailey had struck me as an eminently worthy enemy, a man with plenty of courage and conviction. Wilson Bailey might need a friend, too.

As I started up the car and pulled out of the parking area, I thought of the guy behind the counter of the gun shop. Either he hadn't read my name off my credit card, or he hadn't committed the SAFE list to memory. I doubted he'd have been so friendly if he'd realized I was such an important threat to his livelihood, even if I did buy a nice Buck knife from him.

I got all my gear put away and took a short glass of ice cubes and bourbon out onto my balcony to think about it all. A moon sliver hung like a thin slice of honeydew melon over the horizon. I lit a cigarette and sipped from my glass. It was very clear to me that some fanatical member of SAFE had tried to kill Wally. The newsletter had given Wally's phone number and post office box number in Fenwick. The SAFE vigilante had called the number and left his message. A few inquiries of the local shopkeepers and gas station attendants would have directed him to "the Palmer place," Wally's cabin.

Probably it was seeing my own name on that list that led me

to my next conclusion. Or maybe it was irrational. But it seemed eminently likely to me that the same crazy man who shot Wally might have gotten it into his skewed brain to work his way down the list, picking off enemies one by one, to the greater glory of God, Country, and the Second Amendment For Ever.

I'd be number seven, if he got that far.

State Senator Marlon Swift was number two. If my logic was sound, he would be next.

There had been two messages on my machine when I got back from my adventures in the Berkshires. The first was from Doc Adams, Sunday afternoon, advising me that Wally was safely ensconced in a private room at Mass General Hospital. Doc had dropped in on Wally and found him sleeping.

Charlie McDevitt had called, asking for a report on the trout fishing.

There were no anonymous death threats.

Not yet, I thought. It wasn't my turn.

I watched the moon rise for the length of time it took me to finish my drink. Then I went inside. I found the SAFE newsletter, sat at the kitchen table, and punched out the phone number for Senator Marlon Swift's home in Marshfield.

A woman answered. I asked for the senator.

"Who's calling, please?" she said. Her voice was pleasant, neutral, efficient, as if she was used to having strangers call on Sunday evenings and knew how to handle them.

"My name is Brady Coyne," I said. "I'm Walt Kinnick's attorney."

"Who?"

"Walt Kinnick," I said. "He testified before Senator Swift's subcommittee on Monday. If it's not convenient . . ."

"I'll see if he can come to the phone," she said.

A minute later a cautious voice said, "Yes?"

"Senator Swift," I said, "it's Brady Coyne. I'm Walt Kinnick's lawyer."

"Sure," he said. "What can I do for you?"

"Have you seen the latest SAFE newsletter?"

He chuckled. "Yes. Walt Kinnick has supplanted me as their

number-one enemy. Damned disappointing. My constituents want me to be at the top of that list. Gun control is a big issue in my district."

"Did you know that Wally was shot?"

There was a long pause. Then he said, "What did you say?"

"Walt Kinnick was shot. It happened Friday up at his cabin in Fenwick. He's—"

"Is he all right?"

"Yes, I guess he's going to be okay. They transferred him to Mass General this afternoon."

"What do you mean, shot?"

"He was in the woods. They got him in the stomach."

"And you think . . ."

"Senator, Wally was number one on that list. You're number two."

He laughed quickly. "And you, if I recall, Mr. Coyne, are also on the list."

"Yes. I'm seven."

"So you're calling—"

"To warn you, I guess."

"You think there's some nut working his way down the list, is that it? First Kinnick, second me?"

"I don't know. Yes. That occurred to me."

"Mr. Coyne," said Swift, "you'd probably be surprised to know that Gene McNiff and I are good friends."

"As a matter of fact, yes, that surprises me."

"We've worked together on several pieces of legislation. As the chairman of the Subcommttee on Public Safety, I need the support and advice of men like McNiff."

"But—"

"We disagree on gun control. But we agree on many things."

"I see."

"You're not into politics much, huh?"

"I've read my Machiavelli."

"Well, if you've read old Niccolò carefully, you would understand that Gene McNiff and I are both politicians. He understands my position. I understand his. We respect each other.

He's damn good at what he does." Swift hesitated. "So am I. That's why I keep getting reelected."

"If I remember correctly," I said, "Machiavelli said that it's better to be feared than loved. Maybe SAFE has taken that piece of wisdom to heart."

"Machiavelli also said that politicians should know how to play both the lion and the fox. Gene McNiff's very foxy. No fox would send an assassin after his enemies."

"Well," I said, "I just thought I'd let you know. Wally had a couple of threatening phone calls before they shot him."

"Phone calls, huh?"

"Yes. I heard one of them. The caller said Wally was an enemy of SAFE and deserved to die."

"And you think one of these callers shot him, is that it?"

"It seems pretty obvious. I mean, the sheriff out there thinks it was a hunting accident, but—"

"If you intended to shoot somebody, would you call them first?"

"I don't know what I'd do if I was that crazy. Sure. Maybe I would."

"I've been on the SAFE list for years," said Swift. "No one has taken a shot at me yet."

"You're not concerned, then?"

"Nope. Damned sorry about Walt. But I suspect that sheriff's probably right."

"Well, I'm sorry to bother you, then," I said. "Just figured you might want to know."

"Look, Mr. Coyne. I appreciate the call, and I'm glad it's not a death threat." He chuckled softly. "But listen. Number seven's pretty far down the list, so I don't think you need to be too concerned. They'll catch up with him before he gets that far."

I hung up, feeling vaguely foolish.

Maybe it *was* a hunting accident.

Nah. No way.

I poured one more finger of Jack Daniel's over the half-melted ice cubes in my glass, then pecked out the Wellesley number.

"Hello?" Gloria's voice sounded sleepy.

"Wake you up?"

"Oh, Brady. No. I was reading."

"Just to let you know that I'm back."

"You didn't have to." She yawned. "I wasn't worried about you. I mean, you didn't fall in, did you?"

"No."

"Catch lots of fish?"

"A few."

"Well," she said, "that's nice."

"The boys okay?"

"I guess."

"You?"

"I'm fine, Brady. Thank you. Shit."

"What?"

I heard her sigh. "I guess I don't know why you called."

"I just wanted to hear a friendly voice."

"Well, I'm sorry to disappoint you." She hesitated. "I *am* sorry. I would just think, after ten—what is it, almost twelve?—after twelve years . . ."

"We can still be friends," I said.

"We *are* friends. I'm glad you're back safe and sound. Welcome home. I'm sorry I'm grouchy."

"It's fine. Your grouchiness. It's comforting."

She laughed. "Good night, Brady."

"Good night, Gloria."

I hung up and went to bed.

Julie, as expected, had a big backlog of phone calls for me to return, conferences to schedule, and papers to go over. I did all the phone business and took a halfhearted swipe at the papers, and it wasn't until mid-afternoon when I finally got the chance to call state police headquarters at 1010 Commonwealth Avenue.

I asked for Lieutenant Horowitz, expecting I'd have to leave a message for him. But he picked up the phone and growled, "Yeah. Horowitz."

"Coyne," I said.

"I'm busy. We're even. No favors."

"You already know that Walt Kinnick was shot over the weekend, then."

*"What?"*

"Walt Kinnick was—"

"I heard you. Kinnick's the television guy, right? His name's been in the papers. What happened?"

"You haven't heard."

"For Christ sake, Coyne. If I knew, I wouldn't be asking, would I?"

"I suppose not."

"So tell me."

I told him.

Horowitz was quiet for a moment after I finished. Then he mumbled, "It's not our jurisdiction. Local cops. Unless they invite us in." Another pause, then, "Lemme see what I can find out."

"Sheriff Mason was the one I talked to," I said.

"Mason, huh?"

"From Fenwick, I assume. That's where the cabin is."

"I can figure it out, Coyne."

"I found three spent rifle cartridges in the woods."

"At the scene of the crime, huh?"

"Yes."

"And you gave them to the sheriff, right?"

"No."

"Why the hell not? You trying to obstruct justice, Coyne?"

"Mason thinks it was a hunting accident."

"And you don't, of course."

"No. That's why I'm calling you."

"Thanks a shitload. What the hell do you want me to do?"

"I don't know. Do you want these cartridges or not?"

"It's not my jurisdiction, I told you."

"I know. They're .223 Remington. Varmint load."

He chuckled. "Varmint, eh?"

"Yes. I talked with a guy at a gun shop."

"You at your office now?"

"Yes."

"Got those cartridges with you?"

"Yes."

"I'll have somebody pick them up."

"I'll be here till six or so."

"Okay."

He hung up without saying good-bye. Horowitz wasn't big on formalities.

I stared at the stack of remaining paperwork on my desk. It failed to inspire me. I looked up the number for the Boston legislative office of the senior senator from Massachusetts. A chipper young woman answered. "Senator Kennedy's office. May I help you?"

"I don't suppose I could talk to the senator," I said.

"He's in Washington, sir. If you could tell me what it's about . . ."

"Well, it's sort of personal. Not political or legislative or anything like that."

"The senator's office checks in with us every day," she said. "If you want to leave a message, I'll see that they get it."

"Well, okay," I said. I cleared my throat. "Perhaps the senator is aware that he's number four on the enemies' list of the Second Amendment For Ever. That's the New England gun lobby. I just wanted to alert him to the fact that the man listed number one has been shot, and—"

"Can I have your name and phone number, sir?"

"Sure." I gave them to her.

"Thank you. As you were saying?"

"Well, Walt Kinnick—that's SAFE's enemy number one—he was shot over the weekend. Not killed, but badly hurt. And I just figured that the senator should be, um, aware of it."

"An assassination attempt? Is that what you're saying?"

"I guess so. Yes."

"I'll see that the senator's office gets the message, Mr. Coyne. Thank you."

I called the junior senator's office and conveyed the same message to the enthusiastic young man who answered. He, too, thanked me.

The rest of my fellow enemies, except for Wilson Bailey way down at number ten, were out-of-state politicians. I decided I'd done my good deed for the day and didn't call them.

I sighed and reached for my stack of paperwork.

I was moving semicolons around on a will when Julie buzzed me. "Alexandria Shaw on line one," she said.

"Who?"

"The reporter, Brady."

"Oh, right. Okay." I poked the blinking red button on my telephone console and said, "Brady Coyne."

"Mr. Coyne, it's Alex Shaw from the *Globe*."

"Sure. Hi."

"I'd like another interview. Can we set something up?"

"Boy, I don't know. I've been away, and—"

"I heard about Walt Kinnick. I know he's in Mass General. I know you were there when it happened."

"You must be a helluva reporter," I said. "There's at least one state police lieutenant who didn't know that."

"I am," she said. "I'm a terrific reporter. Look. I think there's an important story here, Mr. Coyne."

I hesitated for a moment, then said, "I do, too."

"I'll buy you a drink."

"One?"

"Sure. Then you can buy me one."

"Fair enough," I said. "Where and when?"

"You know Papa Razzi on Dartmouth Street?"

"Italian, right?"

She laughed. "Good for you. Six-thirty okay?"

"Six-thirty's fine. And Ms. Shaw?"

"Yes?"

"Don't expect too much from me."

"I understand. You're a lawyer. I never expect much from lawyers, Mr. Coyne."

I dictated some letters to Julie. The state trooper arrived right after she left at five. I gave him the plastic bag containing the three spent rifle cartridges I had found in the woods near Wally's cabin and told him that I had not handled two of them so they might get fingerprints off them.

He nodded quickly and said, "Thank you, sir," by which I figured he meant, "We know our job, dummy."

After he left I tried to call Charlie, but he had already left the office.

No one answered at Doc Adams's house.

I stirred legal papers around on top of my desk. After the events of the weekend, practicing law felt frivolous and make-believe. It felt—well, it felt like *practicing*, and I had trouble concentrating on it. I alternated glancing at my watch and swiveling my chair around to gaze out the window behind my desk. The slanting late afternoon sun glowed against the brick buildings and reflected gold on the glass, and I mourned another precious day in May that had been sacrificed to the ungrateful gods of Earning a Living.

On the Deerfield, trout would be eating insects off the surface of the water.

Wally Kinnick lay in a hospital bed, bristling with plastic tubes.

I was willing to bet that somebody, somewhere, was plotting another assassination.

At six-twenty I switched on the answering machine, locked up, and strolled over to Dartmouth Street. I tried to remember what Alexandria Shaw looked like. All I could remember was big round glasses perched low on her nose and her habit of poking at them with her forefinger.

And her legs. She had good legs. I knew better than to remark on them. But I remembered them.

*Very* good legs, in fact. Smooth, tanned, shapely legs.

The Monday after-work crowd was sparse at Papa Razzi's Trattoria, and I spotted Alexandria Shaw's legs astride a barstool. She was wearing a blue and green print dress. It had ridden up several inches above her knees. She was holding a cigarette in one hand and a whiskey sour glass in the other.

I took the empty stool beside her. "This wasn't taken, I hope," I said.

She turned and smiled at me. "Saving it for you. Had to fight off about a hundred hunky guys." She put her cigarette into an ashtray and held her hand out to me. "Thanks for coming."

I took her hand. "I rarely turn down a free drink," I said. She wasn't wearing her big round glasses. Her eyes were the same blue-green color as her dress. They were widely spaced and tilted slightly upward at the corners. She had high, pronounced cheekbones.

She smiled. "You're staring at me."

"I almost didn't recognize you," I said. "You're not wearing your glasses."

"The magic of contact lenses."

"I didn't know you were beautiful."

She shrugged. "Beauty usually gets in the way."

I pondered that one. With me, apparently, she did not expect her beauty to get in the way.

The bartender came over and took a cursory swipe in front of me with his rag. "Sir?"

"Bourbon old-fashioned, on the rocks. And another sour for the lady."

"I want to hear all about your adventures," she said.

I remembered my strained Sunday night phone conversation with Gloria. Gloria hadn't wanted to hear anything about my adventures.

Alex Shaw is a reporter, I reminded myself. Not an ex-wife.

"I imagine you do," I said.

She smiled.

"I'm not sure I trust you," I said.

"You're a lawyer, Mr. Coyne. You're not expected to trust anybody. I'll bet you can take care of yourself."

"And you're a reporter, undoubtedly skilled at dealing with people who think they can take care of themselves."

She smiled in an obvious burlesque of seductiveness, lifting her chin and drooping her eyelids. Then she laughed and crossed her eyes. "You're an eyewitness to a murder attempt," she said. "I've already got the facts of the story. But I want . . ." She shook her head. "There's a *real* story here. I don't know if you can help or not."

Our drinks arrived. We clicked glasses. We sipped. She took out a cigarette. I held my Zippo for her. She steadied my hand with hers, dipped her cigarette into the flame, and looked up at me through the smoke she exhaled. I had the sense that Alex

Shaw was accustomed to getting men to tell her things, regardless of how well they thought they could take care of themselves.

I snapped the lighter shut and dropped it onto the bar. "What are you trying to do?"

"Interview a source."

"Why didn't you wear your glasses?"

She shrugged.

"You're not going to, um, try to seduce me into saying something I don't want to say, are you?"

"Seduce? Oh, my."

I smiled.

"Make it Alex, okay?"

"Sure. And I'm Mr. Coyne. Fair?"

She rolled her eyes. "Fair."

"Tell me, Alex," I said. "What's your angle?"

"Angle, Mr. Coyne, sir?"

"On gun control. On the Second Amendment For Ever. Are you trying to make a case?"

"A case?" She snorted. "Lawyers make cases. Reporters make stories. I want to know what happens, and why it happens, and who's responsible for it happening, and where it happens, and when. That's it. The story. Gun control? I could give a shit. Honestly. I'm reporter, not a columnist. SAFE? Hey, if they make stories, I love 'em."

"Fill up your space."

"Right," she said. "Survival of the vulgarest."

"Well, you're probably wasting your time with me."

"I seriously doubt it," she said. "Look. Can't we just relax, have a couple drinks, and talk? Like friends? How could that be a waste of time?"

"I don't know anything," I said.

"In that case, you certainly can relax."

I sipped my drink. "I didn't really see anything," I said. "I was inside when I heard the shots. So I—"

"How many shots?"

"I'm not sure. Four or five, maybe. There was one, then a pause, then several in rapid succession. Anyway, I ran outside and we found Wally on the ground in the woods. He'd been hit in the stomach. It looked bad. There was a lot of blood. I really thought he was going to die. Diana ran back in and—"

"Diana?"

"I didn't say that."

"Who's Diana?"

"Goddess of the hunt. Nobody. Forget it."

She shrugged. "Okay. Continue."

"That's it, really. The ambulance came, they took Wally to the hospital in North Adams. He made it through the surgery and now he's in Mass General. It looks like he's going to be okay."

"You didn't see who did it?"

"No."

"Did Kinnick?"

"I don't know."

"What did the police say?"

"To me? Nothing. The sheriff interviewed us. He was clearly going through the motions. He wanted it to be a hunting accident. It's spring turkey season. Popular sport in the Berkshires."

"Who's the sheriff?"

"Guy named Mason. Fenwick, that's the town."

"Hunting accident, you said?"

I shrugged.

"You don't believe that, do you?"

"No."

"Why?"

"They hunt turkeys with shotguns. Wally was shot with a rifle."

"Really?"

"Yes. I found some empty cartridges."

"Do you have them?"

I shook my head. "I turned them over to the authorities."

"That sheriff?"

"No. The state police."

"But they don't have jurisdiction."

"No. Not unless . . . "

"Unless Kinnick dies," she finished.

"Right."

"So what *do* you believe, Mr. Coyne, sir?"

I spread my hands. "It seems obvious."

"Somebody from SAFE, huh?"

"It could be," I said. "That's what I think, but I guess it could be anybody. Someone like Wally, a public figure and all—who knows what nutcakes out there think he's a bad guy?"

"You're both on that enemies' list of theirs."

I touched her wrist. "Look," I said. "You've already got your story. I haven't told you anything you don't already know, or suspect. Am I right?"

"You haven't told me anything. Right."

"I mean, that business about the rifle cartridges . . ."

"What rifle cartridges?" She smiled.

"Exactly," I said. "So when you write your story, there's no reason why I should appear in it."

Her free hand touched mine where it lay on her wrist. She leaned toward me. "Listen, Mr. Coyne. If I've got the chance to interview the victim of an assassination attempt before he's assassinated, it would make one helluva story. Don't you agree?"

I took back my hand and used it to pick up my drink. "One helluva story, indeed," I said. I took a sip. "Maybe you wondered why I agreed to meet with you."

She smiled. "You wanted to see what I looked like without my glasses."

"Actually, I didn't know you were ever without them," I said. "No, I just decided that if it *was* some whacko from SAFE . . ."

"A big newspaper story might get the organization to crack down on its membership."

I nodded. "Something like that, I guess. And it would alert any potential, um, targets."

She tilted her head and gazed at me solemnly. "There seems to be one target who's already alert. Maybe even a little frightened."

"He might not actually admit it," I said. "But it could be true. And you might as well make it Brady, I guess."

She smiled.

“And if you want to talk some more,” I said, “maybe we ought to get a table and have some dinner.”

“I’ve got a better idea,” she said. “I live just around the corner, on Marlborough Street. Why don’t I make something for us?”

“Yeah?”

“Sure.”

“You really know how to treat a source,” I said.

Her apartment was halfway down the Berkeley-Clarendon block, on the third floor. Tall windows admitted the sun’s soft setting afterglow into her living room. Both side walls were lined with floor-to-ceiling bookshelves. There was a big sofa with a patchwork quilt rumpled on top of it, a pair of ummatched leather chairs, a coffee table piled with newspapers and mugs and ashtrays. In the corner stood a scarred cherry dining table with a typewriter and stacks of books on it.

Terri Fiori and Sylvie Szabo, my former loves, both kept messy apartments, I remembered. Hell, I kept a messy apartment. And Alexandria Shaw’s place was messy.

Gloria, my ex-wife, kept a decidedly unmessy home.

There was probably something significant in that.

A stereo system had its own table by the front windows. Alex flicked it on. Somebody was playing the saxophone. It could have been Stan Getz.

She took my hand and led me into the kitchen. She waved at a cabinet. “Booze,” she said. “Help yourself. I want to liberate myself from panty hose.”

I found a bottle of Old Grand-Dad, a glass, and a tray of ice cubes in a freezer that needed defrosting. I made a drink and took it back to the living room so I could study her library.

It was a random collection, randomly organized. I found nothing on the subject of fly fishing. The closest thing was a paperback entitled *Breeding Tropical Fish.* I took it to the front window and stood there looking at the pictures and sipping my drink.

Her cold hand on the back of my neck made me jump. I turned around. She had changed into a white T-shirt advertising the Walk for Hunger and black sweat pants. Her feet were bare.

She reached up and tugged at my necktie. "If you don't get comfortable I'll feel obliged to wrestle my panty hose and bra back on," she said.

I took off my tie and jacket and handed them to her. She tossed them onto the sofa.

She tiptoed up and kissed my chin. "That's better." She turned and went into the kitchen, trailing behind her the scent of soap. "Hope you like pasta," she called back over her shoulder.

A red candle burning in an old wine bottle. Fresh plum tomatoes and onion slivers, boiled down into a sauce, poured over linguini, and sprinkled with grated Parmesan cheese and dill. Sliced cucumber with a few drops of vinegar and fresh basil. Two bottles of chianti.

The dill gave the pasta an eccentric flavor. I liked it.

Alex Shaw was thirty-seven, never married. "Sequentially monogamous," was how she put it. Her relationships tended to end when the man of the moment wanted to move in with her, or wanted her to give up her own place to live with him. "That's how I know it's not going to work permanently," she told me after we had taken the second bottle of chianti to the sofa. "I figure, if giving up my space doesn't feel right, then there's no future in the relationship."

"And now?"

She smiled. "That's *not* why I called you."

"Nobody?"

She shook her head.

"Me neither," I said.

She looked at me for a moment. "You've been divorced for twelve years," she said softly. "Two boys. William, a junior at U Mass. Joseph, senior at Wellesley High. Ex-wife, Gloria, professional photographer. One-man law office, catering to prominent wealthy Bostonians. Mostly family law and probate. Avid trout fisherman. You once shot and killed a man."

"He was—"

"He was a criminal. You were not charged."

"Alex—"

She burrowed her head against my shoulder. "I'm a good reporter, Mr. Coyne, sir," she mumbled into my chest.

I stroked her hair. "I'm still not sure I trust you," I said.

"Does that mean you won't kiss me?"

"It means that's all I'll do."

And I did.

And as difficult as it was, that was all I did.

After the noontime recess on Tuesday, I took a cab from the courthouse in East Cambridge over to Mass General. Wally had a private room with a view of an air shaft. A vase of spring flowers sat on the table beside his bed. A television on an adjustable shelf flashed silent color pictures overhead.

His bed was cranked up under his knees and behind his head, folding him into the shape of an N. A plastic tube was trickling clear fluid into the back of his hand. His eyes were closed.

I poked his shoulder. "Hey, are you awake?" I whispered.

He opened his eyes, blinked once, and focused on me. "What time is it?" he croaked.

"Noon."

"Day?"

"Tuesday."

"City?"

"Boston."

"Correct." He grinned. "You win another spin at the wheel."

"So how're you feeling," I said, "aside from that chronic pain in the ass?"

He hunched his shoulders and rotated his head. He winced, then smiled quickly at me. "They wake you up every three hours to shove things into your orifices and then they ask you how it feels. With a thermometer in your mouth, all you can do is mumble, which is what they want to hear, because they don't like to know that your worst problem is all the gadgets they're sticking into you. All I want is a good night's sleep. I try to sneak in naps between interruptions. Mainly, I feel tired, Coyne. Other than that, I just feel stupid."

"Huh?"

"I can't keep track of things. I can't tell whether I'm awake or asleep. I have dreams."

"Drugs, huh?"

"I guess." He yawned. "You just missed Diana, I think."

"You think?"

"She was here. Or else I dreamed it. Or else it was yesterday." He grinned through his beard. "A certain part of it I dreamed, I'm pretty sure, because I don't think I really jumped her. I'm not used to being tethered to a bed."

I pulled a wooden chair up next to him, turned it around, and straddled it. I rested my forearms on the back. "What do you remember about it?" I said.

"It?"

"Your . . . accident."

"The last thing I remember is kissing Diana and taking Corky into the woods. He got to chase a rabbit, and we flushed a grouse." He shrugged.

"You don't recall hearing anything or seeing anything."

"No."

"When we found you, you said, 'They got me.'"

"They?"

"That's what you said."

He shrugged. "I don't remember seeing anything."

"Are you sure?"

He turned his head and glowered at me. "Jesus, Coyne."

"I'm sorry, Wally."

"Enough of the fucking interrogation."

"Okay. I just hoped maybe we could figure it out. You do know what happened."

"Sure. I got bushwhacked."

"Have you thought about it?"

He grinned crookedly. "In what the nurses quaintly call my 'moments of lucidity,' it's about all I do think about."

"Somebody tried to kill you, you know."

"Sure. I know." He cocked his head at me. "Have you and I already discussed this?"

I nodded. "Sort of. Back when you were in North Adams. You were heavily sedated."

"What'd I say?"

"You said, as I recall, that you were sleepy."

"I didn't mention anybody then?"

"No. The sheriff out there is calling it a hunting accident, you know."

He smiled. "A hunting accident."

"Yes. He thinks a turkey hunter let off some wild shots in the woods that you got in the way of."

"Sure," he said. "That's probably what happened."

"You don't believe that."

"Of course not." He reached up, grimaced, and adjusted the pillow behind his neck. "I don't believe much of anything, Brady. But here's what I think. I think if *anybody* was hit by a stray bullet, the first thing he'd do would be to try to figure out all the people who'd have a motive to murder him. And he'd sure as hell come up with a few names, and then he'd feel better about it, because, when you think about it, accidents are a helluva lot scarier than murders."

"In this case," I said, "I personally would prefer it if what happened to you was an accident."

He grinned. "Sure. Because if it was, it'd mean nobody would be after you."
"You know about the SAFE enemies' list, then."
He jerked his head at the vase of flowers. "Gene McNiff sent them. A copy of the newsletter came with them."
"By way of reinforcing the threat?"
Wally smiled. "Nah. By way of telling me it wasn't them."
"What do you think?"
"I don't think McNiff had anything to do with it."
"But somebody else from SAFE?"
He tried to shift his position in the bed. The effort caused him to bite his bottom lip.
"Pain?" I said.
He nodded. "Listen," he said. "I don't like the idea of an accident. I mean, random things just—happen. People invented a wrathful God to account for randomness, because the most arbitrary, vengeful God of man's imagination is easier to accept as a cause than—than no cause at all. We want logic, motive, cause and effect, purpose. Without purpose, life is chaotic and meaningless. Nobody likes to think that bullets fly randomly around the woods hitting people who happen to be in the way. It's a hell of a lot more comforting to believe in rational explanations than in randomness. Having an enemy out gunning for you—at least it makes a kind of sense. If things just happen randomly, that means they're out of our control and the world's crazy. Nobody likes that."
"Thank you Sören Kierkegaard." I smiled at him. "You *have* been doing some thinking."
"It's the best thing to do with a moment of lucidity."
"So you don't *want* it to've been an accident. Does that mean you *believe* you have an enemy who wants to kill you?"
Wally chuckled. "That's not especially comforting, either, is it?"
"You were shot with a rifle, not a shotgun, you know."
"It felt like a bazooka."
"It was a rifle. I found some empty cartridges not far from where you were hit. They were .223 Remington."

"Varmint load," he muttered. "Were they fresh?"

I shrugged. "I don't know."

He shook his head. "I just don't think SAFE was behind this."

"You think it *was* a hunting accident?"

"I kinda believe in randomness," he said, "even if I don't like it."

"But you said, 'They got me.' I assumed you meant SAFE."

He shrugged. "I don't know what I was thinking. I don't remember seeing anything."

"What about their enemies' list? You're number one. Hey, I made seventh place myself. Seems to me some whacko out there sees that, figures he's going to answer the call."

He frowned at me. "Work his way down the list, you mean? Is that what you think?"

I shrugged.

"You were thinking of those phone calls," he said.

"Sure. That one I heard. He sounded pretty serious."

"He'd have to bump off a couple of United States senators to get to you, you know."

"I know. I was thinking he might skip over the hard targets. Paranoid, huh?"

Wally reached over and squeezed my arm. "Shit, Brady. I'm sorry I dragged you into this."

"Yeah. Me, too."

"Jesus, though," he said. "It'd be incredibly stupid for SAFE to send out a hit man to shoot their enemies."

"Of course it would. I doubt that they voted on it in executive session, took nominations, elected an assassin. I just figure there's one warped mind out there somewhere . . ."

"I don't know." Wally squeezed his eyes shut and sighed. "I'm sorry I can't shed more light on this, Brady. All this thinking's hurting my head. This moment of relative lucidity is deserting me."

"Okay." I stood up, then leaned over and gripped his shoulder. "I'll be back."

"Good. We can do more philosophy."

"I'll see what I can find out."

"Track down that turkey shooter."

I got back to the office around one-thirty. Julie was on the phone. I poured myself some coffee and sat on the edge of her desk to sip it. When she hung up, she said, "Where've you been?"

"I visited Wally after court."

"How is he?"

"He seemed pretty good. We had a long philosophical discussion. He's out of ICU, so I guess that means he's coming along."

"Want me to have some flowers sent over?"

"I don't think Wally's the flowers type. I'll bring him a book next time I see him."

I spent most of the afternoon on the phone, with frequent visits to the coffee urn, and it was nearly five when Julie poked her head in. "Lieutenant Horowitz has arrived and I am departing," she said.

"Horowitz is here?"

"Yes. And I'm out of here."

I blew her a kiss. "Send him in."

He was wearing a green blazer with gold buttons over a pale blue button-down shirt, chino pants, loafers. No tie. He was working on a wad of bubble gum, as usual.

He didn't offer to shake hands. Horowitz wastes little time on ceremonies. He went over to the sofa and sat down.

"You want some coffee?" I said.

"Julie offered me some. I declined. Can't chew gum and drink coffee at the same time."

"Nasty habit, that gum."

"So you keep telling me."

"You'll get yourself a case of TMJ."

"Yeah." He grinned. "I keep trying cigarettes. But I'm hooked on the gum."

I sat across from him. "What's up?"

"Nothing, basically. Which bothers me. I talked to a friend of mine at the headquarters in Springfield. Like I told you, it's not a state police case. They got a report from the local cops, who're calling it a hunting accident. No suspects. Presumably they're investigating it. The local guy, this sheriff . . ."

"Mason," I said.

Horowitz shrugged. "He interviewed the witnesses, which were you and the lady and the victim, and none of you saw anything, and he went up and looked around the crime scene, which had already been rained on by the time he got there and where he didn't see anything, and when you cut through all the bullshit in those reports, he got nothing."

"You came all the way over here to tell me this?" I said.

"I *didn't* come all the way over here. I had some business downtown. So I was already over here, figured I'd drop in. You know, out of deep and abiding friendship, all that shit. Listen, Coyne. This stinks, as you know. There's thousands of guys out there who confuse their guns with their peckers and who've most likely decided that Walt Kinnick is trying to emasculate them. It doesn't take a particularly vivid imagination to build scenarios."

"That's what I've been doing," I said. "Building scenarios."

"You don't buy the hunting accident theory, either, huh?"

"Of course not. It's stupid."

"Figure it this way," said Horowitz. "Our guy sneaks up on the cabin like he used to sneak up on VC villages and never quite got it out of his system. Turkeys are okay, but the rush just isn't the same, right? I mean, Kinnick is the first certified enemy he's had in twenty-five years. So he scouts it out, learns Kinnick's habits, knows he goes for a walk first thing in the morning. Same basic route every day. We're all creatures of habit. So our assassin lays in wait, and . . ." He shrugged.

"That's more or less how I see it," I said. "It's pretty obvious it wasn't any accident. The question is, who's the shooter?"

Horowitz rubbed his chin with the palm of his hand. "Those cartridges you gave me?"

"Yeah?"

"Proves it was no turkey hunter. They use shotguns."

I nodded. "I knew that."

"You were thinking an Uzi or something?"

I shrugged. "An assault gun of some kind. Yes, that occurred to me."

"Not an Uzi. An Uzi takes 9 millimeter. The .223 Remington is a 5.56 millimeter load. The 5.56 works in an FNC Paratrooper, a Valmet, a Beretta AR-70, a Galil Model 223 AR, a Steyr AUG-SA, though. There's some others."

"Are those what they sound like they are?"

He nodded. "Semiautomatic paramilitary weapons. Assault guns. But before you get all excited, keep in mind that the .223 is a common varmint load. Winchester and Remington, among others, make rifles chambered for the .223. They probably hunt varmints up in those hills, but they don't use varmint rifles for turkey hunting."

"Whatever kind of gun it was," I said, "it was no accident. Find any fingerprints on those cartridges?"

He shook his head. "A few smudges. Nothing useful."

I shrugged. "Too bad."

"These shots," said Horowitz. "They came close together? Like about as fast as a person could pull the trigger?"

I nodded. "There was one shot, then a pause, then several. Yes, about as fast as you could pull the trigger. Like a semiautomatic."

"All the lab could tell us," he said, "was that the same gun fired those three cartridges. They can't tell us anything about the gun. Of course, if they had the gun, they could match it with the marks of the firing pin and the ejectors on those cartridges." He pushed himself to his feet. "Well, anyhow, it's all academic," he said. "Unless the local cops want to invite the state cops in, it's their case. Of course, if Kinnick should die . . ."

"Then it would be your case."

"Right. Then it would be a homicide. We've got plenty of cases already. Probably not worth it, having him die."

"Probably not," I said.

I was watching the ball game that evening when my intercom buzzed. "What's up, Tony?" I said into it.

"There's a couple of people here who want to see you, Mr. Coyne."

"Who are they?"

I heard a murmur of voices. Then Tony said, "They told me to tell you it's government business."

"Shit," I said. "The IRS this time of night?"

"I don't think they're IRS, Mr. Coyne."

"Well, in that case I guess you can send them up."

"They're on their way."

A couple of minutes later there was a discreet knock on my door. I padded stocking-footed to it and opened up. A man and a woman stood there. He wore a conservative gray business suit with a blue tie. She wore a green pants suit. She appeared to be in her mid-thirties. He was a few years younger. They had grim faces, trim bodies, and short haircuts. They could have been big sister and little brother, and I thought for just a moment that they were handing out copies of *The Watchtower*.

"Special Agent Krensky," said the woman. "This is Agent Tilson."

She held up a leather folder and let it fall open. I squinted at it. The words "Secret Service" jumped out at me.

"You sure you've got the right apartment?" I said.

"You're Brady Coyne?"

I nodded.

"May we come in?" she said.

"Sure."

I stepped aside. They hesitated, so I turned and walked back into my living room. They closed the door and followed behind me.

"Want some coffee or something?"

"No, thank you," said Agent Krensky.

"Have a seat." I gestured at the sofa.

"That's all right, thanks."

So the three of us stood there in the middle of my living room. I reached over and turned off the volume on the television. The Sox had a one-run lead in the eighth, and I figured I could at least keep an eye on the action.

"So what can I do for you?" I said.

"We take all assassination threats very seriously," she said.

"Oh well—"

"You *are* the Brady Coyne who called Senator Kennedy's office on Monday?"

"Yes."

"And you did leave a message threatening him with an assassination attempt."

"Yes. Well, no, not exactly. You see—"

They were both staring at me.

"Oh, Jesus," I said. I began to laugh. Neither Agent Krensky nor Agent Tilson so much as smiled. I took a deep breath. "Look. I didn't threaten the senator. I *warned* him. I called Senator Kerry's office, too. They're on an enemies' list, and the person at the top of that list has already been shot. So I was trying to be a good citizen."

"You didn't threaten the senator?" This was Agent Tilson, speaking for the first time.

"Shit, no. What did that girl tell you, anyway?"

The two of them exchanged glances that defied interpretation. Then Krensky said, "What's this enemies' list?"

"Hang on. I'll show you." I went over to my rolltop desk. Tilson followed right behind me. I rummaged among the papers until I found the SAFE newsletter. I handed it to Tilson.

He turned it over to Krensky, who frowned at it and then arched her eyebrows at me. "You better explain," she said.

So I explained about SAFE and Wally's testimony, the confrontation in Dunkin' Donuts and the phone calls Wally had received. I told them about how Wally got shot in the stomach and how he was doing okay at Mass General. I told them that, personally, I found it a bit unnerving to be on that enemies' list, and I figured that the senator might want to know that he was on it, too.

Agents Krensky and Tilson shrugged at each other. "How about that coffee, Mr. Coyne?" said Krensky. "Is it already brewed?"

I poured three mugs of coffee, and we sat in the living room sipping it. "Didn't figure you for an assassin," said Tilson. "Nothing in your files."

"You've got files on me?"

He smiled. "Why, sure."

"But you know the senator's history," added Krensky. "And that of his family. The word 'assassination' sends up a red flag, as you can imagine."

"That girl I talked to must've garbled my message."

She shrugged. "If it's any comfort to you, Mr. Coyne, you should know that the senator's name is on many enemies' lists. SAFE is only one of them. We've investigated the organization very thoroughly, of course. They are under constant surveillance. There is absolutely no hint of subversion or conspiracy or any illegal activity whatsoever."

"Plenty of paranoia, though," I said. "Hell, they publish a list of enemies and distribute it to guys with guns. What do they expect? It doesn't need to be the organization. It could be an individual. A vigilante. Some nutcake acting on his own."

She nodded. "We take these things very seriously, I assure

you. This—um, this incident with Mr. Kinnick—we'll certainly see that it's followed up." She paused to sip her coffee. "I expect that Mr. Kinnick does have his enemies. Perhaps one of them learned that he is on the SAFE list and figured that suspicion would fall on them."

"I thought of that," I said.

"I assume the local police are investigating."

"Yeah, the sheriff out there in Fenwick is all over the case."

She smiled.

"You should talk with Lieutenant Horowitz. He's with the state police. Friend of mine."

"Sure," she said.

"Look, if you think I'm overreacting—"

"No," she said. "You're not. And neither are we. You should always react. Ninety-nine percent of the time there's nothing to it. But if you react quickly and alertly at that one-hundredth time you can prevent a tragedy."

While Krensky talked, Tilson casually picked up his mug and began wandering around my apartment. Somehow I didn't think he was studying my decor or admiring my profoundly untidy housekeeping habits. No, he was taking inventory, applying his training, drawing inferences about my character and stability from what he saw, comparing all the pieces of evidence with the classic assassin profiles he'd studied.

And it suddenly occurred to me that these Secret Service agents were trained to mistrust people, and they knew exactly how to handle people whom they mistrusted. Chat with them. Be friendly. Sip coffee with them. Make them drop their guard. Get them talking. See what they reveal.

It gave me a small insight into paranoia.

"You believe me, don't you?" I said.

"About what, Mr. Coyne?" said Krensky.

"That I wasn't threatening the senator."

"You weren't, were you?"

"Of course not."

"Why shouldn't we believe you?"

"You *should* believe me. My friend was nearly killed."

She smiled. "Of course," she said. Then she plunked her mug

down onto the coffee table. As if that was a cue, Tilson came back and put his mug down, too. Krensky stood up. So did I. We walked to the door.

Krensky turned and held out her hand. "We're sorry to disturb your evening, Mr. Coyne."

"That's okay. It's good to know you folks are on the ball."

I shook Tilson's hand, too.

"We'll keep in touch," he said.

For some reason, that struck me as ominous.

I spread open the Wednesday *Globe* on my desk and found Alex Shaw's story on page twelve.

The headline read, KINNICK SHOOTING CALLED HUNTING ACCIDENT.

> Local police in the western Massachusetts community of Fenwick have no suspects in the shooting that left Walt Kinnick, the famous sportsman and television personality, hospitalized with a gunshot wound.
>
> Kinnick was shot in the abdomen early Friday morning at his Berkshire retreat. Visiting with him at the time were his attorney, Brady L. Coyne of Boston, and his

> friend Diana West, of Cambridge. Neither witness could be reached for comment.
>
> "It's spring turkey season," said Sheriff Vinton Mason in a prepared statement. "Kinnick's cabin is right in the middle of some good turkey country. Our office is attempting to determine who was hunting in that area on Friday."
>
> Ironically, four days prior to the incident Kinnick testified on Beacon Hill in favor of legislation that would restrict the ownership and use of certain paramilitary firearms known as "assault weapons." Kinnick's testimony opposed that of the Second Amendment For Ever (SAFE) pro-gun lobby, with whom Kinnick was thought to be allied. Subsequently, the bimonthly SAFE newsletter ranked Kinnick number one on its list of "enemies."
>
> Kinnick is the host of the cable television program "Walt Kinnick's Outdoors" and a prominent environmental activist.

I smiled after I read it. Alex's use of the word "ironically" was inspired. Otherwise, her piece was a model of journalistic objectivity. Just the facts.

And yet she had managed to plant the implication that Sheriff Mason was either a dumb hick law officer or a clever obfuscator, that Diana and I had seen something, and that SAFE had powerful motives to kill Wally.

Or maybe I was giving Alex too much credit. It was just a small news item on page twelve. It gave the who, what, where, and when of it without editorializing about the why.

No. That "ironically" made all the difference.

Besides, I knew that Alex lusted to learn the "why" of the story.

She lusted, I recalled, quite literally. It had been a sensational kiss.

She called me in the middle of the morning. "Did you see it?" she said.

"Yes. Loved that 'ironically.'"

She laughed. "I rather liked it myself. My boss is bullshit that he didn't catch it. Listen. I'm on the fly, but I've got a proposition."

"Okay. Shoot."

"Jesus, Brady, don't say that."

"Sorry."

"I've set up an interview with Gene McNiff—you know, SAFE's executive director?—for tomorrow afternoon. I'd love some company."

"Moral support, you mean."

"No," she said. "Your company. I don't need moral support, or any other kind. I'm supposed to meet him at the SAFE headquarters in Clinton at four."

"I don't know, Alex. I'm a big enemy of theirs. I would think my presence could make for a rather hostile interview."

She chuckled. "I thought of that. It wouldn't hurt."

"I thought you just wanted company."

"I do. It's a pretty drive out there in the spring. Lots of apple orchards. Maybe they'll be in blossom now. Tell you what. I'll buy you dinner afterward."

"Four o'clock, huh?"

"I'll pick you up around three."

"Okay."

"Good. See you tomorrow, then."

"Hey, Alex?"

"Yeah?"

"Thanks."

"For what?"

"For how you handled the story."

"I couldn't very well not mention you or Ms. West at all. I corroborated everything, of course."

"I understand."

"I left out those cartridges you found. But that's because nobody at State Police headquarters would talk to me and corroborate it."

"Which," I said, "comes as no surprise to this reporter."

"And," she added, "I did omit the fact that you're on their enemies' list. That's what you mean."

"Yes. I don't need that."

"The last thing I want, Mr. Coyne, sir, is people shooting at you. I've got other things in mind for you."

"Yeah," I said. "So do I."

"Tomorrow at three, then."

In the middle of the afternoon, Julie buzzed me. "Brady," she said, "Senator Swift's office is on line three."

"Okay," I said.

"Hey!" she said quickly.

"Yes?"

"What's this all about?"

"Well, shit, I don't know. Let me talk to him, okay?"

"You don't have to bite my head off."

"I'm sorry," I said.

"You'll keep me informed?"

"Of course. You're the boss, remember?"

I punched the blinking button on the console and said, "Brady Coyne."

"Mr. Coyne," came a male voice, "this is Senator Swift's office."

"Yes?"

"The senator wonders if you'd be able to meet with him."

"Why?"

"He'd rather discuss that with you himself, Mr. Coyne. If at all possible, he'd like to get together with you at the Commonwealth Club at six this evening. Does that work for you?"

"The Commonwealth Club . . ."

"It's on Berkeley Street, sir. Just around the corner from—"

"I know where it is," I said.

"Six o'clock, then?"

"Sure."

The Commonwealth Club is one of those exclusive anachronisms that continue to thrive in Boston: a private men's club, membership rigidly restricted. WASPs only. Republican WASPs. Wealthy Republican WASPs, preferably those whose fathers and grandfathers were also wealthy Republican WASPs.

Because my clientele is skewed to the wealthy, it also tends to be skewed to Republican WASPs with inherited money. I've been inside several anachronisms like the Commonwealth Club. I'd rather have a beer at Skeeter's, but business is sometimes business.

Senator Marlon Swift and I did share membership in a different, even more exclusive, club: the SAFE Top Ten Enemies' club. It gave me a fraternal feeling for the senator. So I would endure the oppressive leather furniture polished by generations of wealthy Republican WASP backsides, the mahogany woodwork stained dark from a century of Cuban cigar smoke, the dusty martinis and the baked finnan haddie served by murmuring old butlers in full livery, and all the dour old bankers and brokers reading their *Wall Street Journals* at the Commonwealth Club to meet with Brother Swift.

When I told Julie I had an audience with Senator Swift at the Commonwealth Club, she arched her eyebrows and said, "Well, la-dee-da."

That's about how I felt about it.

I'd agreed to meet the senator at six, but I waited until six-fifteen to lock up the office for the ten-minute stroll over to the Commonwealth Club. It's not my habit to be late for appointments. Julie thinks it's important to keep people waiting, on the theory, probably sound, that it puts them at a psychological disadvantage. I sometimes defer to her judgment, but I don't agree with it. It's a game. I don't like to think of my law practice as a game.

But in the case of my engagement with Senator Marlon Swift, I wanted him to be there when I arrived, because I didn't feel like having to wait for him. I didn't know if he subscribed to the same theory Julie did. In my experience, the more important a man thinks he is, the more likely he is to play the keep-'em-waiting game.

Politicians generally think they're pretty important.

A small brass plate over the doorbell read "The Commonwealth Club." Elegantly understated. I pressed the buzzer. A shriveled-up little man with sharp blue eyes pulled open the door a moment later. He was wearing a tuxedo that hung a little loosely on him. He appeared to be at least eighty years old. "Sir?" he said, looking me up and down.

"Brady Coyne," I said. "Senator Swift is expecting me."

"Of course."

He stood aside for me. I walked into the foyer, which was as big as my entire apartment. White Italian marble, dark wood wainscoting, textured wallpaper, massive oil portraits, brass sconces, and a crystal chandelier.

I looked around appreciatively. "Pretty nice," I said to the old guy.

His eyes twinkled, but all he said was, "Yes, sir. Right this way, please."

I figured the butler lived in a triple-decker in Southie and had been taking the T over here to his job every day for the past fifty years. If he answered the door, he sure as hell wasn't a member. Probably an Irish Democrat. I wanted to ask him about himself, but he had already begun to lead me through the foyer and into the spacious sitting area.

Leather furniture, dark woodwork, subdued lighting, exactly as I had imagined. Some of the chairs were occupied with men smoking and drinking and studying newspapers. Television sets glowed silently here and there, tuned to a cable channel that flashed Dow Jones numbers. What conversation I heard was soft and conspiratorial.

On the back wall a large window with tiny panes overlooked a small courtyard. Senator Marlon Swift sat in a leather chair gazing out at the tidy gardens.

"Senator?" said the butler.

He looked up, saw me, and pushed himself to his feet. "Mr. Coyne," he said, extending his hand. "Thank you for coming on such short notice. What will you drink?"

I shook his hand. I was tempted to ask for a Bud, no glass necessary, but decided I had no reason to offend. "Jack Daniel's on the rocks, please," I said.

The old butler made a tiny bow and left. The senator gestured to the chair opposite his. I sat, and he did, too.

"Another beautiful spring day," he said.

I smiled and nodded.

"Sox are off to a good start this year."

"Yes," I said.

"How's Walt doing?"

"He seems to be out of danger. It was touch and go for a while."

He nodded. "Good. Nice guy, Walt. I've fished with him, you know. His friend Ms. West worked with me on some legislation a while back. His testimony last week was courageous. Didn't really surprise me, though. Walt's a straight shooter." Swift glanced at me and grinned. "Poor figure of speech, I guess."

I smiled and waited.

He shifted uncomfortably in his chair. He was, I guessed, about my age. He didn't look particularly senatorial. His sandy hair was thinning on top, and he wore dark-rimmed glasses. He was a little shorter than me, on the thin side. "Um, Brady," he began. "Can I call you Brady?"

"Sure."

He grinned shyly. "My friends call me Chip."

"Okay."

"This is difficult," he said.

I shrugged and waited.

"I live in Marshfield, and—oh, thank you, Albert."

The old butler set my drink on the table beside me. I looked up at him. "Thanks," I said.

"Sir?" he said to Swift.

"Not now, thanks."

After Albert had slid away, the senator leaned back in his chair and stared out the window. Without looking at me, he said, "You and I have some mutual friends, Brady. They speak highly of you. They say you're a man of your word. You can be trusted."

I said nothing.

"Discreet," he said. "That's the word they all use. 'Brady Coyne is discreet,' they tell me."

"I'm also a pretty good lawyer."

"Um." He turned his head. "They say that, too. Brady, I want to share something with you."

"And you want me to give you my word that I won't tell anybody what you're going to tell me."

"Yes. Exactly."

"You're not my client, Senator. Privilege is not operative."

"I know. Your word is good enough."

"I think I know what you're going to tell me," I said. "You're putting me on the spot."

He shrugged. "I understand that. My choice is not to tell you. I just figure that you're the one person who can use what I have to say—"

"Without involving you," I finished.

"That's it."

"Okay." I nodded. "You've got my word."

He held his hand out to me and I shook it. Then he returned his gaze to the courtyard outside the window. "I commute from Marshfield," he said quietly. "I own a real estate office down there. My brother runs it. My, um, my Senate duties occupy me. But I drive up and back every day, because I love the peacefulness of the country." He shrugged. "It's not exactly rural, but the air smells of salt and you can see the stars at night. I have several acres that abut conservation land, and every evening, regardless of what time I get home, I change into my running togs and take my two setters out for a slow jog through the fields and woods." He smiled, still looking out at the courtyard. "I don't pretend that it really keeps me in shape. But it cleans out my head."

"Senator—"

"Chip," he said. "Please. Anyway, it was after sundown before I got out with the dogs last night, and we had nearly finished our run, when . . ."

He turned and looked at me, and I saw the fear in his eyes.

"They tried to shoot you," I said.

"Christ, yes," he said. "I was in the Army, Brady. I know a gunshot when I hear it, and my reflexes took over. I fell to the ground and flattened myself out. It was only an instant, and then it was over. There were several rapid shots. I heard them zipping through the trees over my head. Then I heard someone running through the woods. I lay there a long time after I couldn't hear him anymore."

"Did you call the police?"

"Hell, no."

"Don't you think you should have?"

He nodded. "Of course I should have. But I didn't. And I won't. That's why I'm telling you. I'm not sure I can explain it to you."

"You really don't have to explain anything to me, Chip. But if somebody took a potshot at you . . ."

"I know. You're on that list, too."

I shrugged.

He smiled. "Politics is a complicated business, Brady. I have nothing to gain, and much to lose, if this—this assassination attempt were to become known."

"I don't understand."

"Like I said. It's complicated. My subcommittee reported favorably on that assault-weapon bill. Mine was the deciding vote. My record on gun control remains unblemished."

"You support it?"

"Yes. Always. My constituents support gun control. So, therefore, do I. I'm in a powerful position. Chairman of the Senate Subcommittee on Public Safety." He shrugged. "SAFE is more powerful than me, though. As I mentioned to you on the phone the other night, I work with them. Their influence is very important to many of the public safety issues that come before my subcommittee. On the subject of gun control, however, I've been at odds with them for years. They always get their way."

"I still don't see—"

"I had a phone call on my machine yesterday when I got home."

"Just one?"

He shook his head. "I've had plenty of phone calls in my career. Many of them hostile. But yesterday's was—it was different."

"What did he say?"

"Well, it was a death threat. He mentioned SAFE. But it wasn't so much the content of it. It was the tone and the syntax."

"Calm," I said. "Cool. Intelligent. Articulate. Not what you'd expect from a gun-crazy fanatic."

"Why, yes," he said. He arched his eyebrows and peered at me for a moment. Then he smiled and nodded. "Exactly. Cool and articulate. Which made it sound—more frightening."

"I hope you saved the tape."

The senator rolled his eyes. "I'm afraid not."

"Walt Kinnick had a message like the one you describe the night before he was shot," I said. "He didn't save that one, either."

He nodded. "We both blew it. Too bad. Anyway, I don't want any publicity on this. I'm telling you because—well, you were thoughtful enough to call and warn me, and you already know what's going on, and you might be able to use the information. And you've given me your word. I've got plenty of enemies, Brady. I guess every politician does. As far as I'm concerned, SAFE is just one of them. Listen. There isn't a politician alive—even an insignificant state senator—who doesn't think about assassination. It's a disease. A communicable disease. The virus is spread through the newspapers, on television. I'm not just concerned about myself—though God knows I'm frightened. Two United States senators, others, are on that list."

"I'm on that list," I said.

"Exactly."

"That's why you wanted to see me?"

"Yes. To tell you that it would appear your fears are well founded. Walt Kinnick, now me. Number one, then number two. To warn you to be careful."

"You should have told the police."

He shrugged. "Maybe. It was a judgment call. If the police know, the newspapers will pick it up thse way they did with the Kinnick thing. With no witnesses, no suspect, no evidence at all . . ."

"Your image, huh?" I said.

"Yes, I suppose so. My image. The war hero. The man who stands up to powerful special interests such as SAFE. The man with the balls to say no. The man of courage and conviction. The man who—figuratively, of course—dares his enemies to take their best shot. That's my image." He smiled. "It's not necessarily *me,* mind you. But I've got an election coming up next fall. The polls are okay. I don't want to upset them."

"Appearances," I said. "Machiavelli. You don't actually need to be brave. But it must appear that you are."

He nodded. "Yes. That's politics. Do you understand?"

I shrugged. "It doesn't really matter if I understand. Personally, I'd just as soon see that our shooter gets nailed. The sooner the better."

"I know. That's why I feel I must apologize to you. I'd like to see him nailed, too. I didn't like lying there with my face in the dirt. It did not conjure up pleasant memories."

"But your image . . ."

"Yes. No politician wants to come across as frightened, or panicky, or overreacting, or vulnerable. All of which," he said with a small smile, "happen to describe me perfectly right now." He waved his hand. "Anyway, I went out to the woods this morning to look around." He reached into his pocket. "I found these."

He opened his fist. It held two empty brass rifle cartridges. "Take them," he said. He spilled them into my hand. "I don't want them."

I looked at them. They were .223 Remington. They looked identical to the three I had found near Wally's cabin. "How did you—?"

"Prudence," he said, "is one of those important qualities that Machiavelli mentions. I have friends at Ten-Ten Commonwealth Avenue, Brady. After I talked to you on the phone, I inquired about the Kinnick shooting. My contact at Ten-Ten told me you had dug up some evidence." He shrugged. "Now you have some more evidence. Please. Do not tell anybody where they came from."

"Christ, I'm supposed to lie to the state cops?"

He waved his hands. "Or do nothing, if you prefer. It would be helpful, I think, to know for certain that we're dealing with the same man with the same gun. But my name must be kept out of it. I have your word on it."

I shrugged. "Yes. You do."

“Thanks.” He glanced around the room. “Want another drink?”

“No, I guess not.” I leaned toward him. “Look, Chip,” I said. “Do us both a favor, huh?”

“What’s that?”

“Talk to Lieutenant Horowitz.”

He gave his head a small shake.

“Horowitz is discreet,” I said, “and maybe you can convince him that the state cops should be involved in this thing. Right now it’s just a hillbilly sheriff out in Fenwick.”

“I don’t know,” said Swift. “I’d like to help you out, but . . .”

“Help us all out,” I said. “He missed you last night. He might try again.”

“Yeah,” he said. “I thought of that.”

The senator invited me to have dinner with him at the Commonwealth Club. Poached salmon. I declined. I told him I’d made other plans for dinner.

My plan—which I had made at the precise moment that Albert admitted me into the club—was to stroll over to Skeeter’s Infield down the alley off State Street, climb onto a barstool, yank off my necktie, roll up my shirtsleeves, and have one of Skeeter’s big burgers and a couple of draft beers. The Sox would be on the tube and I could argue speed versus power with a banker or a broker or an electrician or an auto mechanic who had seen Ted Williams launch one into the bleachers and who would remember Billy Klaus and Al Zarilla.

I like poached salmon. But I couldn’t wait to get out of the Commonwealth Club.

It was after eleven when I got back to my apartment. I undressed my way to my bedroom. I pulled on a pair of sweat pants and a T-shirt, then went into the living room. I eyed my answering machine cautiously. A steady red eye stared back at me. No messages.

It felt like a stay of execution.

I made myself a mug of Sleepytime in the microwave and took it to the table. I found the SAFE newsletter and sat there with it, sipping my herb tea and trying to read between the lines.

Walt Kinnick was alive, but he was lucky. All but one shot missed him. But that one bullet could have hit him an inch to one side or the other, ripped open a big artery and minced a vital organ or two, and he'd have been dead in three minutes.

Senator Swift had not been hit at all. He had his Army-tuned reflexes to thank for his life, and now he was too scared to talk to the police.

Maybe our assassin was a lousy shot. I found scant consolation in that possibility.

Horowitz wasn't at his desk when I called the next morning. It was nearly noontime when he got back to me.

"What now?" he said.

"I got a couple more empty rifle cartridges for you. They're .223 Remington."

"Our shooter again?"

"Yes, I'd say so."

"Where'd you get 'em?"

"I can't tell you."

"What the fuck do you mean, you can't tell me? I'm a cop, for Christ sake."

"I'm a lawyer, for Christ sake."

"Well, why don't you take your cartridges and pretend they're suppositories for your hemorrhoids, then, Coyne. I ain't got time for games. You trying to pull some kind of privilege shit on me?"

"Yes." I took a deep breath. "No. Listen. I gave my word. If I hadn't, I wouldn't have gotten the cartridges."

"You think you've got evidence about a felony?"

"Yes. I know I do."

He was silent for a moment, except for the sounds of gum chewing. I waited for him.

"Okay," he said. "What *can* you tell me?"

"These cartridges were fired at a different place and at a different time from those that came from the woods in Fenwick."

"And at a different person, huh?"

I said nothing.

"If the lab tells us they were fired by the same gun, you know what that means, Coyne?"

"It means you guys would have jurisdiction on the case."

"Correction," he said. "It means we *could* have jurisdiction. We need more than some fucking cartridges."

"I know. You need evidence of where they came from and that they are linked to attempted assassinations."

"That's right, Mr. Lawyer. And without that evidence—say, in the form of reliable testimony—hell, I could get by with hearsay testimony—we can't do squat."

"I gave my word."

"So it's your ass, Coyne."

"I know. I'd feel better if you guys were on the case. But at least you could take a look at these cartridges."

He sighed. "Fine. Okay. Someone'll be over." And he hung up.

A young female state police detective arrived less than an hour later. I handed her the two empty cartridges. I made sure that I had smudged Senator Swift's fingerprints on them.

I tossed the last of the day's paperwork into the Out box a minute before three. Alex Shaw would be over, and I was eager to get out of the office. So when my console buzzed, I assumed that Julie would tell me Alex had arrived. But she said, "You got a call on line two, Brady."

"Shit," I said. "Who is it?"

"It's your wife."

"My *ex*-wife, Julie. Gloria's my ex-wife."

"I know that," she said sweetly.

I depressed the button and said into the phone, "Hi, hon."

"Brady," she said, "why didn't you tell me?"

"Tell you what?"

"I saw that article in the *Globe*. It said you witnessed a shooting. Is that true?"

"Well, more or less. I—"

"So you called me Sunday night and never even mentioned it?"

"You didn't seem exactly—"

"Brady, I *do* care about you, you know."

"Sometimes I don't know that," I said. "Sometimes I can't tell."

She was silent for a moment. I lit a cigarette.

"I know," she finally said. "I teased you about checking in and out with me. You've got to understand, though. You seem much more conscientious about doing that now than you ever did when we were married. It makes me angry. Does that make any sense to you?"

"As much as anything makes sense, I guess."

"Then when I have to read in the paper that you—you might've been killed, *that* makes me angry, too."

"I wasn't really in any danger, Gloria. They were after Wally."

"What makes me angry is that I had to read it in the paper. Brady, I worry. It's my nature. I imagine bad things. I worry about William and Joseph all the time. And I try to imagine what would become of them if . . ."

"If something happened to me?"

"Yes."

"They'd be fine, Gloria. They're strong young men."

"Or me."

"Huh?"

"What would become of me?" she said. "I mean, if something . . ."

"To quote you, we're divorced, remember?"

"Does that mean we're no longer—connected?"

"I never thought it meant that," I said. "No."

"That I can't still care about you?"

"No."

"Then why didn't you tell me?"

"I didn't think you cared."

"Really?" she said. "You really didn't think I cared?"

"Actually," I said, "I thought you did care. I was going to tell you when I called. I *wanted* to tell you. To talk to you about it. But when we started talking . . ."

"I was bitchy."

"Yes."

"But you know me," she said. "You know that doesn't mean anything."

I sighed. "Gloria, listen."

"What?"

"I know you, yes. I guess I understand your—your moods. Just like you understand mine. But if you recall, we don't like them. Each other's moods. They upset us, make us angry. They make us not want to communicate with each other. It's the way we've always been. It's why we're divorced."

"Which we should be," she said.

"Sure."

"It still . . ."

"It's over, anyway," I said. "It happened. Wally got shot, but he's going to be fine, and I'm fine. Okay?"

There was a hesitation. "Okay." Her voice was small and strangled. "Fine."

"Are you crying?"

"Of course I'm not crying. Why should I cry?"

"It sounded as if you were crying," I said.

"I'm *not* crying. You think—"

"I'm sorry," I said.

"You make me so angry, sometimes."

"I know," I said. "I don't mean to. It's how we are."

"We didn't used to be that way."

"No. It's too bad. I don't have any wisdom on it."

She laughed softly. "There's a first."

"What?"

"You admitting you don't have wisdom on something."

"You—us—you're much too complex for my simple brain, hon."

"Anyway," she said after a moment, "you're okay, huh?"

"Yes. Thanks. I'm okay."

"Well, good. Next time . . ."

"I hope there won't be a next time."

"Me, too," she said quietly.

Julie tapped on my door and stepped into my office just an instant after I hung up with Gloria. "The light went off," she said. "I know you're off the phone."

I sighed and nodded. "I'm off the phone."

"Are you all right?"

"Fine."

"She really cares about you, you know."

"Who?"

"Gloria."

I nodded. Julie believed in marriage. Hers with Edward appeared to be working well. She was happy. She wanted the same happiness for me. Julie believed that my divorce from Gloria was a mere aberration, a pothole in the highway toward marital bliss.

Julie figured that eventually Gloria and I would recognize the error of our ways and reunite.

Actually, Julie believed that the errors were in *my* ways. She believed that Gloria would take me back instantly, and I had learned that there was no sense in trying to explain to her that things were much more complicated than that.

"You love her, don't you?" she would say.

And I would admit that yes, in certain peculiar ways, I loved Gloria.

"And she loves you?"

I would nod and shrug.

"So?"

And I would say, "Well, you never know what might happen," because that was the only thing I could say that would get Julie off the subject. But it also convinced her that she was right, and that Gloria and I shared a destiny.

"So," she said, standing in front of my desk with her fists placed on her slim and shapely hips, "did you get things worked out?"

"With Gloria?"

"Yes."

I nodded. "Yes. Everything's fine."

"Well, good. She was upset."

"I know. Things are fine now."

Julie sat in the chair across from me. "There's somebody here to see you."

"Why didn't you say so?"

"Brady," she said, "I felt so bad. I mean, there you are, talking with Gloria on the phone, and she's all upset and needing you, and right there in our office is this gorgeous woman who you have a date with."

"That's Alexandria Shaw."

"I *know* who she is."

"She's a reporter, Julie."

"So? Everybody's got to be something, no matter how—how *predatory* they are."

I smiled. "The last time she was here, you insisted I see her. You said she had a job to do and I should help her."

"The last time she was here," said Julie, "she wasn't gorgeous. She had these big goofy glasses down on the end of her nose, and if you don't think I understand what's going on when she comes in here in her tight pants and perfect cheekbones and no glasses . . ."

She sputtered to a stop. I smiled.

"You're such an old letch," she mumbled.

"You're worried about Alex's virtue?"

"No." She allowed herself to smile. "Yours."

I reached across the desk and gripped Julie's hand. "Gloria and I really are divorced," I said.

"Yeah, well that's just stupid."

"Go tell Alex I'll be out in one minute, will you?"

Julie nodded. She stood up and started for the door. Then she turned to face me. "I hope you were nice to her," she said.

"Gloria?"

"Yes."

I nodded. "I think I was, yes."

Julie was hunched over the keyboard. Alex Shaw sat across from her with her knees pressed together and her briefcase on her lap.

The two women were studiously ignoring each other.

"Hi," I said to Alex.

She looked up without smiling, then stood and moved toward the door.

"See you tomorrow," I said to Julie.

She glanced up at me, nodded once, then bent back to the keyboard.

Alex drove a small Toyota sedan. She had double-parked in front of my building. We climbed in. She started up. A Bonnie Raitt tape was playing. Alex hummed tunelessly as she cut expertly through the city streets. Soon we were on Route 2, heading west toward Clinton.

We didn't talk.

When we turned onto Route 62 in Concord, I finally said, "What's the matter?"

"Nothing."

"You haven't spoken to me since we left my office. Something's the matter."

She shrugged.

When we got to Maynard, I said, "Stop the car, please."

Alex turned to me. "Why?"

"Please. Pull over."

She did. She turned to look at me. "What's this all about?"

"I want to get out."

"Huh?"

"I don't need this."

"This what?"

"This silence. I'll catch a cab back to the office."

"It's not you," she said.

"Who, then?"

"Me, I guess."

"You better tell me about it."

"Actually," she said, "it's your secretary."

"Was she rude to you?"

"Oh no. Friendly as all getout. Tells me you'll be ready in a minute, but you're on a very important phone call. Your wife. 'He's on the phone with his wife,' she says. Like I'm supposed to understand this is a major priority for you. Now, I know she means ex-wife. But she says wife, and even though I know what she's trying to do, I'm still thinking, what's he doing talking with his ex-wife and keeping me waiting when he knows I've gotta be in Clinton by four, and your secretary keeps chatting away, telling me what a terrific father you are and how devoted you are to your family—she calls it family, see, implying, that it's not just your sons but her, too—your wife—and by the time you come out I'm—aggravated. Aggravated with your secretary for fucking with my head, angry with myself for letting my head be fucked with so easy, and mainly angry at you, because . . ."

"Because?"

"Because, God damn it, I'm a woman and I'm entitled to be angry with a guy if I want."

"Aha!" I said. "My first insight of the day."

She smiled. "Insight, huh?"

"Yes. I know men are no smarter or more competent or anything than women. But I've always maintained that we're different."

"Well, jeez. Of course we're different." She reached over and put her hand on my leg. "Thank God," she said.

"Most women," I said, "seem to think it's an insult to make note of differences between the genders."

"We're different, all right."

"I wish I understood it better."

"Don't try," said Alex. "Just enjoy it." She drummed her fingers on the steering wheel, then said, "Well?"

"Well what?"

"Are you gonna get out?"

"Guess not," I said. "It's an expensive cab ride back to Boston from here." I reached over and touched her hair. "I'm sorry about Julie."

"That's okay," said Alex. "She's a woman. I understand."

She pulled away from the curb. A minute or so later we passed a car that had pulled to the side of the road. I turned to look at it. It was a blue Ford Escort. A classically nondescript vehicle.

"What's the matter?" said Alex.

"That car back there."

"That little Ford?"

"Yes."

"What about it?"

"I think it was behind us on Storrow Drive."

"There must be a million of those cars on the road."

"I know," I said. "That's what bothers me."

Ten minutes later we picked up Route 117, a country road that wound past meadows and newly planted cornfields and apple orchards. The apple trees had already dropped their blossoms and were bursting with shiny pale green leaves. I turned and looked out the back widow. There was no blue Ford Escort in sight.

"I tried to reach Senator Swift," said Alex.

"Senator Swift, huh?"

"I wanted an interview." She glanced sideways at me. "He's next on the list, you know."

"Um," I said.

"I got the brushoff."

"Figures."

"Yeah, I guess. Still, if he gets assassinated, I'll really be upset."

"Hell, so will I."

"I mean," she said, "what a story."

And a few minutes later she said, "I wonder why he wouldn't see me?"

"Who?"

"Chip Swift. I've interviewed him plenty of times. Politicians usually fall all over themselves for reporters. Publicity is their nourishment."

"He's probably just busy."

"Maybe." She was silent for a moment. "Still, I wonder . . ."

I didn't ask her what she wondered. I had the uncomfortable feeling that she knew I had met with the senator at the Commonwealth Club, and somehow she had managed to make me feel guilty that I wouldn't tell her all about it.

Women can do that.

SAFE headquarters occupied the first floor of a converted Victorian house on Route 110 in Clinton, not far from the Wachusett Reservoir. The upper two floors appeared to be apartments.

We pulled into the dirt parking area and got out. As we did a blue Escort cruised past. I couldn't see the driver's face.

"Did you see that?" I said to Alex.

"That car?"

I nodded.

"You think it's the same one?"

"I don't know. If it is . . ."

She squeezed my arm. "Brady," she said.

I shrugged. "Paranoia. Forget it."

We climbed onto the porch. A sign over the doorbell instructed us to RING AND COME IN. So we did.

We walked into the first room off the narrow hallway. It was dominated by a long conference table which was piled with magazines and newspapers and file folders. Two men in T-shirts and jeans were standing by the window drinking Cokes from cans and talking. They stopped their conversation when they saw us. Both of them looked familiar. One of them was tall and gaunt, with close-cropped black hair and gray stubby teeth. The other one was twentyish, with an earring and a blond ponytail and a red face. I couldn't recall his name, though I knew I'd heard it. I had met both of them in the Dunkin' Donuts on Tremont Street.

The younger one hesitated for just an instant, then smiled at us. "How ya doin'?"

Alex and I smiled back. "Just fine," I said.

"Kin I help you?"

"I'm here to see Mr. McNiff," said Alex. "I'm Alexandria Shaw from the *Globe*. I have an appointment."

"Hang on a sec. I'll get him for you."

He disappeared into an inner room. The other guy brushed past us and went out toward the front door without saying anything.

Alex nudged me with her elbow. "Those two guys . . ."

"Right. Dunkin' Donuts."

"Do you think they recognized you?" she said.

"Sure."

"But—"

At that moment Gene McNiff came into the room. His short-sleeved shirt hung untucked over his stomach. If he was surprised to see me with Alex, he didn't show it. "Miz Shaw, welcome," he said, holding out his hand to Alex. She took it. Then he looked at me. "And Mr. Coyne. Hello."

"Hello," I said. We shook hands, too.

"Let's go into my office where we can talk," said McNiff. "Want a Coke or something?"

Alex and I both declined. We followed him through the doorway into a cluttered office. Several metal file cabinets and bookcases stood against the wall. There was a big oak desk with two telephones and several messy stacks of papers. A table held a computer and printer, a copier, and a fax machine. Four unmatched chairs sat randomly on the floor.

The guy with the ponytail was there, too. "Dougie," said McNiff to him, "did you meet Miz Shaw and Mr. Coyne?" To us he said, "This is Douglas, my oldest son. He does a lot of work for SAFE. Sort of my right-hand man."

Dougie nodded to us and gave me a lopsided smile. "I guess we already met, actually. No hard feelings, huh?"

"No problem," I said.

"Well," said McNiff, "we've got some things to discuss, so . . ."

Dougie hesitated for a moment, then left the room.

McNiff gestured at the empty chairs. "Sit, please."

Alex and I sat.

"So," said McNiff after he had settled himself behind his desk, "how is he?" He was looking at me.

"Who?"

"Walt. How's he coming along?"

"He's okay," I said. "It was touch and go for a while."

"Damn shame. Accidents like this shouldn't happen. It only takes one or two irresponsible people to make all gun owners look bad. You know," he said, cocking an eye at Alex, "SAFE has been lobbying for better safety training programs for years. I take every hunting accident personally."

She smiled and nodded. "Mr. McNiff—"

"Gene," he said. "Call me Gene."

"Sure." She cleared her throat. "Mind if I tape this?"

He waved his hand. "Not at all."

She took her little portable tape recorder out of her briefcase, tested it, then put it onto McNiff's desk between them. Then she flipped open her notebook. "Okay," she said. "Now, can we—?"

"Miz Shaw," said McNiff quickly, "I'd like to tell you some things you might not know. Would that be all right?"

"Sure. Fine."

"I'll give you some of our pamphlets, and I hope you'll read them. I mean, I know why you're here." He glanced at me and smiled. "I'm not sure why *you're* here, Mr. Coyne." He dismissed me with a wave of his hand and looked back at Alex. "Anyway, I know your reputation. You're a fair reporter. That's why I welcomed this chance to talk to you. See, SAFE has this unfortunate image, and it stems from our unrelenting battle on behalf of the Second Amendment. But we do a lot more than just fight against the unconstitutional abridgement of the right to bear arms. We teach young people gun safety. We hold special classes all over New England for women who want to learn how to defend themselves. These programs are very popular, Miss Shaw. Women are feeling that they've been the victims of violent crime for too long. They're upset—as we are—about the lack of protection they get from the police and the courts. So they are learning how to defend themselves." He paused and leaned toward us. "And that is precisely what the Second Amendment is all about. It's what SAFE is all about."

McNiff paused, then leaned back and folded his hands on his desk. I had the impression that he had given this speech more than once.

He smiled at Alex. "I hope I'm not boring you."

"Not at all, Mr. McNiff. Please continue."

He shrugged. "We lobby not just for the right to own firearms, but also for tougher penalties for gun-related crimes. See, we know that if the right to own guns is curtailed, then law-abiding citizens will do what the law requires. But criminals don't obey laws. The politicians can disarm the good citizens. But they can't disarm criminals." McNiff shrugged. "End of lecture." He picked up a handful of pamphlets and gave them to Alex. "I hope you'll read them, Miz Shaw. It will help you to understand."

She took them and put them into her briefcase. "Mr. McNiff," she said, "four days after dramatically testifying in favor of gun control, Walt Kinnick was shot. You were seen publicly threatening him. Your newsletter named him the number-one enemy of your organization. It came out two days before the shooting. I'm sure it's obvious to you how that looks."

McNiff nodded. "I'd have to be an imbecile not to see how it looks. It looks like an attempted assassination. But I guarantee that no member of SAFE shot Walt Kinnick." He hesitated. "*I* certainly didn't."

"I didn't mean—"

"Listen," he said. "I publish a newsletter every two weeks. A regular feature is our enemies' list. There's *always* a number-one enemy. Before Walt Kinnick, none of our enemies had ever been shot at. Not one. Ever. And believe me, we've had some pretty big enemies." He leaned forward on his desk and stared hard at Alex. "Look. Our members come from all walks of life. We've got policemen, salesmen, mechanics, schoolteachers, housewives. Lawyers and newspaper reporters, too. You name it. Some of them are highly educated. Some are dropouts. Some are smart, and some, probably, aren't so smart. But they all share our belief in the Second Amendment. And they all know that assassinating our enemies with guns is the worst possible thing for our cause. It's absolutely unthinkable that any SAFE member would do this."

Alex was scribbling in her notebook. She looked up at McNiff. "But you do advocate harassing your enemies with boycotts and so forth. You do publish their phone numbers and addresses." Alex glanced at me, then said, "Walt Kinnick received some threatening phone calls the day before the shooting. The callers mentioned SAFE."

"Sure," said McNiff. "Anybody would. Good way to deflect suspicion, huh?" He shrugged. "We advocate legal, nonviolent activities that help us make our point and demonstrate our influence. Sure we do. All organizations do those kinds of things to promote their cause. We also try to get our friends elected and our enemies defeated. We play by the rules. We believe in the Constitution. Sometimes our members make phone calls. Nothing illegal about that. Maybe some of them are angry. But we don't go around shooting people who disagree with us."

"Walt Kinnick was expected to testify against gun control. Instead, he testified for it. You have been quoted as calling him a traitor."

McNiff nodded quickly. "Yes. He was. That's why he's our number-one enemy. But that doesn't mean we want him to be shot."

"But doesn't that make him different from all your other enemies?"

"We've been betrayed before," said McNiff with a shrug. "Politicians betray our cause all the time."

"Don't you think it was sort of inevitable that sooner or later some nut with a gun would try to serve the cause by shooting an enemy?" said Alex.

"I think," said McNiff slowly, "that the least likely nut to do that would be a member of SAFE. Every one of our members knows that the irresponsible or criminal use of firearms is our worst enemy. Hey, it's obvious someone shot Kinnick. Whether it was an accident or not, I don't know. But I'll tell you this. Maybe it was an attempted assassination. But it wasn't any member of SAFE."

"What are you doing about it?" she said.

"Doing?"

"How are you addressing what happened to Kinnick?"

McNiff spread his hands. "I'm not. There's nothing to address."

"But—"

"I assume the police are addressing it. I hope they catch whoever did it, and I hope they prosecute him and punish him. But it's none of our business. SAFE has nothing to do with what happened to Walt Kinnick. We're always upset when accidents and crimes with guns occur. But accidents or irresponsible behavior or criminal acts do not change our views about guns, any more than drunk-driving accidents change anybody's mind about automobiles."

Alex was frowning into her notebook. "There are other enemies on your list," she said.

McNiff looked at me and smiled. "Yes. There are always ten enemies. Every two weeks, ten enemies. Most of them are perennials. Now and then we have some new ones."

"Like Walt Kinnick," she said.

He nodded. "And Brady Coyne."

"Why is Mr. Coyne on your list?" she said.

"He obviously helped convince Kinnick to reverse his position on gun control. Kinnick came to town prepared to testify against that bill. After meeting with his lawyer, he testified for it." He looked at me. "You must be a very convincing man. A convincing man who opposes the Second Amendment is an enemy of SAFE."

"If you think I convinced Wally to change his mind, you don't know him very well," I said.

"Good lawyers make a living convincing people to change their minds," said McNiff.

I shrugged. "I'm not that good."

Alex glanced at me and gave me a little nod. She was inviting me to plead my case more fully. I realized that was why she had invited me to join her on this interview.

"I have no public position on gun control," I said to McNiff.

"Only through Kinnick," he said.

"I never even heard of SAFE before I picked up Wally at the airport that night."

"I bet you had opinions on gun control, though," said McNiff.

"I have opinions on lots of things. Now and then I even express them. That's the First Amendment. Comes right before the Second."

McNiff smiled.

"If it matters to you, I wouldn't have considered myself your enemy."

"Not me," said McNiff. "SAFE."

"Whatever. I generally see too many gray areas in complicated issues to make anybody a worthwhile enemy."

"If you're not for us," he said, "you've gotta be against us."

"No, I don't," I said. "I can just not give a shit one way or the other, like most people."

He shrugged. "There'll be another newsletter in a week or so. I'll be making a new enemies' list. Maybe you won't make it this time."

"I'm only an enemy," I said, "of those who make me an enemy."

"And a friend to those who have no friends," said McNiff with a grin. "I remember Boston Blackie, too."

"What about those others?" said Alex to McNiff.

"Which others?"

"On your list."

"The others have been there before. Politicians. Our biggest enemies are politicians who don't think for themselves, who take polls before they decide what they believe. Fortunately, we have lots of friends in government, too."

"Those who vote your position," said Alex. "People who do think for themselves."

McNiff shrugged. "Politics is politics."

She glanced at her notebook. "What about Wilson Bailey?"

"What about him?"

"He's not a politician."

"No. He's been on our list before. He's made a career out of testifying against us. It's a tragic thing, what happened to his family. But his is a tired old argument. Unfortunately, it has a lot of emotional punch. So far he hasn't hurt us."

Alex and McNiff talked for another fifteen minutes or so. Nothing new was said. Finally Alex glanced at her watch and said, "I've taken enough of your time, Mr. McNiff." She shut off her tape recorder and stowed it and her notebook in her briefcase.

He walked us out to the porch and held out his hand to Alex. "I hope you'll look at those pamphlets I gave you," he said.

"Sure. I will."

He turned to me. "Mr. Coyne, please convey to Walt my wishes for a speedy recovery."

I nodded. "Okay."

"And I hope you're enjoying your brief appearance on our list."

I smiled. "Oh, it's a lot of fun," I said. "I always wanted to make somebody's enemies' list."

He touched my arm. "We're *not* after you, you know."

"It's comforting to hear you say that."

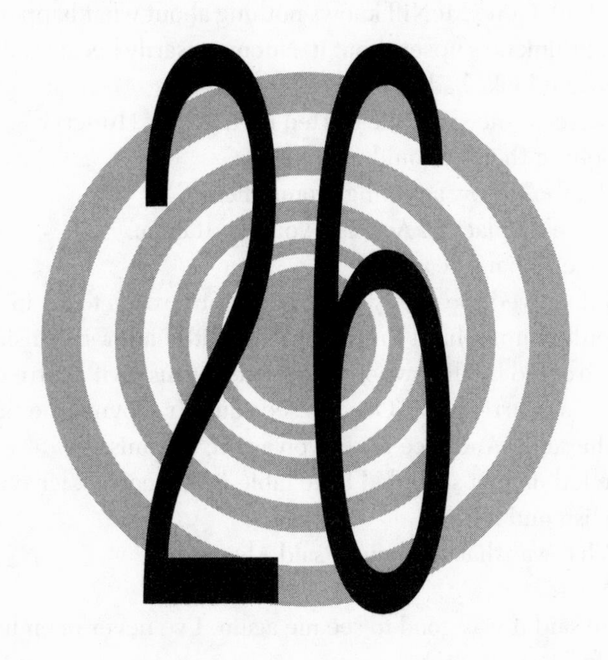

We got into Alex's car. I lit a cigarette. "Thanks," I said.

"Huh?"

"For giving me a chance to tell McNiff my side."

"I think he heard you."

"We'll see if it gets me expunged from his list."

"I hope it does," she said. "Even if it costs me a helluva story."

"I hope it does, too."

"He's good, isn't he?" she said.

"Yes. Very convincing, I thought. Get anything useful?"

She shrugged. "Everything's useful. I'll get a story out of it.

"'SAFE Leader Denies Group's Responsibility for Kinnick Shooting,'" I said.

"Something like that. What'd you think?"

"I think Gene McNiff knows nothing about what happened to Walt. I think he's upset about it. Not necessarily because of Walt. Because it looks bad for SAFE."

"I agree," she said. She started up the car. "Hungry?"

"Getting there. I could use a drink."

"Me, too. Know anything around here?"

"There's a place in Acton, if you like Italian."

"I like Italian. Lead on."

We followed the pretty winding country roads to 2A in Acton and pulled up behind the restaurant a little after six. Inside we were greeted by the owner, who served as his own maître d'. He gave us a courtly bow. "Good to see you, Mr. Coyne," he said. To Alex he said, "And nice to see you again, too, miss."

He led us to a secluded little table in the corner, gave us the wine list, and left.

"What was that all about?" said Alex.

"What?"

"He said it was good to see me again. I've never been here in my life."

"You picked that up, huh?"

"Oh yes. We reporters are quick that way."

"I never told you about Terri."

"Want to?"

I shrugged. "We ate here a lot. She lives right down the street. This was our table."

"Do I look like her or something?"

"Well, aside from the fact that her hair's long and black and yours is short and kind of auburn, and her eyes are practically black and yours are greenish-blue—yes. I mean, you're both very beautiful. I can see why our host is confused. Another man blinded by beauty."

Alex smiled. "What happened?" she said.

I lit a cigarette and exhaled slowly. "She dumped me."

"Why?"

"I'm still working on that one."

Alex put her hand onto mine. "In my experience," she said, "I've found it's a lot easier to be the dumpee than the dumper."

"Yeah," I said. "Easier. But it hurts more."

She leaned forward. I met her halfway. She kissed me on the chin, then the cheek, then the mouth. We held that one for a moment. Then she pulled back. "It still hurts, huh?"

"A little."

"It's good to see."

"What?"

"That you hurt. I mean, that you *can* hurt. That you admit it."

I reached across the table, touched her jaw, and gently steered her mouth close enough that I could kiss it again. "I'm feeling a tiny bit better," I said.

"Maybe we can work out a rehabilitation program for you," she said. Then she turned her head, looked up, and grinned.

A young waitress was standing beside us, smiling. "Wine," I said. "A good first step on any recovery program. Let's have some wine."

When we left the restaurant, it was nearly ten. There were only a dozen or so cars left in the parking lot. One of them, parked by itself at the dark end of the row, was a blue Ford Escort. When we climbed into Alex's car, I gestured at the Escort and said, "Drive around that way."

She frowned for an instant, then nodded. She backed out of the space, then swung around past the Escort. Her headlights briefly lit the other car's interior. Nobody was sitting in it.

She continued out the driveway. "Just another blue Escort," she said.

"Driver slides down so we don't see him," I said.

She reached over and touched my leg. "It must be scary," she said softly.

"Yeah, it kinda is. There's a little shopping mall just over the hill. Why don't you pull in there and douse your lights."

"Sure." She hit the accelerator, zipped over the hill, darted into the lot in front of an all-night convenience store, and switched off her headlights.

We watched the road. A couple of minutes later a blue Escort rolled past us, beat the yellow traffic light, and continued east on 2A toward Boston. We watched until its taillights disappeared.

I sighed. "Millions of Escorts on the road."

"Yeah," said Alex, "but now you've got me paranoid, too."

"Hey," I said, "you're not on any enemies' list. You just hang around with the wrong people. Let's go home."

Alex pulled up in front of my apartment building a little before eleven. "Nightcap?" I said.

"Oh, Christ," she grunted.

"What?"

"'Nightcap.' That's beneath you. You mean, do I want to go up with you and make out on your sofa. Right?"

"'Make out'? I haven't heard anyone say that that since I was sixteen."

"Isn't that what you mean?"

"Something like that, I guess." I smiled. "Something *exactly* like that. Yes."

"And if things progress nicely, maybe you can persuade me to spend the night."

"I didn't—"

"Well, I'm warning you," she said. "I have to get up early, and I'm very grouchy in the morning."

"I can live with that," I said. "Let's have that nightcap."

I woke up abruptly. Alex was sitting astride my hips shaking my shoulders. In the dim light from the hallway, I saw that she had put my old Yale T-shirt back on again. "Hey," she said. "Wake up for a minute."

"Was I snoring?"

"No. Listen. I want to know something."

"What time is it?"

"Three-ten."

"Jesus, Alex."

"If you knew more about this, would you tell me?"

"About what?"

"The Kinnick thing."

"No."

"No what?"

"No, I wouldn't necessarily tell you."

She rolled off me and lay on her back beside me with her hands under her head. I turned onto my side. She rolled over to meet me, and I slid my arm around her. My hand snaked under the T-shirt and traced the curves and angles of her back, down over her smooth rump, than back up again. "There might be things I couldn't tell you," I said into her hair.

"Lawyer stuff."

"Kinda."

"I understand."

"Well, good."

She was silent for a moment. Her fingers moved on my back. Then she said, "But do you?"

"Do I what?"

"Know something? Have some facts?"

"Yes."

"That you can't tell me."

"Right."

"Like who's following you around in a blue Ford Escort?"

"No," I said. "I don't know who's doing that. Assuming I'm not imagining it. Which I probably am."

"You think you're paranoid," she said.

"I don't know. Do you?"

"It depends."

"If somebody really is following me for purposes of finding a propitious moment to shoot me, and it scares me, is that paranoia?"

"I don't think so. I think that's just sensible." She burrowed her face against my shoulder. "What about ideas?" she mumbled. "Hypotheses, scenarios? Do you have ideas you aren't sharing with me, too?"

"Not really."

"What does that mean?"

"It means I haven't come close to figuring it out, but I'm thinking about it."

"But you don't want to share your thinking with me."

"Right."

"Why?"

"Because it's tied into what I know. I can't separate them. You should understand this."

"I do," she murmured. "I was just wondering."

I hugged her against me. The T-shirt had ridden way up over her hips. "Let's go back to sleep, then."

Her hand crept onto my thigh. "Fat chance," she said.

◎

"Your coffee's on the table."

I opened my eyes. Alex was sitting on the bed, fully dressed. Her hip pressed against mine, separated by the blanket that covered me. I reached up to touch her face. Her hair was damp. She bent down and kissed me quickly on the forehead. "I'm out of here," she said.

"What time is it?"

"A little after seven."

"What's your hurry?"

"I got a story to write."

"'Veteran News Hound Seduces Vulnerable Attorney,'" I said.

"That's the one."

I reached up, hooked my arm around her neck, and pulled her down to me. I nuzzled her throat.

"Oh, shit," she mumbled. "Again?"

A half-hour later she was sitting on the side of the bed pulling on her pants and I was propped up in bed sipping lukewarm coffee. "I think I'm going to try to reach Wilson Bailey today," she said.

"Poignant human interest story," I said, drawing circles on her bare back with my forefinger.

"That's not the story I'm after. That's an old story that I should've written when it happened but didn't. Now the man is the number-ten SAFE enemy."

"I forgot. You're collecting interviews with potential assassination victims." She was hunching herself into her bra. "I give you a lot of credit," I went on. "You really throw yourself into your work."

"Mr. Bailey," she said, "might be more forthcoming if I sit on him in the middle of the night."

"Worth a try."

She stood up and buttoned her blouse. Then she smiled. "I'll call you later."

"I've heard that one before."

"I will." She waved and headed for the door. "Have a good day."

"Come give me a kiss."

"No way, buster," she said. "You saw what happened last time I did that."

My bathroom mirror was still foggy. Alex had written "Hi" in the condensation with her finger. I was relieved to note that she did not dot the "i" with a little heart or a happy face.

While I showered, I thought about being followed by a nameless assassin in a blue Escort and wondered again if I were imagining it. Alex had reminded me that Wilson Bailey was number ten on the list. And from there my mind took a convoluted route to the realization that if I did get shot, there was nobody who knew what I knew who could warn Wilson Bailey that he was a logical target, too.

So before I left for the office I found my copy of the SAFE newsletter and dialed Bailey's number in Harlow, Massachusetts. It rang four times before I heard the click of an answering machine. A cheerful female voice said, "Hi. You've reached the Bailey household. I guess no one's home right now. Please leave a message and we'll get back to you."

It was, I guessed, the voice of Bailey's dead wife. She had been gunned down in the public library. But her voice still lived on an answering machine tape. Wilson Bailey, I imagined, could not bring himself to eradicate this last surviving vestige of her.

She had used the pronoun "we." There was no longer a "we" at Wilson Bailey's house.

I had to clear my throat before I spoke to his machine. "Mr. Bailey," I said, "this is Brady Coyne. I saw your testimony before the Senate Subcommittee on Public Safety last week. I have some important things I'd like to discuss with you. Please call me." I left my home and office numbers.

Then I went to work.

Julie buzzed me in the middle of the morning. "It's Lieutenant Horowitz again," she said. "Line one."

Got it," I said. I pressed the button and said, "Hey."

"Where'd you get those cartridges, Coyne?" he said.

"I can't tell you. I already told you that. What'd you find out?"

"Why the fuck should I tell you what I found out if you won't tell me where you got them?"

"Because I might be able to figure something out, and then I could tell you and you could capture a vicious criminal and you'd be a hero."

"Gee whiz," he said. "Golly. You'd let me take all the credit?"

"Sure. You need it more than I do."

"They were shot from the same gun," he said. "I bet you knew that."

"I suspected it. Can you say anything about the gun?"

"Can you say anything about how they came into your possession?"

"No."

"God damn it, Coyne."

"Somebody took some shots at somebody and left those cartridges behind. That's all I can tell you."

"Who? Where? When?"

"I can't tell you."

"Because you gave your fucking word."

"That's it."

"Well, the fingerprints on those cartridges were all smudged and I can't tell you anything about the gun, and if I could, I wouldn't, and fuck you very much," he said, and he hung up.

Around noon Julie buzzed me again. "It's her," she said.

"Her?"

She chuckled. "Her with the cheekbones. Line one."

"Thanks, kid." I switched over and said, "Hi."

"Hi," said Alex. "How are you?"

"I didn't sleep that well last night."

"Me neither, actually. But I feel just fine."

"Did you get your story written?"

"Yep. Funny thing. As I thought about it and listened to the interview, I became more and more convinced that McNiff was straight with me."

"I thought so, too."

"My story doesn't have much to do with the Kinnick shooting. It's just about SAFE. What they do, what they believe. Those pamphlets are pretty convincing."

"So you buy their line?"

"Hey," she said. "I'm a reporter, remember? I tell the story, that's all. SAFE's in the news. What they stand for is newsworthy. Whether I buy it or not is irrelevant. Wanna do lunch?"

"Can't. I've gotta be in court at one. How about later?"

"I've got an editorial meeting that'll drag on till eight or nine. We generally order up pizzas."

"You could come over for a nightcap afterward."

"Hoo, boy. Another nightcap, huh?"

"Sure. A nightcap."

"I might not get there before ten."

"That's okay."

After court that afternoon I took a cab over to Mass General. I didn't notice any blue Ford Escorts following us, which only convinced me that he had either changed vehicles or was lurking back there somewhere in the traffic.

Wally was wearing a bathrobe and sitting in a chair. He was not attached to any plastic tubes.

Diana was sitting cross-legged on his bed.

"Hi, folks," I said. I shook Wally's hand and Diana and I exchanged pecks on the cheek. I sat beside Diana. "How's it feeling?" I said to Wally.

"Better and better." He glanced sideways at Diana and said,

"About ready for strenuous exercise. How about you? Been fishing?"

"Not since the Deerfield."

"Well shit, man. The month of May's passing you by." He smiled. "I was just telling Diana. I had a visit from a friend of yours today."

"Friend of mine?"

"Yeah. State cop named Horowitz. Said you've been bugging him about me. He complained a lot. He respects the hell out of you."

I nodded. "I respect him, too. Crabby son of a bitch. What'd he have to say?"

"He didn't say much of anything. Asked me some questions. Just, basically, what I remembered. Which isn't much of anything. Wanted to know if I could think of anybody who'd want to shoot me. I mean, aside from the SAFE connection."

"What'd you tell him?"

Wally shrugged. "I mentioned the animal rights crazies. I mean, they're at least as fanatical as the SAFE guys. They've been convicted of burning down medical laboratories and issuing death threats to scientists who use animals in their research. Otherwise, I guess I've probably stepped on a hundred sets of toes over the years. Anybody who builds dams on salmon rivers, clear-cuts forests, dumps poisons into trout streams, votes the wrong way. I can think of a dozen politicians and CEOs who'd probably like to see me in an urn."

"Did you mention Howard?" said Diana.

Wally turned and looked at her. "Yes, honey," he said. "I had to."

She nodded, then turned her head to stare out at the air shaft.

"What about poachers with expensive bamboo fly rods?" I said.

"I forgot that one."

I smiled. "I'm sure Horowitz found the interview helpful."

"I don't know. He just sat there chomping on his gum."

"It's not even a state police case," I said.

"I know. It's officially a hunting accident. Your friend Horowitz doesn't seem to buy it."

“Neither do I,” I said.

He cocked an eye at me. “You seem pretty emphatic about that.”

I nodded. “I am.”

“Do you know something?”

“Not much.”

“Well, shit, man. What?”

“I can’t tell you.”

“You playing lawyer with me, Brady?”

“Not really.”

“Somebody else get shot at?”

I shrugged. “Maybe something like that.”

“A listed enemy?”

I nodded.

“Christ,” mumbled Wally, and I knew he was thinking that I was a listed SAFE enemy, too, and it was his fault.

“Don’t worry about it,” I said. “I talked with Gene McNiff yesterday and got everything straightened out.”

“Sure,” said Wally. “Good.” He sounded dubious.

I stayed for about an hour. The three of us talked mostly about fishing. Wally planned to recuperate back at his cabin once they released him from the hospital. Diana was going to stay with him. Neither of them seemed worried about returning to the place where the shooting had occurred.

His producers had assured him that they would adjust their filming schedules to accommodate him. They had even started renegotiating his contract with his agent. Walt Kinnick had become an even more marketable commodity since the shooting. The sponsors were lining up. The SAFE threat of a boycott had not, apparently, scared anybody away.

When I stood up to leave, Wally said, “Brady, do me a favor.”

“Sure.”

“Take Diana out to dinner.”

“You trust me with this beautiful woman?”

“Course not,” he said. “But I trust her.”

“You do?” she said.

“Absolutely.”

She grinned at me. “I can’t stand it.”

"How's tomorrow?" I said to her.

She nodded. "Terrific."

"Where?"

"Do you know Giannino's?"

"Behind the Charles Hotel?"

"Yes. We can eat out on the patio. It's nice outdoors this time of year, and they have good Italian food there. If you don't mind coming to Cambridge."

"Sounds fine. Seven?"

"Perfect. I'll meet you there."

"Thanks," said Wally.

"It'll be my pleasure," I said.

I decided to stop at Skeeter's on the way home for a giant burger and a glass of beer. It was one of those May evenings when even in the city the air smelled clean and fresh, and it wasn't until I turned off Cambridge Street onto Court Street that I became aware of my tail.

He had been lounging by the entrance to the hospital, and when I stepped outside after my visit with Wally and squinted into the slanting late afternoon sunshine, he had looked away from me a little too quickly. I noticed it, but it didn't register. I might have noticed a blue Escort, but I wasn't looking for an undistinguished thirtyish man wearing khaki pants and a brown sports jacket.

But when I turned off Cambridge onto Court Street I glimpsed that same man sauntering along in the same direction on the opposite side of Cambridge Street. I kept walking, and from the corner of my eye I saw him cross Cambridge and head down Court Street. He stayed behind me and on the other side of the street.

When I got to Congress Street, I stood on the corner waiting for the light. I glanced back up the street, but couldn't spot the guy in the brown sports coat. The light changed, I crossed Congress to State, and continued along until I came to Skeeter's alley. When I turned in there I had another chance to look behind me. My tail, if that's what he was, had disappeared.

I went inside and hitched myself onto a barstool. The TV over the bar was playing "Wheel of Fortune" with the sound turned off.

"Hey, Mr. Coyne," said Skeeter. "By yourself tonight?"

I had once met Gloria at Skeeter's, and he had been completely charmed by her. "Yes, I think so," I said, remembering my tail. "How about a draft Sam and a burger?"

"Medium rare, right?"

"The burger, not the beer."

Skeeter poured my beer and slid it in front of me. I lit a cigarette and took a sip, and as I did I glanced in the mirror over the bar. A man in a brown sports coat came in, looked casually around without letting his eyes linger on me, then took a seat in a booth near the door.

I stared openly at him through the mirror. He picked up a menu, studied it, then lounged back and looked up at the television. He was as nondescript as a blue Ford Escort—thinning brown hair cut neither short nor long, medium build, blue Oxford shirt open at the neck. Just an average working stiff happy that another day at the office had ended.

I finished my cigarette, stubbed it out, picked up my half-empty draft of beer, and took it to his booth. "Mind if I join you?" I said.

He turned his head, shrugged, and gestured to the seat across from him. Then he resumed looking at the television. "That Vanna White," he said, still staring at the screen. "Some nice-lookin' broad, huh?"

"A little on the thin side," I said.

"She'd look good to you, if you see my old lady. How do you get waited on in this place?"

"You've got to order at the bar. It's just Skeeter. No waitresses."

"What're you having?"

"Skeeter's burgers are the best in town."

"Burger and a beer," he said. "Sounds good."

"Why are you following me?" I said.

"It's my job." He continued watching the television.

"You're not that good at it," I said. "I saw you in the Escort last night. I picked you up about halfway over here from the hospital."

"Actually, that was another guy in the Escort. But I did follow you from your apartment to your office this morning. Then to the courthouse, then the hospital, then here. You didn't catch on to me until you come out of the hospital? That's not bad, huh?"

"I don't get it," I said.

He swiveled his head around and smiled at me. "It doesn't matter whether you get it or not, Mr. Coyne. And it doesn't matter whether you know we're watching you or not, either."

I sat back in the booth and laughed. "Oh, shit," I said. "You're not an assassin, are you?"

"Not on this assignment I'm not."

"Secret Service, right?"

"Bingo," he said. "You win a night with Vanna."

"Are you protecting me?"

He rolled his eyes. "Not hardly."

"Oh," I said. "I get it. You're making sure I don't assassinate somebody."

"Or conspire with somebody," he said. "Like Gene McNiff."

"Is that what you think I was doing out there yesterday?"

"Me?" He laughed. "I don't think, Mr. Coyne. I keep track of you and report it to the lady who does the thinking."

"Agent Krensky."

"Her own self. My boss."

"Will you report this conversation to her?"

"Sure. That's my job."

"What will you tell her?"

"I'll tell her you and I shared a burger at Skeeter's Infield from seven-oh-nine until whenever, then I tailed you home."

"Would you mind telling her that I'm no assassin and she's wasting a lot of taxpayer's money?"

"I'll tell her," he said. "But she don't listen to me."

We ended up eating together at his booth and watching the first few innings of the Red Sox game. He didn't tail me home. He strolled along with me. We ended up talking baseball. He was a

Cubs fan and his name was Malloy. That's all he would tell me.

I couldn't decide whether to be relieved or annoyed that the Secret Service was following me around.

I kicked off my shoes inside the door, dropped my jacket and tie onto a kitchen chair, and sat on my bed to divest myself of the rest of my lawyer duds. I pulled on a pair of jeans and a T-shirt, then went into the living room.

My answering maching was winking at me. Wink-wink, pause. Two messages. I pressed the button. The machine whirred, clicked, and then came Alex's voice. "I'm running a little late over here," she said. "It's gonna be closer to eleven. Assume that's still okay. I'm pooped. Can't understand why. I might want to skip the nightcap and go straight for the nightshirt. I'm on the fly. Bye."

The machine clicked. Then a voice that I had heard once before on an answering machine tape said, "Brady Coyne, you have betrayed the Second Amendment For Ever and you deserve to die a just and ironic death."

The machine rewound itself. Its red eye stared unblinking at me. I stared back at it.

I'd heard that message before. It was the same one Wally got the night before he was shot. The same precise syntax. I remembered the word "ironic" in Wally's message, and I recalled that Alex had used the word "ironically" in her article. People who understand irony always impress me. Gene McNiff had said that all kinds of people belonged to SAFE.

Still, the man who left me this message didn't fit my image of a typical SAFE redneck bent on shooting his enemies.

I replayed the tape. Alex sounded warm and sexy. It occurred to me to tell her not to come over. I didn't want her to be in the way if something was going to happen. But I didn't think anybody would try to shoot me in my bed behind a brick wall six stories above the Boston Harbor. About the only way to accomplish that would be from a helicopter.

Besides, I knew I'd appreciate having someone to hold on to.

My answering machine was old. I figured the heads needed cleaning or something, because the fidelity was too poor to attempt to identify the speaker by his voice. He might've even attempted to disguise it, I couldn't tell. It could have been anybody. If it was a voice I'd heard before, I couldn't determine it by this brief recorded message.

I removed the tape and replaced it with a new one.

I poured myself a finger of Jack Daniel's and stood by the open sliders. The moon shimmered on the corrugated water of the harbor six stories down. Somewhere out there a bell-buoy clanged quietly, and the air smelled of old seaweed.

I tried to figure out what to do. Or not do. Call Horowitz? And what would he do? Tell me to stay in my apartment, probably. And for how long? Until they caught the shooter? And what if they never caught him? The peculiarity of American law enforcement is that it cannot act until a crime has been committed. Horowitz couldn't do a damn thing to prevent me from getting shot.

If Agent Malloy continued to tail me, he probably wouldn't be able to prevent an assassination, either. But he'd be in a good position to catch the shooter. That offered me a little consolation. Very little.

I couldn't decide what to do. In the end, I did nothing.

I was glad Alex was coming over.

I finished my drink and picked up the clothes and magazines and fishing gear that were strewn around my apartment. I didn't want her to think I was a slob.

I was sitting out on the balcony sipping another shot of Daniel's when the intercom sounded. I buzzed Alex up, and when she came in I hugged her hard for a long time.

"What's wrong?" she said.

"I'm just really glad to see you."

She pressed herself against me, then tilted her head back and grinned. "I'll say you are."

I didn't tell her about sharing a burger with Agent Malloy, and

I didn't mention the telephone message. It didn't seem quite that ominous anymore. Besides, she wanted to get into her nightshirt.

So did I.

◎

I felt her mouth on the back of my neck. I hugged my pillow. "I'm out of here," she said.

I rolled onto my back. Alex was standing beside the bed smiling down at me. I lifted my hand to her, and she backed away. "Oh no you don't," she said. "I gotta get to work."

"What time is it?"

"Seven-thirty. I'm late."

"It's Saturday," I said.

"I work on Saturdays. You want some coffee?"

"I don't work on Saturdays," I said. "I sleep on Saturdays. No coffee."

"Call me?" she said.

"I will."

I heard the door click shut behind her. I lay there with my eyes closed, feeling vaguely edgy and depressed. Then, with a jolt, I remembered the phone call. Somewhere out there a man had threatened my life. I thought about it. He had bushwhacked Wally in the woods in the early morning and Senator Swift in the woods at night. Perhaps he'd wait to nail me in the woods, too. If I stayed in the city I'd be all right.

At least I hoped so. The thought consoled me enough to allow me to drift back to sleep.

I woke up around nine. Ah, Saturday. I love Saturdays. I pulled on a pair of jeans, wandered into the kitchen, poured a mugful of coffee, and took it out onto the balcony. I sat there sipping and smoking and tilting my face up to the sun. I thought about a faceless man who thought I was his enemy, and I decided not to let him ruin my day. So I turned my thoughts to all of the good things I could do with a beautiful Saturday in May. Most of those things involved rivers and trout.

Then I remembered that I had agreed to meet Diana in Cambridge for dinner, and that spoiled my trout-fishing reverie.

Fishing for me is, among other important things, an escape from time. Having to leave a river because my watch tells me to takes a lot of the fun out of it.

Anyhow, I decided it might not be such a good idea to go fishing on this day. An out-of-the-way trout river would make an excellent location for an assassination. I wasn't going to cower behind my apartment door for the rest of my life. But there was no sense in doing something foolhardy.

I retrieved the *Globe* from outside my door, refilled my mug, and went back out onto the balcony. I read the lead paragraphs of each of the front-page stories, folded the paper back to the Friday-night box scores, found the chess problem and solved it, then paged through the whole paper, back to front.

Alex's piece was buried in the middle of the Metro section. I noticed it because it was accompanied by a stock photo of Gene McNiff. GUARDIAN OF THE SECOND AMENDMENT was the headline. I read it through and smiled. I figured her editor, alerted by the "ironically" that Alex had slipped into her previous piece, had wielded his blue pencil with a vengeance this time.

It was a puff piece. The Second Amendment For Ever organization had earned the grudging respect of political insiders by their success in stonewalling antigun legislation. They had some sound constitutional and sociological arguments to support their position, which Alex summarized nonjudgmentally. SAFE also supported get-tough anticrime legislation, ran hunter-safety programs, conducted self-defense seminars. Gene McNiff was a real estate attorney who received a tiny stipend from SAFE for his service as the group's executive director.

Alex had made McNiff sound thoughtful, dedicated, sincere, tolerant, sane.

Her article did not mention Walt Kinnick.

I wondered what her first draft had looked like before her editor took his swipe at it.

Lots of lawyers work on weekends. Big high-powered firms expect it, especially from the young associates. Partners feel obliged to work weekends, too, in order to set an example for the associates.

But not me. One of the main advantages of working in a one-man law office is not having to impress anyone or set an example for anybody. I only have to impress myself, and I'm easily impressed.

I know I don't set a very good example.

I respect the law. I give my clients their money's worth. But the law is not my life. I rank family and friends and fishing and the Red Sox above my law practice.

Julie, even after all the years we've been together, doesn't respect my personal hierarchy of values. She keeps telling me that my business should come first—or maybe second, after family—which, of course, is one of her functions. I need her to question my priorities, because if she didn't, it wouldn't get done.

Julie's my conscience, and as I loafed around my apartment her voice kept nagging at me from inside my head. "Get to work," it said. "Catch up."

In the end I did what I do about three Saturdays a year. I went to the office.

It felt good to stroll leisurely across the Common and up Boylston Street to Copley Square in jeans and sneakers and a polo shirt, and although I failed to spot him, I suspected that Agent Malloy or one of his counterparts was somewhere behind me, and that felt good, too. I liked unlocking the office at noontime and making a vat of coffee and leaving the answering machine on. A few uninterrupted hours and I could get a lot done. That would shut up Julie's voice in my head.

Then I might enjoy a truly carefree Sunday.

Except I kept thinking about being number seven on the SAFE list, and how, after Senator Swift, the only enemies above me were out of the state. And I remembered that calm, cultured voice on my answering machine telling me that I deserved a just and ironic death. It's hard to be carefree when you figure you're the next target of an assassin.

I still managed to plow through a large stack of papers.

# 30

I locked up around five, went home, showered and changed, and took the T to Harvard Square. I was at the bar inside Giannino's at ten of seven, sipping a glass of Samuel Adams, Boston's own beer. I had seen nobody who looked like a Secret Service agent all day.

I told the hostess that I was expecting somebody, and when she arrived we'd like a table out on the patio.

Diana got there fifteen minutes later. She climbed aboard the barstool next to mine and kissed my cheek. "Hi," she said.

"Hi."

"I just came from the hospital. Sorry if I'm late."

"You're not. I was early. How's Wally?"

"All grabby and talking dirty. I'd say he's on the mend."

The bartender came over and Diana ordered a glass of white wine. I asked for another Sam.

"And how are you?" I said.

She smiled and shrugged. "I guess I'm all right. I mean, sometimes when I don't expect it I suddenly remember hearing those shots, running out and seeing him lying there. He's safe now, don't you think?"

"As safe as anybody ever is, I guess."

She slapped my arm. "You are such a comfort, Brady Coyne."

The hostess appeared. "Your table's ready now, sir," she said.

She escorted us outside, described the day's specials in delicious detail, and left menus with us. We studied them, debated the offerings, and watched the mix of Cambridge folks prowl around the patio. We had placed our orders and started to talk about fishing when Diana suddenly said, "Oh, shit."

"What?"

"You've got to excuse me for a minute."

She got up and strode across the open area to one of the outdoor bars. I saw her stop beside a man who was seated there. He was a lanky guy with thinning brown hair and pale skin. He was wearing a sports jacket, a tie pulled loose at the collar, chino pants, and a hangdog expression.

They held a brief but animated conversation. It looked pretty one-sided. Diana jabbed with her forefinger and shook her fist at him. He folded his arms and looked down at his lap. After a few minutes, Diana put her hands on her hips, and the man slowly climbed off the barstool and ambled away. Then she came back and sat across from me.

She tried to smile, shook her head, and let out a short laugh. "Sorry about that," she said.

I shrugged and said nothing.

"That was Howard."

I nodded. "That's what I figured."

"He followed me here."

"Why?"

"That's what I asked him."

"And?"

"He loves me. He wants me to come home. He forgives me. He's worried about me."

"Worried?"

She nodded quickly. "I hang around with dangerous people."

"Wally."

"Yeah. And you." She sighed heavily. "Shit, anyway."

I touched her arm. "What are you going to do about it?"

"Do? What are my choices?"

"I don't know. The usual, I guess."

"Restraining order, you mean."

"That's one."

She shook her head. "I just can't. It's not as if he wants to hurt me."

"Has this ruined our evening?" I said.

She smiled. "Hell, no."

Our salads arrived. We ate them. Diana said, "I guess I mainly feel sorry for him."

"Sounds to me as if that's his objective. To make you pity him."

"I guess it is."

She had a spicy chicken dish. I had scallops and mushrooms in a cream sauce. We didn't talk much.

Afterward we wandered around the Square. We browsed through bookstores. I looked for old first-edition fishing books at bargain prices. I found a few books, but there were no bargain prices on books in Harvard Square.

We watched a street performer juggle five basketballs.

A girl with bare feet and a braid down to her waist sang and played acoustic guitar in front of the Coop. She sounded exactly like Joan Baez, and I asked her if she knew "It's All Over Now, Baby Blue," the Dylan song. She sang it beautifully, and I dropped a five-dollar bill into her guitar case.

Diana and I had a beer at Grendel's. We didn't talk about Wally's shooting or Howard or SAFE. She told me about trips she'd taken with Wally, steelhead fishing in Oregon and British Columbia, a two-week river float in Alaska, tarpon fishing in the Keys and Belize. I countered with tales of the trout that live in the spring creeks of Montana's Paradise Valley.

I didn't tell her about the phone message I'd received the previous evening or the fear that gnawed on the margins of my consciousness. Being with her comforted me. Our assassin only went after his enemies when they were alone in the woods.

Diana's condo was on one of the little side streets that connect Broadway with Cambridge Street, a fifteen-minute walk from the square. We cut through the Harvard Yard. It was deserted, which I found strange for a Saturday night until I remembered that nowadays the ever-shrinking college academic year ends sometime around the first week of May.

Her tree-lined street was quiet. Old houses stood shoulder to shoulder, separated from each other only by the width of a driveway. Cars were parked solid on both sides.

We stood on the porch. Diana fumbled in her purse for her keys, found them, and unlocked the door. "I'll put on some coffee," she said.

"Thanks, no," I said.

She turned to me and put her hand on my arm. "Hey," she said softly.

"It's okay," I said. "No misunderstanding. It was a nice evening."

"You sure?"

I nodded. "Thanks anyway."

She tiptoed up and kissed my cheek. "Well, thanks. It was fun. I'm glad to have you as a friend."

"Me, too," I said.

She opened the door and went inside. She turned and smiled. "Good night, Brady," she said.

"Night, Diana."

The door closed. I heard three locks engage. I went down the steps to the sidewalk. I touched my cheek where Diana had kissed it. I decided when I got back to the square I'd call Alex from a pay phone. I could take the subway to her place on Marlborough Street, or she could meet me at my place. Either way—

No sound registered. If there was the click of a safety being released, or a shoe scuffling on concrete, or a harsh breath being exhaled, I don't remember hearing it. But something made me flinch an instant before the shot cracked from across the street at the same instant that glass exploded beside me, and I lurched sideways and stumbled onto the pavement and pressed myself flat between two parked cars. Several shots boomed in the night air, one after the other, so close together they sounded like a single extended explosion, and I huddled there, wedged under the front bumper of a car with my arms around my head.

It was over as abruptly as it started, and the street was quiet. I lay there, reluctant to move. I listened, but heard nothing. No clatter of running feet, no squeal of tires. Just the hum of the evening and the whisper of the spring breeze in the trees.

I crawled out and knelt behind the car that had probably saved my life. Cautiously I peered over the hood. I saw nothing.

"Brady?" Diana was standing on the porch. "Brady!" she yelled.

"I'm okay." I stood up.

"What—?"

"He missed."

"Oh, Jesus!"

She came down the steps to me. I put my arms around her. She was trembling, and I felt myself beginning to shake, too. She hugged me hard, and I held on to her. After a minute we went to the steps and sat down. I fumbled out a cigarette and got it lit.

"Diana," I said, "I'm sorry."

"Huh?"

"I'm sorry. He could've . . ."

"He wasn't after me," she said. "If he was, he wouldn't've waited till I went inside. He was after you. He must've followed us."

"Unless he knew where you lived."

"But if he was after you . . ."

"You're right," I said. "He must have followed us."

"What do we do?"

"We don't sit out here," I said. "We go inside. You make some coffee. I call the police."

By the time I got the 911 operator I heard sirens in the distance. When I told her that there had been gunshots, she said they'd already had two calls on it and a cruiser was on its way. I gave her Diana's address. She said she'd radio it to the cruiser.

A few minutes later there came a knock at the door. Diana answered it and led two uniformed Cambridge police officers into the kitchen. One looked like a high school freshman and the other was about my age. The older one took out a pen, flipped open a notebook, and asked what happened. I told him. He took a lot of notes.

Was I sure it was gunshots I'd heard, not fireworks or a car backfiring?

I was sure. One of them had broken a car window, if he'd care to check outside.

And did I think the shots were aimed specifically at me?

I believed they were.

Why?

I told him about the SAFE enemies' list, and Wally, and the identical phone calls we'd both received. I did not mention Senator Marlon Swift, or the fact that I'd been under Secret Service surveillance, or that I had apparently been abandoned by Agent Malloy.

Was there anybody else I could think of who'd want to shoot me?

I tried to make a joke of it. I mentioned Gloria.

The cop looked up and frowned at me.

I told him I was kidding.

He said he supposed they'd go outside and look around.

I suggested that he should contact Lieutenant Horowitz at 1010 Commonwealth Avenue.

The cop looked at me sharply.

I told him Horowitz was a friend of mine.

He shrugged and asked how he could get ahold of me in case they needed to talk to me again.

I gave him my card.

The two cops left.

Diana and I sipped coffee at her kitchen table. "Are you all right?" she said.

"Yes. How about you?"

She shrugged.

We sat in silence for a few minutes. Then she said, "I was thinking . . .

"Howard?"

She looked at me and nodded. "First Walter, now you. You were with me."

"Where does he live?"

"Out in Westwood."

"Why don't you call him?"

"What will I say?"

"It's about a forty-five-minute drive from here. If he's there . . ."

She nodded. She stood up and picked up the kitchen phone. She pecked out a number from memory, then shifted with the telephone wedged against her ear and gazed at the ceiling. After a long minute she hung up. She looked at me. "No answer," she said.

I shrugged. "All it means is that he's not home."

Tears brimmed in her eyes. "I just can't believe it."

"It doesn't mean anything," I said. "It just means he's not home."

I finished my coffee. Diana walked me to the door. "I'm sorry," she said.

"You didn't do anything wrong," I said. I kissed her forehead. "Wally once mentioned to me that you knew Senator Swift."

"Chip Swift? Sure. I worked with him on a bill he was sponsoring. It was pretty exciting, actually. At the time, it helped me get my mind off Howard. We got the bill passed and Chip had a big party for all of us who had worked on it at his place down in Marshfield." She looked up at me and frowned. "Why? Why are you asking about Chip?"

I touched her arm and smiled quickly. "Nothing, really. I just wondered."

I took a cab back to my apartment. Alex had left a message on my machine. She said, "Oh well. Guess you've got a date tonight. Too bad."

I poured myself two fingers of Daniel's, no ice, and took it out onto my balcony.

Wally had been shot once, not fatally. He could have been

killed, but all the other shots had missed him. A wounded man lying on the ground would make an unmissable target for an assassin bent on murder.

Marlon Swift hadn't been hit at all.

Neither had I.

Whoever had fired at me had stood somewhere across the street, no more than fifty feet from me. He had shot the window out of a car, missing me by several feet. He was either the world's worst marksman, or his intention was not to kill me. And if it wasn't murder—then what was it?

No answers came to me out there in the night air.

Maybe my turn had come and gone. He hadn't tried to finish off Wally. As far as I knew, he hadn't taken another crack at Chip Swift. Maybe no murders would happen. Maybe this man with the gun was just working his way down the SAFE list trying to scare the shit out of his enemies.

In that case, the shooter had achieved his goal. He *had* scared the shit out of me.

I went inside and called Horowitz's number. He wasn't there. I asked to be patched through to him and was told he was unavailable, would I like to leave a message. "Tell Lieutenant Horowitz that Brady Coyne called," I said. "Tell him that the guy who shot Walt Kinnick took a crack at me and missed."

I disconnected, then called Alex. It rang several times before her muffled voice said, "H'lo?"

"It's me. You were sleeping."

I heard her yawn. "Yup. You okay?"

"Sure. I'm fine."

"Miss me?"

"Yes."

"Tomorrow, 'kay?"

"I'll talk to you tomorrow," I said. "Sleep tight."

"You, too, sweetie."

My dreams were jumbled and vivid and continuous. When I awakened on Sunday morning, though, I could only remember one of them. I was wrestling in the woods with Bobby Farraday. It was night and the ground was muddy and a flock of crows perched on the low limbs above us. The crows didn't make any noises. They had their heads cocked down and they watched us with their shiny black eyes. Bobby seemed much stronger than me, and I didn't fight back. I just lay there and let him twist my arms and legs. It didn't hurt me at all. I kept wanting to ask him why he was trying to hurt me, but I couldn't seem to speak. Bobby didn't say anything at all in my dream.

Bobby Farraday was a kid I'd known in grammar school. We

hadn't been friends. He was a frail, somber boy, frequently absent. When the rest of us frolicked on the playground during recess, Bobby would sit and watch us with his round sad eyes. He died of leukemia sometime in the summer after fourth grade. I hadn't had a conscious thought of Bobby Farraday for more than thirty years.

Sunday was a brilliant May day. It would be wasted if I didn't take myself fishing. But the Bobby Farraday dream lingered. It was a death dream, of course. One might logically expect to have a death dream or two after hearing a volley of gunshots whiz overhead on a quiet Cambridge street.

And somewhere on the fringe of my consciousness, I was aware that there were other, deeper levels to my dream. I struggled to decipher it. But try as I would, its meaning eluded me. It made me feel edgy and vaguely depressed, and it dampened my enthusiasm for fishing.

Horowitz called a little before eleven. "What the hell happened last night?" he said.

I told him.

"I got a call from the Cambridge cops," he said. "They called it an alleged shooting."

"It wasn't alleged," I said. "It happened. There were two witnesses."

"The only thing they came up with was a broken windshield on an old Chevrolet."

"No empty cartridges?"

"Nope." He paused, and I heard his bubble gum snap. "Listen, Coyne," he said. "Your name has been popping up around here lately."

"What do you mean?"

"For one thing, this goddam Secret Service agent was asking questions."

"They were following me," I said. "Not doing a particularly good job of it, either."

Horowitz laughed. "Yeah, I heard you made one of 'em. Of

course, they'd been on your tail for a few days by then. They dropped you."

"I figured they did. Otherwise they would have witnessed an assassination attempt."

"On you," he said. "Right. Anyway, I also got a call from a certain state senator, and—"

"What state senator?"

"I think you know, Coyne."

"Swift?"

"None other. He told me all about it, on account of you told him I could be trusted, which I can, though I don't like playing these fucking games. Both Swift and this female agent tell me you suggested they give me a jingle. Then this thing last night."

And?"

"And nothing, if you mean do we know who's taking potshots at SAFE enemies. Far as I know he took a whack at numbers one and two and then moved on to number seven which, as you know, is you. Doesn't look like he wants to tangle with big-name politicians. You got any ideas?"

I hesitated for a moment, then said, "Well, I can give you the name of someone with a motive to shoot at Walt Kinnick, and maybe at me."

"But no motive to shoot a state senator, huh?"

I hesitated. "Maybe him, too."

"Who is it?"

"His name is Howard West. He's the estranged husband of Walt's lady friend."

"A stalker type, huh?"

"Maybe. Yes."

"Okay," said Horowitz, "that would certainly explain Kinnick. But why would he shoot at you and Swift?"

"He saw me and Diana having dinner together. And Diana used to work with the senator and went to a party at his house. If West is really crazy jealous . . ."

"Hm," said Horowitz. "That's a motive, I guess. What about means and opportunity?"

"I don't know. He was in Cambridge last night. He saw me and the lady together."

"Where's this guy live, do you know?"

"Westwood. But—"

"But what?"

"But I guess I still think SAFE is behind it."

"Yeah," said Horowitz. "Probably. Still, I guess we ought to check this Howard West out."

"What about protecting other people on that list?"

"On the basis of what?"

"Three of them have been shot at already."

"Yeah," he said. "Be nice if we could protect everybody. Unfortunately, it doesn't work that way. You're not having any other useful thoughts, are you?"

"Yeah," I said, "I'm having thoughts."

"Well?"

"They're pretty vague," I said. I didn't think Horowitz would place much credence in my dreams. "I haven't figured out if they're useful or not yet. When I do I'll let you know."

"Make it snappy, Coyne. One of these days this nut might kill somebody."

"That," I said, "is certainly one of the thoughts I've been having."

After I hung up with Horowitz, I retrieved the SAFE newsletter with its enemies' list from the rolltop desk in the corner of my living room. After Wally and Senator Swift, enemies number three through six—the Connecticut governor and the two United States senators from Massachusetts and the Congressman from Rhode Island—had apparently been skipped. Brady Coyne, the seventh enemy, had been next.

Eight was the senator from Vermont, and nine was a United States congresswoman from Maine. If Horowitz was right, the next target of the assassin would be Wilson Bailey, enemy number ten.

I didn't want to underestimate this shooter. He *had* shot Wally, and it almost killed him. Senator Swift had saved himself by his reflexes. I had been plain lucky, although, as I remembered it, I must have heard or sensed something, because I had flinched and ducked behind a car an instant before the first shot was fired. Otherwise, maybe I'd have been killed.

That's what my Bobby Farraday dream was all about.

I dialed Wilson Bailey's number. His answering machine picked it up. "Hi," came the woman's cheery voice. "You've reached the Bailey household. I guess no one's home right now. Please leave a message and we'll get back to you."

I swallowed hard before I responded to the dead Mrs. Bailey's invitation. "Mr. Bailey, it's Brady Coyne again," I said. "If you're there please call me right back. It's very important." I left my phone number.

I skimmed through the Sunday *Globe* while I waited for Bailey to return my call. There was a long piece by Alex comparing safety procedures and evacuation contingencies at the Seabrook and Plymouth nuclear power stations. It was strong, frightening journalism. I told myself I should call and congratulate her. But I didn't want to tie up the phone in case Wilson Bailey tried to reach me.

I remembered the man's testimony. His wife and daughter and unborn child had been murdered in an utterly random act of violence in a small-town library. I tried to imagine being Wilson Bailey, the horror of it. I found it unthinkable.

Two o'clock came and went. No call from Bailey.

I found a map and located the town of Harlow, where Bailey lived. It was near the Ware River, a decent trout stream in the middle of the state that I fished occasionally. It looked as if it would take about an hour and a half to drive from Boston to Harlow.

I went to the phone and dialed Alex's number. Her answering machine invited me to leave a message. "Good article," I said. "You're a helluva reporter, lady. I'm going fishing. I'll call if I don't get in too late. I'm feeling a bit hug-deprived."

I gathered together my fishing gear. I found myself wanting very much to talk to Wilson Bailey. After that, maybe I'd feel more like trying to catch a trout.

# 32

I pondered my Bobby Farraday dream all the way out to Harlow. The more I thought about it, the more ominous it seemed. I knew enough about dream interpretation to understand why I'd had that dream. But that didn't help me to figure it out.

The SAFE enemies' list told me that Wilson Bailey lived at 78 Aldrich Street. The kid at the 7-Eleven store in Harlow had never heard of Aldrich Street. But he had a town map, and together we located it. I bought a can of Pepsi, thanked the kid, and followed the directions I had written down from the map.

Harlow appeared to be a typical old New England mill town whose mill had long since been closed down and which now survived as a bedroom community halfway between Springfield and Worcester. It was a reasonable commute to either city, and as I navigated the streets I saw considerable evidence that optimistic real estate developers had targeted Harlow during the boom of the seventies and abandoned it in the collapse of the eighties. There were many building lots that had been cleared but not built on and unoccupied homes with piles of raw dirt and For Sale signs in front.

The dwellings on Aldrich Street were small and neat and of the same vintage, all cut from the same half-dozen architectural plans. They were set back from the road among tall pines on large lots. I drove slowly, checking the mailboxes out front for street numbers. Kids pedaled their bikes in the street and played basketball in the driveways. Men rode mowers back and forth across their front lawns. Young matrons wearing cotton gloves and T-shirts and shorts knelt on the edges of flower gardens.

It was a pleasant residential street, the kind of place where the neighbors got together for barbecues on summer Saturday evenings, and the kids swam in each other's pools, and the grown-ups pitched horseshoes and played volleyball. A nice street for raising a young family.

Aldrich Street was a dead end. Number 78 was the last house on the right. Number 76 next door had a For Sale sign out front. The house appeared empty. On the dead-end side of Bailey's house lay undeveloped woodland.

A Plymouth station wagon was parked in his driveway. His lawn had been mowed within the past few days. The gardens were neatly edged and mulched. The foundation plantings of azaleas and rhododendrons rioted in full pink and red bloom.

I parked behind the wagon, got out, and slammed the door. I walked up to the front door and rang the bell. I heard it jingle inside. I waited, then rang it again. A minute or two later a fat old golden retriever came sauntering around from the back of the house. He sat at the foot of the steps and looked up at me.

I descended the steps and scooched down beside him. I scratched his ears. "Do you live here, boy?" I said to him. "Is your master out back?"

He cocked his head at me as if he understood what I was saying. I stood up, and the dog stood, too. He started around the side of the house. I followed him.

It was a typical suburban backyard, with a swing set and a small above-ground pool and a metal toolshed and a flagstone patio with a gas barbecue grill and a picnic table and some folding aluminum lawn furniture.

I squinted into the afternoon sun and saw Wilson Bailey sleeping on a chaise on the patio. He was wearing sneakers and chino pants and a white polo shirt. The dog went over and lay down beside him. I followed him.

"Mr. Bailey. . . ?" I began. But I stopped. Because I saw the dark puddle under the chaise and I knew Wilson Bailey would not answer me.

He was lying on his back. His eyes stared up at the sky. His mouth was agape and a trail of crusted blood ran from the corner of his mouth and made a dark stain on the front of his shirt. The back of his head had been blown away. The weapon lay on his chest. It was short and ugly. Bailey's right thumb was curled inside the trigger guard.

His left arm was folded over the gun and across his chest. He was clutching something in his left hand. I bent to look at it. It was a photograph of a plain round-faced young woman and a very pretty little girl.

I wedged two fingers up under his jawbone. His skin was the same temperature as the air. I felt no pulse.

I backed away from him and sat heavily on a lawn chair. The dog came over and laid his chin on my leg. I stroked his nose for a moment, then lit a cigarette. I stared at Wilson Bailey lying rigidly on the chaise while I smoked the Winston down to the filter. Then I stood up and went to the back door. It was unlocked. I went into Wilson Bailey's kitchen and dialed 911.

I sat on the front steps to wait. The dog waited with me. Within a couple of minutes I heard the sirens, and then two cruisers skidded to a stop in front of the house. I waved toward the backyard, and two of the cops jogged in that direction. One stayed out front to talk to the kids on their bikes and the neighbors who began to gather there. The other cop came to the front steps where I was waiting.

"You called it in?" he said.

I nodded.

"The detectives are on their way." He turned his back on me, folded his arms, and stood there watching the street.

A rescue wagon arrived a minute later, and then another cruiser, and then a couple of unmarked vehicles. I continued to sit on the front steps patting the dog and smoking, and the cop stood there ignoring me.

The uniformed cops kept the curious neighbors in the street and off the front lawn. They draped yellow crime scene ribbon all the way around the yard. Official people kept moving back and forth from the back of the house to their vehicles parked in front. Distorted voices crackled from police radios. After a while a graying man in a green plaid sport coat came along and said something to the uniformed cop who was guarding me. The cop sauntered away and the guy in the sport coat sat beside me on the steps. "You're the one who called it in?" he said.

I nodded.

"Lieutenant Morrison, state police." He held his hand out to me.

We shook. "Brady Coyne. I'm a lawyer."

"Mr. Bailey's lawyer?"

"No." I shook my head. "It's a long story."

"You better tell me."

So I did. I began with Wally Kinnick's testimony before the state Senate subcommittee where Wilson Bailey had also testified, the SAFE enemies' list, Wally's getting shot, my conversation with Senator Swift, the Saturday night gunshots on the Cambridge street. All of it. Except I didn't tell him about my Bobby Farraday dream. It was beginning to make sense to me, but I didn't think it would to the lieutenant.

"So you came out here to warn Mr. Bailey?" said Morrison.

I shrugged. "Warn him. Or ask him why he was doing it. I wanted to talk to him. I thought I understood what he'd been living with. It seemed like a better reason than most to try to shoot people."

"It looks like he shot himself."

I nodded. "I know."

"Stuck the muzzle in his mouth and pulled the trigger."

I nodded again.

"How do you figure it?"

"Me?" I said.

"Yes."

I shrugged. "I guess he felt he just had to do something."

"So he was number ten on that list, huh?" he said.

"Yes," I said. "It was his turn."

Morrison nodded.

After a minute, I said, "That gun . . ."

"It's a Valmet," said the lieutenant. "Pretty common assault weapon. Made in Finland. Semiautomatic. Modeled after an automatic military weapon they make. Fifteen-round magazine."

"What's the caliber?"

"It's 5.56 millimeter."

"That's .223," I said.

He looked at me and shrugged.

"You should talk to Lieutenant Horowitz in Boston," I said.

"Horowitz has been on this case?"

"Sort of."

Morrison was silent for a moment. Then he said, "We got a little problem here, Mr. Coyne."

I looked at him.

"No note," he said.

I remembered that Bailey had spoken without notes at the subcommittee hearing. When asked to hand in his written statement, he had instead given the committee members a photograph of his wife and daughter. "That photograph he had in his hand," I said.

"Yeah?"

"I think that was his suicide note, Lieutenant. I think he believed that photograph says it all."

He smiled quickly. "Yeah, I guess maybe it does at that, doesn't it?"

Lieutenant Morrison sat with me for a while longer. We didn't talk anymore. I figured he was just keeping track of me. Or maybe I was some kind of suspect. I didn't really care.

A rescue wagon drove across the lawn and around the side of the house. A few minutes later it returned and disappeared down Aldrich Street. It didn't bother to sound its siren.

Gradually the onlookers in the street went back to mowing their lawns and playing basketball in their driveways and pedaling their bikes and weeding their gardens.

I rode with Lieutenant Morrison in the backseat of a state police cruiser to headquarters in Springfield. Another cop followed behind us in my car. I gave my deposition to a tape recorder, telling my story and answering the lieutenant's questions.

It was after dark when I got home. There was one message on my answering machine. Alex's voice said, "I'm glad you had a chance to go fishing. Nice day for it. Call me when you get in, if it's not too late, huh?"

I went out and sat on my balcony and decided I didn't want to talk to anybody.

When I got to the office Monday morning, I said to Julie, "Hold my calls, kid. And cancel anything on the calendar. I don't want to be disturbed."

She opened her mouth, gave me a quick hard look, then closed it. She nodded. "Okay, boss."

I fiddled around with paperwork all day. There was plenty of it. But my mind kept wandering, and I frequently found myself swiveled around in my chair with my back to my desk, staring out the window at the concrete and glass of Copley Square.

My console didn't buzz and my phone didn't ring all day.

At five o'clock Julie tapped on my door, then opened it. Without speaking, she came to my desk and laid a sheet of paper onto it. "Your calls," she said. "You'll notice that Alexandria Shaw called several times. You should call her back."

"I thought you didn't like her."

"I do like her. And I wish you'd call her. Maybe you'll tell her what you're not telling me."

"Okay," I said. "I'll call her, then."

"Good." She turned and went to the door.

"Good night," I said to her.

She stopped and frowned at me. "Good night, Brady."

"I'll tell you about it when I'm ready."

She nodded. "I know you will."

I stared at the phone for the length of time it took me to smoke a cigarette. Then I tried Alex at home. Her machine answered again. I hung up without leaving a message, then called her number at the *Globe*. She answered with a brusque, "Alex Shaw."

"Hi," I said.

"Oh, geez. How are you?"

"I'm okay."

There was a pause. Then she said, "No, you're not. I can hear it in your voice."

"You're right," I said. "I'm not. I want to talk to you about it. But not now."

"Want me to come over tonight?"

"I don't think so. I wouldn't be very good company. Give me a couple days, okay?"

"Okay," she said. "Whatever you say."

"Are you upset?"

"Should I be?"

"No. I do want to see you. I've just got to sort out some things."

"Call me when you're ready, then, all right?"

"I will," I said.

I fooled around with paperwork the next day, too. No calls, no visitors. When Julie gave me my messages that afternoon, I saw that one was from Wally. "Getting discharged tomorrow," it said.

So I walked from the office over to Mass General. Wally was dressed in jeans and a flannel shirt and sitting in a chair. Diana was sprawled on the bed. When she saw me she scrambled up and hugged me. "Are you okay?" she said.

"Sure, I guess so. Why not?"

"I called several times. Your secretary wouldn't put me through. After what happened Saturday night, and then you found that poor man . . ."

"Your friend Horowitz was in," said Wally. "He told me all about it."

"I bet he had some questions for you, too."

Wally smiled. "Why, sure. But he did smuggle in a quart of Wild Turkey."

"I suppose it's all gone by now," I said.

"Not quite. We probably ought to find a way to get rid of it. It'd be risky to try to smuggle it out again."

So Diana slipped out of the room and came back a couple of minutes later with three water glasses and a pitcher of ice. We closed the door and Wally retrieved the bottle from his duffel bag and we toasted each other's good health.

He and Diana were headed straight to the cabin in Fenwick the next day. They planned to unplug the telephone so they could fish and read and eat and sit in the sun and make love without interruption, and from the way they kept looking at each other, it wasn't hard to deduce which activity held the highest position on their order of priorities.

They planned to stay for at least two weeks. They hoped I'd join them.

I shrugged. I was behind on my office work. Maybe I could get away for a weekend.

They didn't press me, but they made it clear they were sincere.

We toasted the trout of the Deerfield River.

Wally said that Gene McNiff had called. The assault-gun bill, which had passed Senator Swift's subcommittee by a single vote, had been buried in committee and was officially dead for the current legislative term. McNiff told Wally that as far as he was concerned, there were no hard feelings.

We toasted Gene McNiff.

Horowitz had said that the state police lab confirmed that Wilson Bailey's Valmet was the same gun that had shot Wally and missed Senator Swift. So we toasted Horowitz.

Wally's doctors had given him a clean bill of health, and we toasted that, too.

When I left the hospital a couple of hours later, I felt peppier than I had for a while.

But by the time I walked into my empty apartment, the effects of the Wild Turkey toasts and Diana's and Wally's happiness had worn off.

I sat on my balcony and stared down at the dark harbor and thought about Wilson Bailey and Bobby Farraday. Then I went to bed.

◎

I got to the office before Julie on Wednesday. When she arrived, I brought her a mug of coffee. "No calls," I said.

"Brady, you can't—"

"Just one more day. Okay?"

She shrugged. "Whatever you say."

Sometime in the middle of the afternoon she knocked and then came into my office. "Listen," she said.

"Julie, please."

"Alexandria Shaw is here to see you."

"Tell her I'll call her later."

"I think you should see her now."

I looked up at her. "Why?"

"She's very upset."

"Shit," I mumbled.

Julie smiled. "Brady, as adorable as you are, I've got the distinct impression that Miz Shaw is not feeling lovelorn."

"What did she say?"

"She needs to talk to you. She says it's a professional matter."

I sighed. "Fine. Okay. Send her in."

Alex was wearing her big round glasses. Behind them, her eyes were red and swollen. I stood up and went to her. She allowed me to hug her. But she did not return my hug. She rested her forehead against my chest for a moment, then stepped back. "I've got something I want you to hear," she said.

"Okay. Say it."

She shook her head. "Not me. It's a tape. Can we sit?"

I gestured to the sofa. She sat down, and I sat beside her. She fumbled in her briefcase and came up with her little tape recorder and a cassette. "It came in the mail this morning," she said. "I've listened to it once." She inserted the cassette, then switched on the machine.

"Miz Shaw," came the recorded voice, which I recognized as the same voice that had left a message on my answering machine, "by the time you get this I will be dead. So you might consider this my suicide note. I have much to say, and I think it will be easier just to talk this way than to try to write it all down. I suppose you'll have to turn this over to the police, and that's okay. But I hope you can use what I've got to tell you. I've tried every other way I know to get this story in front of the public where it belongs, and so far I've failed."

His voice was soft. But it was firm and conveyed strength and conviction. "Oh, this is Wilson Bailey, and it's Saturday evening. I've just returned from Cambridge where I shot my Valmet in the general direction of Mr. Brady Coyne. A few nights ago I did the same thing to Senator Marlon Swift down in Marshfield. I know this isn't coming out very logically. I hope you'll bear with me."

He cleared his throat. "See, Miz Shaw, you wrote the story about the massacre in the Harlow public library two years ago. Maybe you don't even remember it. I know that every day you have a different story to write, and I imagine that yesterday's news is something newspaper people quickly forget. But in your story you mentioned the fact that two bystanders were wounded by a man with an assault weapon. The man killed his wife, the librarian. That was your story. But my wife Loretta and my daughter Elaine were those two anonymous bystanders who were rushed to the hospital. Elaine died that night. They tried to operate on Loretta, but she didn't make it. Neither did the baby she was carrying.

"I kept looking at the *Globe*, waiting for your story about Loretta and Elaine. I thought that was a much more important story than the one about that man killing his wife. I still do. I mean, the story is very obvious. That horrible weapon was the criminal, not that crazy man who shot it. He intended to kill his wife, okay. That was his crime. But it was the gun, that AK-47, not the man, that killed my family. Don't you see? So I waited for that story, and it never came. The true criminal, that gun, that AK-47, was never accused or indicted or convicted of the crime. Loretta and Elaine—they just—they just died, Miz Shaw. Like it was an accident or a disease or something. Just one of those things that happens all the time."

There came the low hum of recorded silence from the tape. Alex reached quickly for the machine and turned it off. I looked at her. Her cheeks were wet with tears. "He's right," she said. "I never followed up that story. I intended to, but I didn't. Other stories came along, newer news. I didn't think of them as people. They were—they were just stories."

"Do you think it would have made a difference?" I said.

She shrugged. "I don't know. Yes. Yes, I guess I do."

I put my arm around her. She rested her head on my shoulder for a moment. Then she cleared her throat, sat forward, and clicked the tape recorder on.

The hum of silence continued for a few seconds. Then Bailey's voice said, "Excuse me, Miz Shaw. I'm trying to think clearly here. I want you to understand."

There was more silence. Then, "Since that afternoon two years ago I have devoted the poor miserable remnants of my life to one thing. Getting rid of those evil weapons. I have written letters to newspapers and magazines. Very few of them have been printed. And when they are, they are edited so that they don't say what I intended. I have harassed legislators with letters and phone calls. Mostly they avoid me. I have tried to testify both in Washington and on Beacon Hill. A couple of times I have been heard. But my testimony—my story, the story of Loretta and Elaine—has been ignored. Ignored by the politicians, Miz Shaw, and ignored by the press. At first I didn't understand. It's all so obvious to me. But then I began to see. It's all about money and votes, and I don't have either. Groups like the Second Amendment For Ever, they have the money and the votes. They get heard. They get their stories in the newspapers. Like today's *Globe*, Miz Shaw. A nice story about SAFE, and I suppose you couldn't very well accuse them of shooting at Mr. Kinnick or Senator Swift, although, of course, they *are* responsible for it. But what about Loretta and Elaine? Where's their story?

"When I testified two weeks ago, what were the stories? They were all about the courageous Walt Kinnick, risking his career as a friend of guns to speak in favor of a very modest gun-control bill. You heard him. What does he know? To Kinnick and to the politicians and to all the others, it's a political issue, an abstraction. They say what they think will serve them, and then they're done with it. When I heard Kinnick, my first thought was: Aha. An ally. But then I realized. He's just another politician. Shallow, uncommitted, cynical, opportunistic. He'll say whatever serves him, reap the publicity rewards, and then go fishing. It's not an issue for men like him, not a cause. It's just an opportunity to advance himself.

Men like Kinnick, they're as bad as the politicians. No. They're worse. We expect cynicism from politicians. We expect more from the Walt Kinnicks of the world. I was naive. Men like Kinnick don't care whether the legislation passes. They only care about what they can get out of it. They test the wind, they take their public opinion polls, and then they decide what they believe. We expect that of politicians. You'd hope for more from someone like Walt Kinnick. So he comes out for the bill. Big deal. The bill meant nothing to him. Just a chance to get his name in the paper. What about Loretta and Elaine, Miz Shaw? Were you there to hear me, or were you one of those who rushed out to interview Walt Kinnick and marvel at his courage? I tried. I did my best. I thought my story would—would make a difference."

Bailey's long sigh hissed in the tape recorder. There was silence for a moment. Then, "It took me a while to figure it out, Miz Shaw. The enemy was not the press, not the government. It was the money and votes of SAFE. It was SAFE that was telling you what to write, telling the politicians how to vote. And after my testimony that day, when I stood out there on the State House steps, I heard Mr. McNiff threaten Mr. Kinnick. And then I knew what I had to do. I knew that SAFE and all their cynical self-serving arguments had to be discredited. It was obvious, once I saw it. And then I read your stories about how they distributed lists of their enemies. What did they expect men with guns to do about their enemies? If you, Miz Shaw, if the press and the politicians believed that SAFE was murdering their enemies—if they were using those evil guns to do it—then you and the politicians and everybody else could no longer ignore them. The entire anti-gun-control argument would be exposed for what it is—a license for killing innocent people.

"I thought about it for a long time, Miz Shaw. I realized that Elaine's and Loretta's deaths were just the beginning. More deaths were needed. And a few days later the names of those victims were given to me on the SAFE list of enemies. Mr. Walt Kinnick was to be first."

Bailey actually chuckled. "Miz Shaw, you would be amazed at something. You understand, I owned no firearms. But several years ago I tried to purchase some Mace for Loretta, because I was concerned for her safety in this awful violent world of ours. And I was told that I couldn't make this purchase without a Firearms Identification Number. An FID, they call it. So I went to the Harlow police station, and in due course I got a card for me and one for Loretta, because she had to have her own if she wanted to carry Mace legally. Loretta and I, we always obeyed the law. So anyway, after I saw the SAFE newsletter, I took my FID card to a gun shop near here and I picked out this weapon. It's very evil-looking. The man told me it was called a Valmet, and he assured me it was an assault gun. He showed me how to use it and he sold me ammunition and I bought that gun. Miz Shaw, I just bought it. It was no different from buying a book or a quart of milk. I walked into the shop with my FID card and my Visa card and I walked out with that wicked gun and a box of ammunition." He paused. "I see I'm close to the end here. I'm going to turn over the tape."

Alex reached forward, ejected the tape, turned it over, and reinserted it into the machine.

"Wait a minute," I said to her.

She hesitated, then sat back on the sofa.

"Come here," I said. "Please."

She turned to me. I held her against me with my face in her hair.

Her arms dangled at her sides, and after a minute she pulled back and poked at her glasses. "Let's listen to the rest of it," she said.

She hit the play button. "Okay," said Bailey's voice. "I bought that Valmet. Probably just the way that David Burton bought the AK-47 that killed Loretta and Elaine. And I drove to Fenwick and found where Walt Kinnick lived, and while they were off fishing I called and left a message for him, pretending I was someone from SAFE. I walked up there that night, and in the morning I waited in the woods outside his cabin until he came out. I wanted to kill him. He was a cynic and an opportunist, and I guess, after two years of getting nowhere with men like him, I hated him. I thought I had to kill him. He was the number-one enemy. If he was assassinated with an assault gun, they couldn't very well ignore the evil influence of SAFE any longer. The influence that made it so easy for me to walk into that shop and buy that gun. Isn't that ironic? Miz Shaw, the hardest thing I've ever done was to aim that gun at Mr. Kinnick. And I pulled the trigger, and he fell, and I thought, Oh, my God, what have I done? And I kept pulling the trigger, but I wasn't aiming, because, you see, I was crying. Crying for Mr. Kinnick, who I thought I had killed, and crying for Loretta and Elaine and all the other victims of these evil weapons.

"But," he continued after a pause, "my mistake was that I didn't kill him. You wrote one piece in the paper. But you failed to implicate SAFE, Miz Shaw, and you said nothing about the weapon that shot him. So I went after Senator Swift. But I didn't have any hate left in me. I couldn't shoot him. I couldn't make myself point that gun at him. I thought maybe if I shot into the air it would be enough. But nothing. Not a word in the newspaper. The next people on that list were out of state. So it was to be the lawyer, that Mr. Coyne, who I would kill. Hate had nothing to do with it. I had to kill somebody, I realized that. Otherwise there was no news. But I couldn't do it, Miz Shaw. I couldn't make myself aim at him."

I reached for Alex's hand and gripped it hard. She gave my hand a quick squeeze. I glanced at her. Behind her glasses she was crying.

Wilson Bailey laughed quietly. "See, Miz Shaw? There has to be a killing. Who's left? Now you know. It's not SAFE that's shooting at people on their list. But if you think about it, it's still their fault. I have this weapon right here, and I walked into a store and bought it because no one has had the courage to stand up to SAFE and tell them it's wrong. Please, Miz Shaw. I *could* have killed Walt Kinnick and Senator Swift and Brady Coyne. You see that, don't you? And I *can* kill myself."

The tape hissed quietly for a long moment. Then Bailey said, "I was there, Miz Shaw. I was in the library. I saw it all. I saw that man walk in. I saw the gun. I saw him raise it to his hip. Loretta and Elaine were there. I saw that gun jump in his hands when he fired. I saw Elaine, little sweet Elaine, lifted off her feet when those bullets hit her. I saw Loretta start to reach toward her before the bullets slammed her backward. I still see these things.

Every minute of my life since that day I see these pictures, over and over again in my head. Miz Shaw, I have thought about this for a long time. There's still one question I cannot answer. It's this: Why in God's name wasn't I standing at the desk with Elaine and Loretta? Why did I have to keep living?"

The tape hissed. Alex reached toward the machine and switched it off.

We sat there, staring at it, not speaking.

"What are you going to do?" I said finally.

She shrugged. "I've got to give it to my editor. I wanted you to hear it first."

"I was the one who found his body," I said.

"I know," she said. "We got the police report. You figured it out, huh?"

"Not really. Certainly not all that." I gestured at her tape recorder. "I tried to call Bailey. To warn him. He didn't answer. It was his wife's voice on his answering machine. It said, 'We're not here.' That 'we,' it got to me, I guess, because there was no 'we.' The woman who had made that recording *was* dead, and he had never changed it. It was just him, all alone, living in the same house with his ghosts. That got me imagining what it must be like to be him, to live with what he'd had to live with. And I got this—it was just a vague indistinct feeling. A discomfort. After I got shot at Saturday night, I was frightened, of course. That night I had a dream, and he was in it, although I didn't recognize him. See, my subconscious was playing with it, making connections that my conscious mind refused to recognize. I tried to reach him again Sunday morning. Still no answer. So I went out there to meet him, and I wasn't sure why. I wanted to know him. I thought it was to warn him. But I think on another level I knew he was the one doing the shooting. Except it was all out there on the fuzzy fringes of my consciousness where I couldn't quite focus."

"So you followed your intuition."

I shrugged. "Something like that, I guess."

"It must have been awful for you."

"Yes, it was. I'm sorry I put you off. It wasn't fair of me."

"I understand."

"I couldn't talk to anybody. It's how I am sometimes."

She touched my arm. "It's all right, Brady."

"I think a hug would've helped more than anything."

She poked at her glasses. "All you had to do was ask."

"Can I have one now?"

She smiled softly. "Sure," she said.

I stood up. She took off her glasses and put them on the table beside the tape recorder. Then she pressed herself against me and wrapped her arms around my waist and laid her cheek against my chest. I held her tight with my face buried in her hair. After a minute she tried to lean back to look at me, or maybe to kiss me, but I held her against me. I didn't want her to see that my eyes were a little watery.

"Um, Miz Shaw?" I said, when I felt I could trust my voice.

"Mm?"

"How would you like to spend a weekend in a cozy cabin in the woods with me and two of my very best friends? We'll keep the phone unplugged, and we can do a little fishing and reading and sitting in the sun and . . ."

"And what?" she mumbled into my chest.

"And . . . and be together."

Her arms tightened around me. "I'd like that very much, Mr. Coyne, sir," she whispered.